THE
WILDING
PROBATE

A BUCKY MCCRAE ADVENTURE

D. J. BUTLER

Immortal Works LLC
1505 Glenrose Drive
Salt Lake City, Utah 84104
Tel: (385) 202-0116

© 2020 D. J. Butler
www.davidjohnbutler.com

Cover Art by Ashley Literski
http://strangedevotion.wixsite.com/strangedesigns

ISBN 978-1-953491-05-3 (Paperback)
ASIN B08KDPQPN2 (Kindle Edition)

*This book is for
Carolyn and Dave Westergard,
who gave me much, much more than just
two characters in a book.*

CHAPTER
1

"**E**ver serve process on a horse?" I asked.

Michael P. Fellows raised an eyebrow at me and twisted his mouth into half a grin. His face was thin and angular, he had a high forehead, and his hair was swept up like a crown. He had the kind of blond good looks and comfortable-in-your-own-skin vibe that can be really useful at trial or at getting new clients in the door. He was also clean—clean-shaven, manicured nails, straight tie, crisp charcoal suit. I mean, you're supposed to look nice for job interviews, right? But this guy looked *too* nice. He looked like the cleanest person in Howard County.

He also looked amused. I got it, I understood. He'd come expecting to talk to a lawyer named James, and instead he was being interviewed by a sixteen-year-old girl with a ponytail."I'm sorry," he said. "The woman outside told me your name was Bucky."

"Rebecca McCrae. Friends call me Bucky."

"I see." He laughed. "Sue a lot of horses here, do you?"

Smart aleck. "No," I said, "but some places around the county you can't get to by car. You get involved in a dispute between ranchers in the Ups, you'll find yourself carrying court papers in your saddlebags."

"No way you've done that, Ms. McCrae." He grinned his grin again. "I bet you aren't even eighteen."

I gave him my hard, shrewd look. "My experience is not the point, Mr. Fellows. If you really want to join the Law Offices of James F. McCrae as an associate attorney, you're going to have to show me you're up to the job."

Fellows's eyes wandered across the framed certificates on the wall behind me. I wished they were a little straighter. "I guess I just expected I'd be talking with Mr. McCrae himself," he said. "And not his...are you his daughter? Kid sister?"

"Office manager." I could have said *paralegal, messenger, billing specialist, secretary, filing clerk, publicist, and sometimes even investigator*, but I didn't. "And recruiter. This is a screening interview."

"Right." Fellows straightened up in his seat and smoothed out his jacket. The gesture was as fake as it could be, like when you pretend to drink the imaginary cup of tea a four-year-old hands you. He was humoring me. "I've never served process on horseback, Ms. McCrae." He pointed at the liquor license on the wall behind me. "Nor have I ever tended bar. I do, however, like to bowl."

As if to punctuate his words, I heard the crash of a ball slamming into pins.

"You think it's funny that Mr. McCrae owns both a bowling alley and a law practice?"

"In the same building. A law practice and a bowling alley. Yes. Yes, I do." The grin was less charming now that he seemed to be laughing at me. "A bowling alley that serves alcohol."

"In compliance with state and local licensing requirements." Michael Fellows was starting to get on my nerves. "Well, I imagine this is all very different from what you're used to in New York City. Maybe you should think twice about whether you really want to be joining this practice."

"Hey, I already said I *like* bowling."

"Around here we have a serious boredom problem. McCrae's Fun Lanes is a business, and it's also a service to the community." I resisted the urge to wag my finger at him like Mrs. Anderson, the Principal at Howard High.

"Yeah?"

"Yeah. When you're sixteen years old in the middle of nowhere, there's not that much to do for fun. If you're lucky, you're one of the nerdy ones who can't get enough Dungeons and Dragons or World of Warcraft, or a car nut who can spend hours in the garage. Otherwise, you can only watch so much television, and after that it's sex, guns, and crystal meth."

"Sounds like a band name."

"Ha," I deadpanned. "So a bowling alley—a *cheap* bowling alley —is a place where kids can stay out of trouble. And before you say anything snarky about the bar, you should consider that the bar means kids and their parents can hang out in the same place on an evening. Everybody bowls a few games, mom and dad have a Bud to unwind. This is an establishment for families."

And now I was in fact wagging my finger. I stopped, sat back, and smiled, trying not to show my teeth.

"And family law." He smiled again, disarmingly.

"Whatever a client needs, Mr. Fellows. Water rights, criminal defense, land disputes, tort or commercial lawsuits, incorporation, writing a stern letter to a tenant, finding a lost dog, writing a will, or yes, family law." I grabbed the open *Howard County Register* with both hands and rustled it, smelling the newsprint smudging onto my fingertips. "This is the kind of practice where I read the newspaper every day to see if anyone is suing any of our clients, or if any of our clients has organized an LLC without us, or taken a job with the County, or died."

"And have they?"

I jabbed my finger into the paper. "Aaron Wilding." I had never seen Aaron Wilding in life, but his photo showed him to be a handsome man, though his face was a bit too angular. "He's a client, and he's passed away. Natural causes—and that's no surprise, the guy had a stroke just a couple of weeks ago, Dad told me—survived by his wife Marilyn, who gets quoted in the story."

Fellows's face grew serious. "Sounds like just the practice for me." He scooted to the edge of his chair and leaned forward, clasping his hands together between his knees. I half-expected him to invite me to huddle and hear him call the next play, or join him in a moment of prayer. Fortunately, Dad's broad, scarred walnut desk—a remnant of his days of being a big firm lawyer in Boise, along with the oversized filing cabinets in the corner that held the Old Files—put some space between us. "I get small towns," he said. "I spent a couple years in Lost Bend as a kid."

Lost Bend isn't even a small town, it's a hamlet. It's a village, above the Dam and out past Hooper, deep in the sticks in pine tree country. We don't have a good word in American English to describe a cluster of trailers and cabins around a gas station as small as Lost Bend. Lost Bend only exists so loggers, hunters, and people who are on their way to better places can stop for a ham sandwich starting to go yellow at the edges, and a Slim Jim for the road. "You could hang out your shingle there," I suggested. "Wouldn't be any competition."

"Wouldn't be any clients, either." He grinned. "Maybe I could set up my law office in the back room of a gas station."

"Don't knock it. People share a lot of news at a corner store."

"And everybody needs gas."

"You know a lot of Native Americans when you were a kid?" I asked him. "Up there in the sticks?"

"Sure." He shrugged. "Why? You practice Indian law, too?"

"When we get the work." It was a lie. Indian law is a specialty, and mostly practiced by lawyers who are connected with the tribal organizations. So mostly Indians, and fair enough. "What were they, Umatilla kids? Nez Perce? Wachigonk?" I did my best to keep a casual expression.

"All of the above." He leaned back out of his offer for a prayer huddle. "But I don't know any tribal law."

"Didn't learn that with the Kings County District Attorney, I guess." Pins crashing again.

"Nope," he said. "Mostly I busted bored kids on drugs. So maybe Brooklyn and Howard aren't so different after all."

"Bet the kids in Brooklyn weren't cooking meth in doublewides."

"Bet the kids in Howard County don't kill each other in gang fights."

"Maybe. When was the last time a tractor in Brooklyn chopped off anyone's arm?"

"Touché." He held his hands up in surrender. "When the moment comes that I have to learn a little Indian law, I'm happy to do it."

"That's the right answer," I said, and it was true. In a practice like the Law Offices of James F. McCrae, you take whatever work comes along and you figure out how to get it done. The learning curve is constant. It didn't matter that he was right about Indian law, though, just like it didn't matter that he was clean and good-looking and had a case-winning grin. I was going to tell Dad not to even talk to the guy.

Because Michael Fellows was an obvious liar.

"I'm staying at the Motor Inn. Probably easier to reach me on my cell than on the land line."

He handed me his card and I tossed it onto the desk without looking at it. I already had his cell phone from his resume, and besides, I only planned to call him later that evening to turn him down. "South end of town. Good choice. You've got Ernie's Pool Hall there, plus the Pie Hole makes a decent pizza. Can't really buy it by the slice here, though." I'd never been, but one thing I knew about New York City was that you bought pizza by the slice there. I stood up to signal that the interview was over.

He stood up too, unfolding a lanky body out of the chair and reminding me that he was a good six inches taller than me—and I've always thought of myself as tall. I caught a glint of black inside his jacket that had to be a pistol. That wouldn't have bothered me at all if I trusted him; Dad kept a pistol in his desk drawer and one in the glove compartment of the Taurus and one under the seat of the pickup truck and carried another with him. You can get rough clients out in the sticks, and sometimes the nearest cop is hours away. Heck, people walk around Howard County openly carrying weapons, and that's fine, too. But Michael Fellows was a liar, and the fact that he was carrying only made me more uncomfortable.

Without meaning to, I rested my hand on the desk surface, just above the drawer with the pistol—Dad's nine-millimeter Beretta.

Fellows looked at my hand and raised his eyebrows. "That's fine," he said. "I'll go run a few miles and then just eat a whole pie myself."

We shook hands and I looked him sternly in the eyes. "I'll give you a call soon to let you know."

"When do I meet your...when do I get to meet Mr. McCrae? Will he be here later?"

"You in a rush?"

"Nope." He shook his head. "I'm booked into the Motor Inn for a few days. Figured I'd do some hiking."

"See old friends." I said it neutrally.

"Yeah," he agreed. "Talk about old times."

The Law Offices of James F. McCrae have their own exit from the building, but Dad saves that for the occasional client who needs to be extra discreet and for the times when he wants to pop out the back without being noticed. I opened the door into the Fun Lanes and Fellows loped out. He nodded to platinum-bleached Gladys, who sat resting her ankles behind the front counter and mending a tear in a kid's-sized bowling shoe with tight little stitches of fifty-pound test line. She nodded back.

"I look forward to the call." Fellows waved to me over the gumball machine and the shoe cubbies. Then the bell at the top of the door tinkled and he was gone.

I heard rattling pins again, and then whoops of joy and swearing. There was a cluster of teenagers on lane eleven—I didn't know them, which might mean they went to St. Joe's instead of Howard, or it might mean they came from out in the county somewhere. Farm kids or sagebillies.

Gladys looked at me over the top of her reading glasses. "That man," she said, "belongs on TV."

I laughed. "That's not what you really mean."

"Nope." She shrugged deeper into her red cardigan and punched another stitch into the shoe. "It ain't. But you're not of age, young lady, so I can't tell you where he *really* belongs." She inhaled through her nostrils with a dreamy expression on her face. "I don't know what that scent is, but you can't get it in Howard."

I drifted over to the door, sucking on my teeth. "Nope. You surely cannot."

"Mind you," she added, "your Evil's none too bad-looking, himself."

"He's not my Evil."

I looked out the glass door at the gravel parking lot and watched Michael Fellows drive off. Blue Corolla; looked like a rental car, no bumper stickers or decals or visible dents; California plates.

I took out my phone and typed out a text. *Nice try, Dad. Guy's a dud.*

I looked up to see a man lurching toward the door. He had long hair and a beard, and both were matted and dirty. He wore a too-small brown corduroy jacket over a long white shirt, both splotched with dirt, jeans, and hiking boots. Loops of colored beads hung around his neck. He might have been a backpacker—June through August, Howard sees a lot of those, and also fishermen—but I didn't see any gear.

He reached for the door, saw me, and stopped, his eyes bulging.

Not a backpacker, I thought. A bum, with a face full of pure crazy.

I grabbed the metal bar across the door. I wasn't one hundred percent sure whether I wanted to push it open or hold it shut, but the bum made up my mind for me. He whipped around to the side, staring at something in the parking lot I couldn't see and twitching like a rabbit that had been mainlining caffeine.

"Bears," he muttered. "Bears and balloons."

Definitely going to hold the door shut.

But I didn't have to. Mumbling something I couldn't quite hear through the glass, he turned and shuffled away, into the thicket and trees behind the Fun Lanes.

CHAPTER
2

I stepped outside and looked after the bum, holding the door open. The bright sun of the August afternoon hit me. It wasn't quite hot, but it was warm enough that the red flannel shirt I wore open as a jacket felt like just a little bit too much.

Yeah, I was wearing a red flannel jacket, like a lumberjack. What can I tell you? Howard is not one of your fashion metropolises. I was also wearing hiking boots.

The bum was gone. He'd disappeared down into the river bottom, and with any luck he was sloshing across it and into the empty land on the other side. I wasn't sure who owned that, probably the Forest Service, but there was nothing over there but pine and tall yellow grass and once in a while a kid on a dirt bike.

There were two new cars in the parking lot with the multi-colored pickup, Gladys's battered old metallic blue Grand Marquis, and the cars the kids from St. Joe's had come in. The drivers had to be here to see James McCrae or bowl in his lanes, because we don't exactly have neighbors. There's the highway, the trees, and the river. We're a little bit out of town on the west side, our nearest neighbors being Yukon Video and the Comfort Lodge, both at least one hundred fifty yards away. There's a denser downtown part of Howard, and we're not in it. Cheaper rent, Dad would joke, and no hassle about zoning restrictions.

One of the cars stood out like ten sore thumbs. It was a canary yellow H3, you know, a Humvee for the rich-people-with-bad-taste market, and as I looked at it the vehicle chunked open a door and spat out a client.

I recognized her from around town. She stared at me. Her face was a little too made up, in that tight way that tells you that someone really wants to put on a good appearance. Well, no wonder. Her husband had died.

"Hello, Mrs. Wilding." I held the door. "I'm Rebecca McCrae. My father is James McCrae."

She nodded. "Is your father here?"

"He's meeting some other clients right now," I said. "Please come in and let's see if I can help you. If nothing else, I can schedule another time that's convenient for you."

A man climbed out of the other car, a white new-model sedan. He was dark-haired and had thick eyebrows and a tan that made me think he might be Greek or Persian. He wore a red turtleneck and sunglasses, that kind that skiers sometimes favor, with leather wrapped around the sides and a string behind the neck. As Mrs. Wilding passed me and entered the building, he stood on the edge of the boardwalk made of two-by-eights and looked it up and down.

Just as I was about to open my mouth and invite him in, too, he grabbed the bar's door and went inside. The bar has its own entrance from the boardwalk, and a glass door connecting the bar itself and the Fun Lanes. The bar doesn't have an official name, but from the way people talk about it I guess its unofficial name is McCrae's.

I followed Mrs. Wilding by the clicking of her heels across the Fun Lanes and into the office. "Gladys," I called. "There's a customer in the bar."

Mrs. Wilding sat. I shut the door behind me and grabbed the bowl of M&Ms. I ordinarily keep them on top of the filing cabinet, because if I left them on the desktop, Dad would absent-mindedly eat his way through a pound of them every time he worked. I set the bowl on the desk and sat down.

"Mrs. Wilding," I began.

"Please call me Marilyn," she said. "*Mrs. Wilding* makes me feel like a widow, and I'm...that is, I don't want to feel like that."

"Of course, Marilyn," I said, and then experience kicked back in.

"This is probably obvious, but I should point out I'm not an attorney. Things you say to me are not privileged." This last bit was a joke, but since Marilyn Wilding's hard look didn't relent, I felt like I had to make the joke obvious. "So if you get prosecuted, I could be called to testify."

"I know what *privilege* means!" she snapped, and then softened. "Sorry. It's been a hard couple of days."

I took a box of tissues from the drawer underneath the pistol drawer and set it next to the M&Ms, making a mental note that we were almost out, and I should stock up on my next Costco run to Yakima.

"Sorry, bad joke. How can I help you, Mrs....Marilyn?"

"Thank you." She ignored both the tissues and the M&Ms and sat quietly for a moment. She wasn't quite as young as she made out— maybe forty? I'd only seen her once or twice before around town, when Dad had pointed her out to me. Her husband had been older. I let her sit, and while we waited I noticed that she had long fingernails, long and curved and as red as her lipstick. Her nails didn't make her unique in Howard County, but they did mean she didn't work with her hands, and around Howard that was unusual among adult women. Two of the nails were snapped off.

Of course, Aaron Wilding had been a rich man. He'd been a feature of Howard County's local color as long as I could remember. Well, less of a feature and more of a ghost, really. He was some kind of Silicon Valley kid genius in the 80s, one of those guys in the original club that invented computers or something. After he'd hit it big he moved out to Howard to get away from the fast lane, was how I'd heard it. He'd bought a couple of adjacent ranches, sold all the cattle, and built a custom solar- and geothermal-powered house out of sight of the highway. He showed up in Howard shops once in a while, or to fill his tank coming in or out of town, and that was it. I'd heard that the only time he'd ever invited anybody from Howard up to his house was when he held a party for some of the local bigwigs (really, medium-wigs, Howard County being officially, after all, the Middle of Nowhere) so he could bounce the idea off them of his running for office as a candidate for the Green Party. When they told him he was more likely to turn into a badger than to win a Howard County election as a Green, he got married instead. That had been maybe fifteen years ago.

I wondered what sorts of things Dad had done for him. Sued trespassers, maybe—Aaron Wilding was a hiss and a byword among local hunters for the barbed wire and *KEEP OUT* signs all around his land. Evil claimed that the deer knew it, too, and would deliberately run on Wilding's land just to taunt hunters.

"Your father helped my husband prepare his will," the widow finally said.

I took a yellow legal pad and wrote *will* on it. "When was that?" I asked.

She hesitated. "After we were married, of course. A few years after."

10 yrs ago? I wrote. "I see."

"I think your father has the will in his files. I'm not aware of any...amendments."

Executor? "Okay."

"And...what comes next?"

I put down the pen. "Well, remember that I'm not a lawyer. But the will needs to be filed with the court so we can start the probate process."

"Probate?"

"*Probate* means a *test* or a *trial*."

"Who's on trial?"

"The will, really. The court tests the will. That will take a few months. The executor and the court will have to work together to give notice to anybody your husband might have owed money to, and pay any debts, and then carry out the instructions in the will. The court also needs to make sure the will we have is the last will your husband made, because it will only enforce his last valid will and testament. People change their minds over their lifetimes."

"Can I see it?" Her lip trembled slightly. It must be rough to lose your husband. I couldn't imagine my lip trembling at the thought of Evil, even if he was dead. Another reason I had to stick to my guns today. "The will, I mean."

"I think so," I said. "If my dad has it"—I nodded at the filing cabinets nearest me, the ones holding the New Files—"then I think he'll bring a copy by to discuss it with you and explain the process." I thought as much because that was exactly what I was going to tell Dad to do, right after I prepared the filing to submit the will and kick off the probate proceedings.

That makes it sound like I'm the lawyer, and I'm not, but a lot of court filings are just form documents. If you know the right form to use and what to attach, you can mostly fill in the blanks. That's convenient, because I can do a lot of administrative stuff to free up Dad for other things. Like landing new clients.

Marilyn Wilding looked at the New Files cabinets too, and then bit her lip. "That will be fine, of course." She stood to leave.

My phone buzzed in my shirt pocket: incoming text message. I ignored it and walked Marilyn to the door. The sunglasses guy had already left, but the two bottle tops and twenty-dollar bill sitting on the small bar told me we'd made a few bucks off him first. I followed Marilyn out to the boardwalk.

"Don't worry about the will," I told her. "That's complicated stuff, and that's what the lawyer is for." It wasn't nice of me, but I secretly hoped that Aaron Wilding owed a lot of tricky debts, or that his heirs would fight over what he'd left. A long and bitter probate could mean good fees for a year or more. It might even mean being able to afford hiring someone else who could help Dad, someone who wasn't a creepy liar from out of state. I shut the idea out of my mind before it could go any further. "Have you thought about funeral arrangements?"

"All in hand." She smiled a little smile at me, got into her yellow monstrosity, and drove off, cutting the corner so tight as she exited the parking lot that she nearly drove off the road. Among the pickup trucks, Jeeps, hammered SUVs, and beaters on the roads of Howard County, the H3 looked like an alien. Straight from Planet California. It couldn't have looked more out of place if it had been flying six feet above the surface of the highway. The fact that it barely fit in the lane didn't help.

I checked my phone. Dad: *Really? Too bad, I thought his resume looked good.*

I sighed and put the phone back in my shirt pocket, just as Evil came stomping up the boardwalk.

Objectively, Gladys was right; Evil Patten was a good-looking young man. He wasn't tall, exactly, but he had a lot of masculine charm in his broad shoulders and narrow hips. He walked confidently. His nose was crooked, but his teeth were good and he smiled a lot. He couldn't ever manage a normal hairstyle—either it was buzz cut like his Marine older brother's, or it was long and ragged, like he was auditioning to play the stoner kid in some 1980s movie about teens making out a lot and finding themselves. There was no middle ground, and his hair seemed to jump from the one state to the other without warning. Right now, it was long, and that was the better situation, because when it was long it hid the fact that his skull was kind of funny shaped, too flat in back. Dad said it was because the Pattens had so many kids, and Evil hadn't been held enough when he was a baby, had just lain in a car seat all day.

His name wasn't really Evil. His first name was Ronald and his *middle* name was Evil. His parents, God bless them, had named Evil after one of their favorite presidents, Ronald Reagan, and their favorite stunt motorcycle rider, Evel Knievel. Only on the birth certificate, they'd misspelled 'Evel,' and by the time they figured out the mistake, it would have been too much work to change it. It could have been worse—Evil had a younger brother cursed with the name Abraham Hulk Patten. On the first day of school, teachers just looked at the boy's name on the roll and laughed out loud.

"Hey," he said. He wore a flannel shirt not so different from mine, over a t-shirt that read *Marines Never Die, They Just Go to Hell to*

Regroup. His boots were steel-toed Redwings. Evil was spending the summer working with a highway crew. He got paid pretty well for standing on the side of the road holding a stop sign, especially since he was willing to work nights and weekends. He waved a DVD at me. *"The Last of the Mohicans.* Your favorite. With that English guy."

"Not my favorite."

He looked surprised. "Really? I could have sworn."

"Not my favorite," I repeated. "Which I already told you, the first three times you rented it."

"I guess we could stream something." He reached past me for the door.

"I think you better not come in, Evil," I told him.

"Gladys will be disappointed." He snickered, but not in a mean way. Evil he might be, but he didn't have a mean bone in his body.

"She'll have to be disappointed," I said. "It's over."

"Aw, man." He frowned. "Are you dumping me again?"

"Yep."

"What is it this time?"

"It isn't anything, Evil. That's the point. Just like it was last time, and the time before. It just isn't anything. You're a nice guy, but there's no reason for us to be anything but friends."

"There's how I feel about you," he protested.

"You're not in love with me." I pointed at the DVD case. "You're in love with Daniel Day-Lewis."

"Ha!" He looked thoughtfully at the case and then shook it in my general direction. "What am I going to do with this?"

"Return it?"

"I won't get my three bucks back."

I sighed. "Fine. You can come over to our house tonight. I'm not going to watch it with you, though."

"Dinner?" He looked hopeful.

"Whatever we're eating, you can have. I can pretty much guarantee it will come either out of a can or out of a box."

"Just the way I like it." Evil turned and ambled back toward his muscle car, a restored Buick GSX he was *actually* in love with. He waved *The Last of the Mohicans* over his head. "Say hello to Gladys for me!"

"Ten o'clock!" I called after him.

"I know when you close!" he yelled back.

CHAPTER
3

Ten o'clock sounds late, but in Howard County in the summertime that's when the sun is just starting to set. Staying open late lets us catch a few extra customers, including the folks who want a tuna melt, a Coke, and a basket of fried mozzarella sticks for dinner. When there isn't actual work to do in the office, I can catch up on course work, which is what I did that night: I took an online mid-term for American History 201. Aced the multiple-choice section, which was graded immediately by the computer, and felt pretty good about the essays. Andrew Jackson is definitely our most underrated President.

The kids from St. Joe's bowled two more games and left, and later there were a couple of families. I didn't know any of them; Howard's not *that* small a place, especially when you take into account all the farms out on the Flats and all the little places like Hooper, Three Pines, Finnegan, and Lost Bend. The smallness of Howard County isn't so much that it's tiny as that it's isolated. When your nearest big cities are Boise and Spokane, and they're both hours away, you know you're in Nowheresville, even if your town has a population of thirty thousand, all in.

Gladys and I closed down at ten. Of course, she had to stay until the end—even in Howard, you can't have a sixteen-year-old running a bar and serving alcohol. She left first, squeezing into a parka as she trundled out the front door. I washed the restrooms and finished cleaning up in the kitchen, and then I did one last circuit to check all the doors and windows. Just because Howard's a small town doesn't mean we don't have break-ins, given that we keep booze and cash on the premises; I locked everything up tight. Throwing on my wool poncho—don't get into your head images of a chic New York girl playing Mexicana, my poncho is dust brown and more Clint Eastwood than Cecilia Prado, I wear it because it's warm—I took the last half cup of coffee from the pot, baked almost solid, and headed out into the parking lot.

Even at the edge of town, with the yellowish hum of light pollution from Howard itself, the stars punched me right in both eyes. That's one of the things about Howard that's hard to explain to someone who's only ever lived in a big city. The stars in the mountains are ten times bigger than they are anywhere else, and there are a hundred times more of them. Drive an hour into the Ups, even less, and you hit what they call Dark Sky country, where there is almost no light pollution at all, and there it's like...well, you know that scene in Star Wars where the Millennium Falcon jumps into hyperspace out of Mos Eisley, and the first time you see it on the big screen it just blows your mind? It's like that, only real.

My truck was the only car in the parking lot. The starlight downplayed the fact that the truck was seven different colors. I actually don't know which was the original—Javier at the Jalopy Graveyard, Howard's pick-a-part auto shop, pieced it together from multiple different wrecks. He claims it's a Toyota Tacoma, but I don't know how you'd know. It was the closest thing to a homemade car I'd ever seen, and getting it a consistent paint job had not yet climbed to the top of my list of financial priorities. It looked like a calico cat.

The truck opened the old-fashioned way, key in the lock. I started the engine and gave the truck and my hands, wrapped around the coffee, both a minute to warm up. This high up, nights are cold in any season. I wondered how far into *The Last of the Mohicans* Evil had gotten. It was true that it wasn't my favorite movie, but it wasn't bad, especially the jumping-through-the-waterfall scene.

I was just about to put the truck into gear when something slammed against the driver's side window.

I spilled the coffee on my leg. "Sheesh!"

It was the crazy bum. He leaned against the window and hammered on it with one fist. "McCrae!" he yelled. "You're McCrae!"

Not worth going for the gun, I decided. My heart was pounding and I was shaking like a leaf, but I kept my head, put the truck into first, and started driving away.

The bum threw himself onto my hood. He dug his fingers under the lip of the hood where the windshield wipers are and yelled again. "The trailer! I went to the wrong one!"

I could have just gunned the engine and driven home. Somewhere along the way, the crazy old guy would have fallen off, for sure. It probably would have killed him, though, and I didn't want that on my record or my conscience. I jammed the truck back into neutral and pulled up the hand brake.

Then, for his sake, I went for the gun.

The gun Dad keeps in the truck's glove compartment is a .38 special. If you're not a gun person, that's a small, lightweight pistol with a short barrel. It's not particularly accurate, but it's got a pretty good-sized bullet and it packs a punch. That makes it a good defensive gun for someone who doesn't have a lot of arm strength and doesn't want to go target shooting. Like me.

It's Dad's gun, because I'm a minor and I'm not supposed to drive around with a gun. It's also loaded, which is a no-no...but "better judged by twelve than carried by six" is a pretty common saying around Howard, and it's one Dad uses mostly when it comes to *my* safety.

I grabbed the pistol. My hands shook a little worse now—I wasn't scared, I told myself, I was royally pissed off.

"McCrae!" the bum roared.

I stepped out of the truck and pulled back the hammer.

"Get away from the car, asshole!" I yelled. The word *asshole* caught in my throat and came out sounding a bit like *gashole*. I don't usually curse, not a lot, anyway. But Dad always tells me that if I'm going to point a gun at someone, I have to be prepared to use it. So maybe swearing was my way of convincing the bum I was serious, or maybe it was my way of convincing myself.

The bum, at least, believed me.

"The trailer!" he yelled, backing away.

"This is no trailer, jerk!" I toned down the cursing because I was clearly winning. "And I don't know anything about your bears and balloons! Stay away from me!" I pointed the gun at the center of his chest.

He turned and ran, past the corner of the building. At the edge of the slope he jumped, disappearing down into the trees and brush around the river.

In the glow of the headlights I couldn't be sure, but it looked like there was blood on the back of his head.

"Crazy old man." I got back in the truck.

No one else tried to jump me on the drive home. We lived even farther outside of Howard than the Fun Lanes, right on the border between the Flats and the Ups. Technically our address was on Ranch Road, but that was the name of the highway that cut up into the hills, and our house was one of half a dozen on an unnamed paved drive that turned north off Ranch just before it entered the canyon. We called the nameless road the Stub. The area had once been pasture, and had been subdivided for something like a hundred houses, and Mom had spent a lot of time with the developer looking at his plans for a playground and a charter school. When only six homes had been built the recession kicked in, house sales went through the floor, and the developer went bankrupt. Dad bought one of the houses cheap because he thought Mom would like it, and then Mom ran off to Texas with the developer.

So, you know, it's not all happy endings and rainbows in Howard County.

I'd decided on the drive not to mention the bum to Dad. I was safe, I didn't think the old man would bother me again, and there was no sense worrying Dad about it when there wasn't anything he could do. When I opened the door, I was hit by the smell of pizza.

Dad and Evil sat on the couch, both in that guy way where you lie on your shoulders and just your head is propped up against the sofa back. Dad's tie was loosened so much he could have worn it as a belt. Evil was gnawing on a slice of mushroom and olive.

"You must have collected on a bill," I said. I threw my poncho over the banister, kicked my way out of my boots, and took a slice of plain cheese. Señor Pepperonio's was the nicer of Howard's two pizza joints, despite the fact that the owners apparently didn't know the difference between Spanish and Italian. The nearest chain pizza parlor was Yakima.

"Nope." Dad kept his eyes on the screen, where Daniel Day-Lewis was running, you know, with his hair all flowing out behind him like a flag in the wind. That guy must use some powerful conditioner; my hair's long, and when I run it just bounces, even when it's not in a ponytail. The crusts of Dad's pizza were piled in a bowl on the floor, next to two empty Michelob bottles and a third bottle that was still half full. "But I got a new engagement. Sally Harris wants me to file a discrimination suit against the County."

"I thought you were golfing with Sam Barlow today." Sam Barlow was Howard County's Magistrate. He held court in a trailer next to St. Joe's, and heard little cases—misdemeanors, suits under five thousand dollars, things like that. He took care of the small stuff, and that lightened the load on the District Court.

"Got confused on the dates." Dad sighed. "Sam's already gone fishing. Guess I ought to let you schedule my social calendar, too. Anyway, gave me time to talk to Sally. Her case is airtight, her supervisor flat out told her he'd denied her raise because she wouldn't go out with him. The County'll settle."

"Nice," I said. "So we can pay for this pizza in, like, eighteen months." I dragged the ottoman over next to the armchair and arranged myself.

"*He* brought the pizza." Dad took his eyes off the TV and jerked a thumb in Evil's direction. "Guy shows up at your door with three large pies, you can't really turn him away."

"Unless it's that alfredo sauce pizza crap, Jim," Evil added around a mouthful of carbohydrates and cheese. He didn't take his eyes off the movie. "Then you *have* to refuse it, because...dude, that isn't pizza."

"I landed a client today, too," I said. It was an exaggeration, at least. I hadn't landed anybody—an existing client had come in to talk to my Dad.

"Oh, yeah?" Dad picked up a pizza crust and licked salt off it.

"Mrs. Wilding."

"Came in about the will, I bet." Dad shook his head. "I should have called her already."

"I told her you'd come by."

"Good. And what's wrong with that guy Follower?"

"Fellows." I chewed on my pizza for a moment and organized my thoughts. "One, he's too clean. His suit's way too nice. I don't buy that he grew up around here, and I don't buy for a second that he's an assistant DA. That's a government job, and those guys make peanuts."

Dad shrugged. "In Howard County. Maybe they get paid more in Brooklyn."

"No way. He was dressed like an assistant DA on TV, not an assistant DA in real life. Two, I don't think he's from New York. He was driving a car with California plates."

"Probably a rental. What's he going to do, drive out from New York City?"

"Yeah, it looked like one. But why not Washington plates, or Idaho, or Oregon?"

Dad shrugged. His grin looked amused, but also pleased. "Rental cars move around."

"True. But also, I caught him in a total lie."

"Yeah?"

"He said he grew up in Lost Bend, and knew a lot of Wachigonk Indians as a kid."

Evil snorted and then made a coughing noise like he had pizza stuck in both his nose and his windpipe. "What the hell is a Wachigonk Indian?"

"There's no such thing." Dad looked at me closely and cocked one eyebrow. "Did *he* say 'Wachigonk Indian?'"

"Well, no," I admitted. "But he agreed to it easy enough."

Evil was laughing so hard he almost fell off the couch.

"In other words," Dad said, "you asked 'did you know any Wachigonk Indians growing up?' and he said 'sure.'"

"*I* wouldn't have said 'sure.'" I pointed at Evil, still laughing. "I would have said 'what the heck is a Wachigonk Indian?'"

"Maybe he misheard you. Or maybe he didn't want to admit he didn't remember the names of the local tribes."

"Yeah, but *Wachigonk?*"

"Or maybe," Dad stretched his face out in his bemused-considering-a-hypothetical expression, "he thought *you* were an idiot, and he was humoring you. It was a job interview, after all."

I felt my face go all hot and I shoved the stub of my pizza slice into my mouth to keep from saying anything embarrassing.

Dad shrugged and reached over to squeeze my knee. "I don't care," he said. "We don't have enough work for another lawyer, anyway. He showed up out of nowhere and left his resume this morning, and I figured you might as well talk to him. I thought it might be interesting to you to meet a big city lawyer. That could be you in six or seven years. Besides," he grinned, "Gladys did say that if he spent too much time at the Fun Lanes he'd make all our beer boil."

"That's not going to be me in seven years," I said. "For one thing, I've never had that nice a manicure in my life."

"You know what I mean." Dad looked at me closely. "You gotta think about your future, Bucky."

"I am," I agreed. "I've almost earned my Associate's Degree through the CWI online courses."

"Wow," Evil said. I guess he'd forgotten about my online classes, too. "You almost have your college degree? We still have two years of high school to do."

"Associate's," I said. "Remember? It's no big deal." It was a big deal. I stayed up late at night to do the online work, even over the summer, and since Howard was giving me credit for some of the courses, I was on track to graduate from high school a year early and earn my Associate's at the same time.

"Next step is your Bachelor's." Dad drained his beer. "I want you out of state for that. I'd like to see you in California or New York or somewhere exciting. Your grades, you should get a scholarship."

"There's time enough for that," I said. "First I have to worry about paying for the next pizza."

"Don't worry about that." Evil pointed at the boxes. "There'll be leftovers."

"I'll call Mrs. Wilding first thing in the morning," Dad said. "I can go see her up at the ranch. Then he frowned. "Kind of sad, some of the wills you have to put through probate."

"What do you mean?" I asked. Dad's sentimentality was endearing, but it wasn't his best trait as a lawyer.

"Well, I recall the will favors our client. So that's a good thing. But if I remember right, it's not so great for everyone else."

"Who else is there?"

"There were two kids. Not Marilyn's, kids from a previous marriage. Or relationship, anyway. They grew up and moved away when you were young. The son went off to military school somewhere, I think, which was kind of a surprising move, given what an old hippie Aaron Wilding was. Kids rebel against their parents, I guess. The daughter... I think she went into politics. Or started her own tech company, or something."

"Do you remember their names?" Not that it mattered.

Dad shrugged. "No. Do you have the will?"

Oops. "I left it at the office."

"Right." Dad belched as he stood, up, scattering crumbs on the carpet. At home he sometimes had the manners of an orangutan, but even with his slight gut and his quickly receding hairline, he was a handsome man. For the thousandth time I wondered what Mom had seen in that developer with the helmet head of pomade and the long horns on the front of his Cadillac. I immediately clamped down on the thought, killing it dead. Dad patted down his pockets, looking for keys. "I'll go get it," he said.

"You've had three beers, Dad."

"Jim's had *five*," Evil corrected me.

I hesitated, thinking of the bum. I'd scared him off, but I still wasn't crazy about the idea of driving back to the office alone.

"I'll come with you," Evil said, as if, just this once, he'd read my mind.

"How many beers have *you* had?" I asked him.

"I am a minor," he said, and then belched.

"Right." I stood up and headed back toward my boots and poncho. "I guess that means I'll drive."

CHAPTER
4

"So I'm thinking," Evil said as I drove up the Stub toward Ranch Road, "about how I can prove my love to you."

"Stop right there." I slowed down for a jackrabbit, and then turned onto the highway. "I have a better idea."

"Yeah?"

"Yeah. Finish high school. Go do some college somewhere, go into business."

"I don't know if I'd be good at that."

"Sure you would," I said. "You're dependable, you're a problem solver, and you're persistent. And ten years from now, when you own your own car lot or software company in Spokane, you can marry your secretary."

"Bucky..."

"See, there's one of the problems. To be clear, one of the many problems. You still call me *Bucky*."

"It's your name."

"No, it isn't. My name is *Rebecca*, which is feminine. *Becca* or *Becky* would also be feminine, but *Bucky* isn't. *Bucky* is a kid name. *Bucky* is what you call someone who isn't masculine or feminine."

"Uh... I'm not sure I get it."

"You're not in love with me," I told him. "You're just comfortable around me. I'm like your cousin, and this town is small enough that you think that's a good enough reason to get married."

Evil was silent for a bit. He's not an abstract thinker. We snaked past a trailer park and the Forest Service station.

"I think being comfortable's important," he said. "Comfort, and trust, and you said I was dependable."

"Yep," I agreed. "That's why I like having you as a friend, Evil. That's why Dad doesn't mind if sometimes you crash on our couch or call him *Jim*. But even if you're going to someday decide that's enough of a basis for getting married...don't you think you owe it to yourself to take your time? Don't you wonder if maybe, just maybe, you might fall deliriously in love with some mysterious, dark-eyed woman, and want to marry her?"

"Maybe." Evil pulled a stick of gum from his shirt pocket and popped it into his mouth. "In the meantime, I suppose I'd better freshen my breath."

"Just in case you meet a mysterious, dark-eyed woman tonight at the Fun Lanes?"

"Just in case you decide that as long as I'm a friend, I might as well be a friend with benefits."

"Don't kid yourself." I laughed. "You weren't even a boyfriend with benefits."

I saw the lights of the Comfort Lodge and slowed down. In the dark, it would be way too easy to miss our gravel parking lot and stick the truck into a knot of trees.

"I'll figure you out yet...Becky," Evil said slowly. "I think I've still got time."

"Sorry, time's up." I pulled into the lot and set the parking brake. "We're here."

Turning off the headlights left the gravel lot in a silvery-blue pool of starlight, with just a splash of moon from the thin waxing crescent. I found the Fun Lanes key on my ring as I crossed the parking lot.

"Beer lights burned out," Evil said behind me. "Both of 'em."

I looked up and saw he was right. McCrae's—the bar—had a Coors neon light in one window and a Budweiser in another. Both were dark.

"Good eye, detective," I said.

He kicked at the gravel modestly. "First rule of deer hunting.

Keep a close watch on the beer."

"Probably a power surge. The box is in the office, I'll check the fuses there." I stepped onto the boardwalk and froze.

The wood of the doorframe next to the lock had been ripped out. It looked as if someone had taken a crowbar and a hatchet to it at the same time, and I could see the exposed deadbolt. "Nuts," I said. I wondered if it might have been the kids from St. Joe's. I could probably give Sheriff Sutherland a decent description of most of them. "Well, I hope the electricity gave out first, and all the beer they stole was warm."

"Bucky," Evil said.

I opened the door.

Something crashed into me, moving fast and hard. In the darkness I saw nothing except a shadow that exploded out of the open door. The shadow barreled me to the ground and then flashed left, away from the road and toward the river.

"Hey!" Evil chased the running shadow.

I rolled to my feet. My head hurt, and I was sucking hard to get cold air back into my lungs, but I was wearing my poncho and it had padded me against the worst of the blow. Light, I thought. I needed to get the lights back up, and maybe put a pot of coffee on while I waited for the sheriff department to show up.

I stepped into the dark cavern of the Fun Lanes.

The main fuse had definitely been tripped; the clock faces and vending machines and safety lights that were normally always on were dark. I hoped Evil caught the jerk who'd done this and gave him a black eye.

I moved beyond the bowling alley to the office. As I pushed the office door open, a voice in the darkness beyond hissed at me.

"McCrae!"

Bang! Bang! Bang! Gunshots, in the office. I saw the flashes and confused silhouettes, and then something heavy hit the floor. A burning smell—sort of like firecrackers, but not quite—filled the enclosed space of the office.

An adrenaline surge filled my body. My heart roared inside me. *Holy crap-holy crap-holy crap—I'm going to die!*

I threw myself to the ground, expecting more shots, but they never came. Something clattered on the floor next to me, and then the office's back door slammed open and starlight flooded in.

For a moment, framed against the starlight, I saw the shooter. I couldn't see his face, but I got a clear look at his body. He wore a khaki shirt, black pants, a utility belt with flashlight and pistol, and badges that identified him by his job.

It was a Howard County Deputy Sheriff's uniform.

Then he disappeared.

I scooted forward to get behind the shelter of the desk, my entire body trembling.

Feet thudded, the deputy running away.

I hoped Evil would get him. But Evil was chasing the other guy. And if they had guns, Evil catching up to one of them might be bad news for Evil.

In the darkness I put my hand on something warm. It took me only a moment to realize it was a pistol, and I wrapped my fingers around the grip.

It was a semi-automatic, like Dad's desk gun, and it felt natural in my hand. I popped up from behind the desk, pointing the gun at the door. The deputy was gone, and that was a good thing. I was shaking like a gum wrapper in a hurricane, and if I'd had to pull the trigger I'd have missed for sure. I'd never had to pull a gun on another person in my life before, and now I'd done it twice in one evening.

I edged around the desk and poked my head out the door. I saw the aspens and scrub bushes whose names I didn't know clustered around the top of the slope; I saw the concrete flagstones that made a slightly irregular path to the parking lot and the highway along the side of the building; no sign of the deputy.

I found the fuse box. In the dark I fumbled around a lot, and for a moment I worried I'd shoot the box and start a fire, but the box's cover was open and after a few moments of prodding with my fingers I found that the main switch was flipped. I snapped it the other way, and the dull green light of the clock face on the wall smudged back into existence.

I shut the door.

Then I remembered that something heavy had fallen to the ground.

"Hold still," I said. I tried to make my voice as hard and cold as I could, but I knew I wasn't doing a very good job. I edged back around to the door and hit the light switch.

The lights in the office are fluorescent tubes, so they flickered a few moments as they came in. The gray snapping light made the office look surreal. I saw the room as if I was seeing it in black and white and through really old film, and the puddle on the floor was black.

Lying on his side in the puddle was the crazy-eyed bum in the corduroy jacket.

"Holy crap!" I shouted.

He said nothing and didn't move.

"Mister!" I prodded him with a toe. "You awake?"

I felt for his pulse at his neck, and found nothing. I held my hand in front of his mouth and nose and felt no breath.

He was dead.

I looked at the gun in my hand.

It was a Beretta, like Dad's.

Just like Dad's.

"Oh no," I said. "No, no, no."

I circled the desk. I watched where I was walking, but I saw that in the dark I had already stepped in the bum's blood and left clear boot prints in the carpet.

The pistol drawer was open and empty.

I looked at the bum again. My mind spun around like a Fourth of July pinwheel rocket, and I forced myself to try to think, focus, notice details. The bum lay on his side, but his lower back was bloody. He had blood on his face too, and on the back of his head. He looked as if he'd been beaten up, quite apart from the shooting. I drew aside a fold of corduroy with the pistol and saw three bullet holes in the jacket, over the small of his back.

He'd been shot in the back. It hadn't been self-defense. He'd been murdered. He'd been murdered in my Dad's office...*my* office. Why? I drew a gigantic blank. He'd been murdered, and my fingerprints were all over the murder weapon, which was a gun I had access to, and my footprints were in his blood.

And he'd been killed by a cop. Maybe by two cops.

Holy crap, I looked guilty.

"Bucky!"

The voice was Evil's, and he was calling from the bowling alley. At least they hadn't killed him, but whatever relief I felt from that realization was overshadowed by the thought that I couldn't let Evil see me like this.

I opened the door and slipped out the back.

"Bucky? I mean...Becky?" I heard him call again.

I ran. Up the flagstone walk, as fast as I could go, and I was almost to the corner of the building before it occurred to me I should be keeping an eye out for the cops, but if they weren't gone they stayed hidden. I pressed myself against the edge of the building, in shadow, as a pair of headlights cruised by.

I was still holding the gun, and I stared at it in shock. It was evidence, but I didn't know if it was evidence that might prove I was innocent, or if it would only be used against me. I almost threw the pistol into the woods before a smarter, calmer part of my brain pointed out that that was the worst of all worlds—the gun would be found, and once the police took fingerprints off it, it would be obvious I was the one who had tried to hide it.

"Becky!"

Evil was still inside the office, and didn't know where I was. I ran.

Across the parking lot, into the truck. Chucked the Beretta into the glove compartment with the .38. Started the engine and rumbled onto the highway, with no idea what in the world I was going to do.

CHAPTER
5

I drove the opposite direction from home, by instinct. I'm not sure I can explain why, except to say that if I was in trouble—and it sure felt like I was—then I didn't want to bring the trouble down on Dad, too.

But that meant I was driving into downtown Howard. I was shaking so bad that I drifted into the wrong lane more than once, so it was a good thing it was late at night, and people were mostly in bed.

Though there would be cops out all night. Howard County deputy sheriffs, the only law enforcement that Howard has, unless you counted the Fish and Game folks. And one of those deputy sheriffs had just shot and killed a man in Dad's office.

And, it occurred to me only as I was stopped at a light in the middle of Howard, I was driving the world's worst getaway car. Not very fast, not particularly good at off-roading, and completely unmistakable.

I'll admit I felt like crying, but only for a second. Then something inside me slapped something else inside me in the face and said, *Cowgirl up, sister. Freaking out will only get you shot.*

I needed to start making better decisions.

I watched the red light and took deep breaths. I needed protection. In a movie, I'd maybe run to the feds if I thought the state police were criminals, but there weren't any feds in Howard County. I wasn't sure, but I thought the FBI's nearest Field Office might be Salt Lake City or Seattle. An APB would surely go out with a description of my truck, and I'd never make it. I could hitchhike, but I still didn't like my chances, and I didn't think I'd feel safe thumbing a ride from some trucker.

Dad...I tried, but I didn't see how Dad could help me.

I had to turn myself in, but not to just anyone.

When the light turned green I had made up my mind. I drove a few more blocks and then turned into the parking lot of the SuperMart. It had closed at midnight, so I knew the lights would be off and no one inside. I parked behind the building, sliding the truck in between a dumpster and the wall so no casual passerby on the street could see it.

I needed to take the Beretta. It was evidence, and bringing it with me would be a sign of my good faith. Also, maybe I hadn't totally wiped out the fingerprints of the shooter. I dug around under the seat, found a bandanna that wasn't too greasy, and wrapped the Beretta inside it. I also took the .38.

So there I was, in the middle of the night, walking around Howard with a gun in each hand. For once, I wished I had a purse; even my school bag would have been convenient. I had to hope no one would stop and ask me what was under my poncho.

But I had chosen my parking spot carefully. Behind the SuperMart was a dirt lane that led between little wood bungalows, the original classic Howard-style home, down to the river. I kept a careful eye on the houses, and other than a couple of blue television glows, there was no sign of life. I stayed pressed up against one wall to keep out of the light of the rising moon and crept down to the river.

At this point the river was a park, mostly undeveloped except for a broad dirt jogging path and a few benches. A mile farther along was a picnic area with tables and swings for the kids, but I turned in the other direction, heading for Wood Duck Island.

Wood Duck Island was where Sheriff Sutherland lived. I couldn't be sure it was safe to go to him, it was a gamble. If there was a plot involving the sheriff department, he might be in on it. But I was pretty sure it wasn't him I'd seen in the office doorway, and I thought he liked Dad. They were shooting buddies, for the same reason Dad tried to be golfing buddies or fishing buddies with all the businessmen in the county—professional connections generated legal work.

My phone buzzed. I awkwardly held both pistols in one hand and checked my messages.

Evil: *Where are you? I'm worried.*

I had to tuck a pistol under my arm to work the phone with one thumb; I didn't want to stop moving. *I'm fine. I'll explain later.*

There was no immediate answer and I trudged on, stepping over the branches and trying to keep quiet. Rustling sounds in the woods around me made me slightly nervous, though I knew they had to be made by squirrels. Evil: *Say something only you and me would know.*

I considered. *I hate The Last of the Mohicans.*

Lol, okay. Be careful. This place is crawling with cops. I think I'm a suspect.

Did you catch the guy?

Nope. Never saw his face, either. Where are you?

Obviously, I couldn't answer that question, because one of the deputies might take Evil's phone. I also wanted to type in *Am I a suspect?*, but I didn't. It wouldn't help Evil, and it wouldn't help me, either. Instead, I put my phone back in my pocket.

And heard a loud *CRACK* behind me.

I whipped around so fast I dropped the Beretta. I kept hold of the revolver, and managed to get it out from under my poncho and pointed in the right direction.

I didn't see anyone. That didn't mean much, because the path wound in and out of the trees, and someone could have been standing on the path thirty feet from me and still hidden from view. Or the sound could have been made by a deer.

I crouched to pick up the Beretta, still in the bandanna, trying not to take my eyes off the woods. I half-wished I had told Evil where I was; at least then, if I was killed, someone would know where to find my body. Or if I disappeared, they'd know where to start looking.

"I have a gun," I said. "So if your idea of a funny joke is to jump out and yell *boo* at me, I suggest you pick someone else for your entertainment."

Silence, except for the gurgling of the river.

I backed up, watching the trail, until I had taken a curve or two and was starting to feel confident that the sound must have been made by an animal. Then I turned and walked on to Wood Duck Island. I walked faster, and I kept the gun out and ready.

Wood Duck Island isn't an island. It's a fancy neighborhood on the river, gated at the front, and lived in by some of Howard County's most prominent residents. I knew which house was his because I'd been over once or twice, with Dad. The sheriff liked to sit inside his home with the windows open and shoot squirrels in his backyard with a .22. He found it even more amusing with company.

I stepped over a muddy little stream and pushed through a stand of aspens to move into that backyard now. I hid the revolver under my poncho again. Getting mistaken for a burglar and shot was not my plan.

Lights were on upstairs in the Sutherlands' house, and in the kitchen. I crossed the narrow strip of grass and just as I reached the steps up to the back porch, a light snapped on. It was strong and white, and shone right down on the steps.

Oops. Motion sensor-activated. That was fine, though; I wasn't trying to hide from the sheriff, and the trees were thick enough to screen me from his neighbors. I tucked one pistol under my arm again, walked up to the back door past the pool and the barbecue, raised my hand to knock—and almost jumped out of my skin.

Someone stood inside the door watching me. The person was in shadow, so it took me a moment to recognize her as Carol Sutherland, the sheriff's wife. She was tall and graceful, and she was wearing a black robe with flowers embroidered into the shoulders. Just as I realized who she was, she flicked a switch to turn on more porch lights, and I was totally illuminated. It might as well have been day. I looked over my shoulder; if someone had been following me in the woods, he could see me clearly now.

She opened the door, one hand down at her side, and looked at me with piercing eyes over a pair of thin reading glasses. "You're Jim McCrae's daughter, aren't you?"

She knew me from my occasional visits, but she'd also seen me at school—Carol Sutherland was an EMT for the county, and a couple of times a year she'd come into Howard High to teach an assembly or a health class about CPR or the Heimlich maneuver.

"Yes, ma'am," I said, looking as respectful and not-weird as I possibly could, given that I was standing on her back porch wearing a poncho in the dead of night. The pistol in my hand and the one tucked against my ribs both felt heavy. "Rebecca. Is Sheriff Sutherland here?"

She looked over my shoulder at the woods. "You must need help. Come on inside." She stepped back to make room for me.

I hesitated. "There's something I need to show you first," I said. "I just want you to know what I'm holding, and I don't want to surprise you."

"Tell you what." She raised her hand and I saw that she was holding a taser. "If you do surprise me, I'll try really hard not to surprise you back."

I moved slow, easing both guns out from under the poncho.

Carol Sutherland laughed. "Honey, if *guns* were enough to put me off my breakfast, I'd be living in a different state and married to a different man." She put the taser away in the pocket of her robe and led me into the kitchen. It was lovely, with high-end appliances, a stone floor, and deep counters. The whole home was about ten times as much house as Dad and I lived in, both for size and for being fancy.

I breathed a sigh of relief. "This one I need to give to the sheriff. It might be evidence." She took the Beretta, holding it carefully in the bandanna, and put it in a drawer. "This one..." I didn't know quite what to say.

"You've had a rough night," Carol suggested. "You brought this one along just in case. Is someone following you?"

"I'm not sure." I shot a glance out the back windows. The whole ground floor wall of the Sutherlands' home seemed to be glass, and I felt very visible. "Could you maybe shut some drapes or something?"

"If I shut the drapes, we won't be able to see anyone who's out there. I've got a better idea." She hit several switches on the kitchen wall; the kitchen itself went dark, and the back yard lit up like a football stadium on game night. "There," she said. "Now you and I are invisible, and the creep following you has nowhere to hide."

"Thanks. Will your neighbors complain about the lights?"

"Let them." Carol Sutherland wasn't done. She whistled once, sharply, and two big German Shepherds padded into the room. She opened the back door, let them out, and then locked it behind them as they rushed into the woods, barking joyously. Finally, she reached into a broom closet and came out with a pump-action shotgun.

"Much better," she said. "Now let's sit down and chat, and see what the dogs turn up."

We sat.

"Thanks," I said again.

She shrugged off my gratitude. "If one of my daughters ran up to Jim McCrae's house in the middle of the night because she was being chased, I'd be downright disappointed if Jim didn't get out his shotgun and sit a little watch."

"I guess the sheriff's not here?" I tried to sound casual about it, though I wasn't sure why. It had been a very un-casual evening.

"He got called out. He'll be back."

I nodded. "I think that might have to do with me. What he got called out for."

"Shall I send him a message?" Carol Sutherland was astonishingly calm, given that I'd shown up on her doorstep armed.

"Please don't. I...I can't really explain, but if I can wait here for him, I would appreciate it."

Her voice softened. "Does your father know what's happening?"

"I'll tell him," I promised. "I just need to talk to Sheriff Sutherland first."

"Coffee while we wait?"

I shook my head. Yawned. The inside of the Sutherlands' house was toasty, especially after the chill of the jogging path and the river. Their couch was deep and comfortable, and my poncho felt more and more like a blanket every second. But I was wide awake, still charged full of adrenaline and trembling. I wasn't worried that I'd fall asleep, I was worried that if I had to shoot I wouldn't be able to shoot straight. And that Sheriff Sutherland wouldn't believe me and I might get blamed for the murder. And if I didn't get blamed, the people who really did commit the murder might come after me because I was a witness. And Evil might get in trouble, and all because of me.

I woke up to the booming sound of Sheriff Sutherland's voice in the darkness.

"Carol tells me you have something to do with the evening's mayhem, Bucky, so which is it? Are you the killer or the burglar?"

CHAPTER
6

I sat bolt upright. The gun wasn't in my hand, but a few feet away from me on the couch. That was a good thing; in my sudden surprise, I might have shot the sheriff. And not in a cool Reggae way. Instead, I wiped a dribble of sleep-slobber off my cheek and made noises that sounded like animal snorts.

"Take your time," Sheriff Sutherland said.

It was still night, and the backyard lights were on. In the indirect white glow, I could see the sheriff's face. Doug Sutherland was a redhead going gray, with bristly hair like a brush and a broad face that could go from scowling to open laughter in split nothing flat. He perched now on the edge of one of his couches, leaning forward and nursing a paper cup of coffee. One of his big Stetson hats sat on the cushion next to him.

"Ugh," I said, rubbing sleep out of my eyes. "Sorry, I've had a bad night. Who got burgled?"

Sheriff Sutherland frowned. "Huh." He set down the coffee. "See, I'd have figured you for the burglar, not the shooter."

"I guess Carol didn't tell you yet about the gun."

"Nope. She likes to surprise me. What gun?"

I hesitated. "Are you alone?"

"Carol's upstairs. No one else in the house. You going to confess?"

"I'm not going to confess," I said. "I'm innocent."

"Well, that's a relief. So I won't arrest you, then. Tell me about the gun."

"It's Dad's Beretta. Someone used it to shoot a man tonight. Not me. But I was there. I...I picked up the gun. Sort of accidentally. Sort of to defend myself. And then I realized I was holding a murder weapon, and I panicked. So I ran. When I could think straight, I came here." I meant my explanation to be complete and calm, but it came out in fits and starts and as I heard it myself I realized it posed more questions than it answered.

The sheriff nodded. "Glad you did. Why not come to my office? Sneaking up through someone's backyard is a good way to get shot in this neighborhood."

I remembered the silhouetted head, the deputy's uniform. "Sheriff, I saw the shooter. He was one of your deputies."

The sheriff's expression, which had been slowly relaxing, snapped into a hard slab. "That's a serious accusation."

A wave of doubt slammed into me so hard it took my breath. I had felt comfortable coming here because Dad knew the Sutherlands, and also because I had been pretty sure that the silhouetted head I'd seen in Dad's office door hadn't belonged to the sheriff. Suddenly, I was much less confident. I looked about in the darkness, groping for my next move. "I'm...not sure. He was wearing the uniform."

"You're worried I'm dirty," Sheriff Sutherland said.

"What?" I turned my head back around and focused on him. I couldn't tell if he meant it as a joke or not.

"You're looking at the furniture and you're thinking, how does this shmuck get such a nice house working for the county? On a sheriff's salary, by rights he ought to be out there with the sagebillies making his own whisky in a can and heating microwave burritos on a hot plate."

"No," I said, but the image of Sheriff Sutherland hunkered over a hot plate almost made me laugh. "Besides, I think the sagebillies go in more for the crystal meth."

"You know this is my second career, right?" he asked.

"I didn't know that."

"I used to be an investment banker. You probably know what that is, you're a smart kid."

"You did deals." I didn't really know what an investment banker was, but I knew they made a lot of money and didn't live in Howard County. And I vaguely knew that they did big, fancy deals. Mergers and acquisitions, initial public offerings, and that sort of thing. I didn't know any details because it wasn't the sort of business that anyone would ever bring to the Law Offices of James F. McCrae.

"Made a lot of money," he said. "But my job satisfaction was low, so I quit and moved to Howard."

"Okay," I said slowly. I wasn't sure where this was going, but I felt myself relax a little bit as he talked.

"You know what drove my job satisfaction down, Bucky?" He squinted at me, and his mouth twitched a little at one corner.

"Long hours?" I guessed.

"I work longer hours *here!*" He snorted. "Nope, that was a job with great pay, full benefits, travel, respect, and excitement. There was just one thing wrong with it."

"They wouldn't let you wear a hat?"

"Damn fools wouldn't ever let me shoot anybody. Not even just a tiny bit. Not even when they deserved it, which was most of the time."

I laughed out loud.

"Look." He leaned closer to me, and dropped his voice to just above a whisper. "I like catching bad guys. Even when I don't get to knock holes in 'em. It's what I do, it's what I'm good at. Help me out here, huh? Tell me exactly what you saw."

I nodded. "I was in the office. It was dark. I heard three shots, then the door opened, and I saw the shooter in the doorway before he ran off."

"Still dark inside? So how good a look did you get?"

I shook my head. "I could see he was wearing a deputy sheriff's uniform. But I couldn't see his face."

"But you must be pretty sure it wasn't me, for instance."

"No offense, but..." I wished I had a better way to say it. "Your head is too big. Also, your hair is bristly, like a shoe brush. This guy had curlier hair, and more...combed."

Sheriff Sutherland laughed. "First time in my life I'm grateful to be told I have a big head." He sipped the coffee again. "Okay, so at some point you picked up the gun."

"It was stupid," I blurted.

"It was certainly sub-optimal," he agreed. "What were you thinking?"

"It was an accident at first." I tried to remember. I was tired, and the night's events had moved so fast. "I'd come into the office to get papers for Dad, and the lights were off—the main breaker had flipped. I heard the shots, really close, in the same room with me, and then a sound that must have been the body falling, and then a sound that must have been the gun being dropped. I saw the...the deputy, and I tried to hide. My hand touched the gun in the darkness. I realized it was a gun, so I picked it up in case I needed it."

Sheriff Sutherland tilted his head back and forth like he was weighing the case. "It may have muddied some evidence," he decided, "but I'm glad you took the gun. Better to have your fingerprints on a murder weapon than to confront a murderer unarmed."

"Thanks," I said.

"Notice anything else about the shooter?"

"Nothing."

"Did you see a car that might have been his? Or hear one?"

"Nope." Then I remembered my conversation with Michael Fellows from that afternoon, about serving court papers in the backcountry. "Not a horse, either."

Sutherland chuckled. "Fair enough. What time would you say you entered the office?"

"Eleven-thirty?"

"Anyone else with you? Anybody who can corroborate your story?"

"Evil. I mean, Ronald Patten."

Sutherland harrumphed. "I know Evil." There was no way the Pattens and the Sutherlands socialized, so I wondered how the sheriff knew Evil Patten. Must have busted him for something.

"He came with me because...because I had to get some papers, and didn't want to do it alone. Because earlier tonight, when I was locking up, I was harassed in the parking lot."

"By anybody in particular?"

"By the guy who got shot in Dad's office. And there was another guy. When we first got to the office, someone came charging out. Evil chased him. And then I went into the office." Wow, this was really coming out in a jumble. "I didn't get a good look at him."

The sheriff nodded. "So...you, Evil, a guy with no description who ran away, and one of my deputies, identity unknown. I think I've just about got my arms around this thing."

"And the bum," I said.

"Bum?"

"The dead guy."

"Ah. The dead guy was Charlie Herbert. He was a queer old hippie, no doubt about it, but he wasn't a bum. Worked for Aaron Wilding, apparently. Must have been a software programmer."

"He seemed...stoned."

"He might have been. I guess the coroner'll tell us. Or he might have been upset because his boss just died and he was out of a job."

"I guess I shouldn't really complain about my day."

"You've had it rough enough. Look, it's too early to tell whether one of my deputies is really crooked. I'll see who was on duty last night, and do some poking around. If it was one of my guys responding to a B and E and accidentally shooting Herbert, I would know it already. On the other hand, maybe the shooter was wearing something that only looked like one of our uniforms in the dark. I'll do some digging, and what we do next will depend on what I find. Might be a line-up, see if you can identify the shooter. By the curliness of the hair on his tiny head."

"I have to tell Dad I'm okay."

"Let me do it," Sutherland said. "I'll tell him I've got you in protective custody, but I won't tell him where...just in case. You stay here, and you stay inside. Got it?"

"Got it," I said, and then curiosity got the better of me. "Who got burgled?"

The sheriff chuckled. "You're not all that shaken up, I see. Well, since you'll probably read about it in the *Register* day after tomorrow, I don't mind telling you it was the District Court. Some jackass messed the place up. Judge Ybarra is going to be really irritated in an hour or two."

"Why would anyone break into the court?"

"One thing you'll see more clearly as you grow older," Sheriff Sutherland said, creaking to his feet, "is that the world is full of dipshits. Every few years someone breaks into a bank somewhere 'cause he imagines if he burns the paper copy of his mortgage, he won't owe any more money on his house. This is probably the same thing...some clown thinks that if he steals his folder out of Judge Ybarra's filing cabinet, he won't have a criminal record anymore."

"There's a logic to that."

"Yep." He picked up his hat. "But it's the logic of morons. I figure I'll start with recent meth convictions. I suppose I should be grateful the fool didn't just light the place on fire." He gestured at the ceiling with his hat. "We got a guest room upstairs. We keep it ready in case any of our daughters drops by unannounced, you should find it comfortable enough. It's the room with the light on and the towels on the bed. I want you to plan on staying here at least through tomorrow, and keep upstairs so you're out of sight. I know you've got a phone, so I want you to stay off MySpace or Twitter or wherever it is you kids play electronic footsie these days, and don't tell anyone where you are. If it looks like you need to stay here past tomorrow, I'll get you some changes of clothes. Got it?"

"Got it."

"Now you go get some sleep. I've got to make a few calls and maybe say a brief hello to my friend Jack Daniels before I get any shuteye myself. Most likely I won't see you in the morning, but Carol or I'll make sure there's food upstairs for you."

"Thanks," I said.

"Thank *you*. You did flee the scene of a crime, but you did the right thing, coming to me instead of running home or skipping town."

He disappeared into a doorway beneath a moose head, shutting the door behind him, and I went upstairs. The guest room must have been their youngest daughter's, because it was still decorated like a teenager's bedroom, though the pop idols on the walls were now five years out of fashion, as were the Vogues and Cosmos stacked in the corner. The room had its own bathroom, but I was too tired to wash my face or even get under the blankets. I threw myself onto a zebra-striped pillow and fell fast asleep, still in my boots and poncho.

The room was still dark when my phone buzzed me awake with a text. It was from Dad: *Don't answer me, kiddo. Glad you're okay.*

I drifted back asleep. When the phone buzzed again the cold gray light of morning shone through the window. Evil: *Get out of there! Fast! You're in danger!*

CHAPTER
7

I stared at the phone for a few seconds, numb. It buzzed again.

Rebecca, wake up! Are you there? Are you okay?

I managed to thumb in a short message: *What's wrong?*

No time to explain. Get out of there!

The words cut through the fog of my brain like a lighthouse beam. In my mind's eye I saw the silhouetted deputy in the office door, and heard Sheriff Sutherland telling me not to go anywhere or talk to anyone. Was he keeping me safe...or keeping me prisoner?

I sat up and looked at the door. It was shut, and I didn't see light underneath it. I crept over to it and listened, grateful that the Sutherlands' house was new enough that the floor didn't creak.

Nothing. The house was quiet. Maybe they were asleep.

Or maybe Carol was standing guard at my door with a shotgun while the sheriff gathered his accomplices. Or dug a hole to hide my body in. But that was crazy, wasn't it?

The sheriff wasn't the man with the smaller head and curly hair... but there had been a second man, a man I hadn't seen. That could have been Doug Sutherland.

Doug Sutherland, who had been anxious to explain to me that he wasn't dirty, and who hadn't wanted me to contact Dad.

Rebecca!

I shoved the phone into my pocket and sneaked over to the window. My feet ached from sleeping in my boots, and I could see that I'd soiled the guest bed's quilt with dirt from my soles, but I was glad not to have to be lacing up my footgear now.

The window slid up smoothly, with very little sound. Below, the narrow yard and the woods were still, blue-gray in the morning light. I could hear the river running back beyond the trees, but didn't see or hear sign of any person, or of the Sutherlands' dogs.

I climbed out the window, easing myself softly onto the shingles covering the roof over the Sutherlands' wraparound porch. I closed the window, wishing I could latch it. At least, I thought, if anyone came looking for me, they wouldn't *immediately* guess I'd gone out this way.

Which was a paranoid thought. But you can be paranoid and right.

I took a moment to plan. If I went left, I'd pass in front of the Sutherlands' bedroom window. The drop in front of me was a little higher than I was comfortable with. So I went right. Somewhere on the street in front of the house I heard the sound of car engines— people of Wood Duck Island driving off to their businesses or jobs. At the end of the building I found myself looking at the top of the Sutherlands' Winnebago.

Perfect. I stepped onto the roof of the RV—paused as the wimpy metal of the rooftop dimpled in and made a single loud *poink!*—then let myself down the ladder in the back, and I was standing on solid earth again. Or a poured concrete pad, anyway, that ran along the side of the garage and had hookups for the motor home. No dogs barked, and I started to breathe easier.

Get out! my phone buzzed.

I didn't need the reminder. I checked the front yard to make sure no one was standing in it and no police cars were parked in front. All clear; the street's big rambling houses were dark and quiet, their SUVs mostly still snoozing in their driveways. Then I walked up the street, away from the Sutherlands' house at an angle I hoped would keep me out of view of the house's windows.

Though suddenly I remembered the cracking branch in the darkness of the jogging path, and wondered whether I was making a wise choice.

And then I realized I'd left the pistol—both pistols—in the Sutherlands' house.

I stopped, feeling totally exposed in this neighborhood of million-dollar houses. I pressed myself against a scabby pine trunk and considered. I could still go back, I thought. I could climb up the RV, across the roof, and probably lever up the window.

And then I couldn't remember where I'd left the revolver. Carol had put the Beretta in the kitchen drawer, but had I left the .38 on the couch downstairs, or had I carried it up with me? I didn't know. Did I dare creep around the house looking for it?

My phone buzzed again, but before I could look to see what Evil was saying, the Sutherlands' garage door rumbled into action.

I turned and ran.

The house next-door to the Sutherlands' was fenced with wrought iron, but beyond that was a vacant lot, hard clay-filled dirt and pebbles but without the contractor debris of fast-food wrappers and beer bottles that you usually see on vacant lots around Howard. I turned left and skedaddled across the lot and into the woods.

The jogging trail crossed the back of the lot, but I skipped right over it, thinking nervous thoughts about the night before and the possibility of still being followed. I crashed through a grove of pines and around a blackberry bramble before I stopped, crouching down beside a boulder and straining my ears to find out if I'd been followed.

Birds chirping, and the low rumble of the river.

Evil. I checked my phone. *Tell whatever lie you need to, or sneak out if you can. Meet me at St. Matthew's.*

St. Matthew's was one of three Catholic churches in town; Howard County had a fair number of Catholics, what with the French and the Basque history of the area, and more recent immigration from Mexico and Central America. There were plenty of Hispanic kids at Howard High, and it wasn't cool to ask what anybody's immigration status was. Sometimes when they needed help with their paperwork, those kids and their families came to the Law Offices of James F. McCrae. And on Sundays, the ones who lived south of Howard, around the clump of warehouses, gas stations, and crumbling office park space sometimes called the Dog Ears after the two electric pylons straddling the highway there, they went to St. Matthew's to pray and hear the good word from Father Rojas.

Coming, I typed into the phone. *Keep your pants on.*

Hat, I immediately thought. I should have typed *hat*. No need to encourage the poor guy in his delusions.

It was a two-mile walk to Dog Ears. I was grateful for my boots, but the feet inside them felt like chicken breasts that had been pounded flat with a hammer and were now ready for breading and mozzarella cheese, so my walk started as a limp. I kept my hands under my poncho, holding my phone so I'd be sure to feel it when it buzzed. I also had the probably totally pointless hope that if anybody was thinking about attacking me, they'd wonder if I was holding a gun under the poncho and think twice.

Crazy, right? But that's where my head was.

I followed the river. After Wood Duck Island the houses disappeared and I tramped through the tall yellow grass of late summer. Low bumps of earth, rises too small to be called hills, hid me from Howard as I hiked. Two miles would mean forty minutes of walking, even with me pushing myself, so I tried to focus and use the time to think.

Three men had been in Dad's office last night. I didn't know whether they'd come there together or separately. I didn't know *why* they'd come there at all. They'd have had to break in, so it couldn't have been accident or coincidence. They wanted something from Dad. I didn't know whether one of the men, or maybe two, were Howard County deputy sheriffs. I didn't know why the one in uniform had shot the bum.

Not the bum, I thought. Charlie Herbert, who worked for Aaron Wilding.

But did I really know that? Sheriff Sutherland had told me that, but now I was terribly afraid I'd make a mistake confiding in the sheriff. He'd said he wasn't dirty, he'd said he would investigate, but so what? Maybe he'd lied through his teeth the entire time. Maybe he was just waiting for a chance to get rid of me quietly. He couldn't exactly shoot me in his own house, not without attracting a lot of attention, anyway. Except, of course, that I was in his house armed, with my fingerprints all over a gun that had already killed someone that same night.

Or maybe the sheriff was dirty, but his wife wasn't. I remembered her sending out the dogs and sitting watch over me, and found it hard to believe she would want to kill me. So he'd needed to wait until later to shoot me, get rid of the witness who knew that one of his deputies had murdered a man. Shot him in the back, and maybe on the sheriff's orders.

I should tell someone else. Just in case.

I typed in a text to Evil. *The guy in Dad's office last night. I think he was a deputy.*

Evil: *The killer, you mean?*

Me: *Yeah. Don't tell anyone for now.* My fingers were cold and numb, though the sun was inching above the Ups and I began to feel sweaty in my poncho. *Just in case...I wanted someone to know.*

Evil: *Jeepers. Be careful.*

Of course, Carol Sutherland might have been watching over me to make sure I didn't escape.

But what would Sheriff Sutherland or his deputies want from Dad that they couldn't just ask for? And why kill Charlie Herbert, if that was his name? Was he just in the wrong place at the wrong time? I felt a twinge of guilt, thinking maybe the wild-eyed computer programmer had come back to the office to see me, and had been shot for his trouble.

But maybe he'd just been wandering around stoned, or out of his mind, and got himself shot by accident. *Bears and balloons*, he'd said.

I saw the electric poles first, poking up over the rise. I climbed out of the river behind Max's, a gas station and rest stop popular with truckers. It had a shower and bunk facility inside; outside, the pavilion over its pumps was tall enough to accommodate a full-sized tractor-trailer, and a triple-sized parking lot held semis lined up neatly, waiting while their drivers were inside.

I scanned for police cars once, and then kept my eyes on the ground. I crossed the parking lot and then Reservoir Road and then I was shuffling past one of Howard's genuine trailer parks. With our almost nonexistent zoning, there were plenty of trailers, pre-fab houses, corrugated metal sheds and other low-end buildings around town, and Serendipity Gates wasn't nearly the worst of it. Serendipity Gates had small lawns and big cottonwood trees, and as trailer parks go, it was pretty genteel. Genteel, and mostly Mexican. A kid at school named Antonio once told me an entire village in Oaxaca relocated to Serendipity Gates, and I don't think he was exaggerating.

On the other side of the trailer park was St. Matthew's. The church was built of brick, had been one of Howard County's first brick buildings, in fact, back before there had been much of a town at all. It was small, but big enough to stretch out in the cross-armed shape the Catholics like to build their churches in. Behind the church was the little building where I assumed Father Rojas lived, along with a shed and a scraggly patch of lawn.

I leaned against a cottonwood, keeping the trunk between myself and the highway. I dug out my phone. Still had a solid charge—that was because all I did was send text messages, which didn't use a lot of battery.

Where are you? I texted.

Inside.

I was definitely sweating now, and the sun stabbed me in the eyes as I moved up the walk to the front door of the church. A tile mosaic in a recess to the left of the double door showed a balding man with long hair down to his shoulders. He sat writing at a desk, and behind him, with arms spread wide like he was ready for a hug, stood a winged and haloed angel.

I was a little surprised to find the door unlocked, though I suppose if you wanted the church to be a welcoming safe haven, being open most of the time probably made sense. And it wasn't like St. Matthew's had a lot to steal—the inside was pretty Spartan, none of the gold and velvet you'd imagine from seeing the *Godfather* movies. There was a stone basin of water, a table in a corner with some pamphlets on it, wooden benches with kneelers, and an altar.

No sign of Evil.

What gives? I texted. *St. Matthew's, right?*

Side chapel. On the right.

If Father Rojas found me, I'd tell him I came to pray. I skirted the benches and came to the little space on the right side. It wasn't quite its own room, but the right arm of the cross that the building's floor plan made. I knew this part of the building had its own name, but I couldn't remember what it was. There was a wooden statue of the Virgin Mary in an alcove in the back wall, with an iron rack in front of her holding lots of stubby votive candles. Only one of them was lit.

I was about to text Evil again when I noticed that the single burning candle sat next to a little rectangle of plastic. A card. I picked it up and saw that it was a driver's license. *Ronald E. Patten*, it said.

Evil? I asked.

In response, a picture appeared in the stream of my text conversation. It was a picture of Evil, wearing the same flannel shirt and *Marines Never Die* t-shirt he'd worn the day before. He sat inside a bathtub; his hands were behind him and he had a strip of cloth tied through his mouth as a gag.

This isn't funny, Evil, I told him. My hands trembled.

This isn't Evil. Pay close attention, now. You're going to do exactly as I say.

CHAPTER
8

My hands shook so bad I couldn't spell. *Pkay,* I typed. *Okay. Dont hrut him!*

That's what I get for turning off autocorrect.

I'm watching you, came the next message. *You try to talk to the cops, or your dad, or anyone else, your pal gets it. Understood?*

Understood. Did that mean he wasn't a cop? Or just that the entire Howard County Sheriff Department wasn't dirty? I had to assume the latter, or I might run and turn myself into the bad guy, or his accomplice. I tried to force myself to think. Couldn't I call Dad? Shouldn't I? But what would Dad do, except call the cops? And if I couldn't trust them, all I was doing by involving Dad was risking his life.

Go outside.

I obeyed. The day was becoming warm. Kids in the trailer park shouted as they played soccer on a patch of dirt and trucks rumbled in and out of the gas station, leaving a faint diesel stink in the air.

What do you want? I asked.

Follow Reservoir Road up into the hills. Don't call or text anybody. If anyone offers you a ride, say no thanks. You're enjoying a nice hike.

I looked up at the beginning of the Ups, yellow in some spots from the dried grass of late autumn, gray in others from exposed rock faces, and elsewhere dark green with evergreen trees. *I won't get recpetino very far up that road,* I typed, hands shaking still.

No answer.

I sighed. My heart was pounding and before doing anything else I took several deep breaths to try to slow it down. Then I put the phone in my pocket and started trudging toward the hills. Grass swished at the cuffs of my jeans and the soles of my boots crunched the dry dirt and gravel beneath loud enough to hear. The sudden tangibility, the boring, plain obviousness of the dry high desert terrain of Howard County made the events of the last twelve hours seem unreal.

This is crazy, I thought. Someone's been killed. A deputy sheriff might have done it, and might have it in for me. And now someone... maybe the same deputy sheriff...or worse, it suddenly occurred to me, maybe *somebody else*...has kidnapped my boyfriend and is making me hike into the mountains.

Ex-boyfriend, I reminded myself. Not even really ex-boyfriend, just a friend who asked me to be his girlfriend for a while and I was bored enough, or merciful enough, to agree.

Evil. I thought of the image of him tied up on my phone and forced myself not to look.

Is this guy going to kill me? He can't ask what I know and then decide to trust me. If he's afraid of me as a witness, all he can really do is get me out of the way.

Why would anybody want to kill me? The question seemed ridiculous in the bright sun, but then I remembered hearing the gunshots and smelling the gunpowder the night before in Dad's office. Killing me because I was a witness to a murder was no more unlikely than committing that murder in the first place. Especially when the victim was a crazy old computer programmer living in the middle of nowhere.

Why would anybody want to kill Charlie Herbert?

I remembered that he'd had a blow to the head when I saw him at the Fun Lanes the night before. So before he was shot, he'd been in a fight. Or anyway, he'd been beaten up.

For a moment a fantasy flashed into my head that I was being led out into the middle of nowhere so that I could be bought off. *Take this cash and don't reveal the identity of the shooter*, a man with an unseen face would say. Since I didn't actually know who the shooter was, couldn't I take that money in good conscience? And then Dad would have some resources and could hire a real paralegal and receptionist, and I could go off to school.

Like I had told Evil *he* should do.

I remembered Evil again, tied up in a shower, and my fantasy seemed small, greedy, and cruel.

I wasn't going to be offered money. I was going to be killed.

I was sweating fiercely now, even though I'd thrown the front of the poncho up over one shoulder. I hit the beginning of the Ups, stepped gingerly over the thick horizontal bars of a cattle guard, and then dropped into the gravelly ditch at the side of the highway and kept walking.

I looked at the reception bars of the phone as the canyon narrowed around me. They dropped down to a slender single bar, with a second flickering in and out, but they didn't disappear entirely. I put the phone away and watched the walls of stone instead. Would this be the place? Would a passing car just slow down long enough for the driver to lean out the window and gun me down? There was nowhere to hide, and unless I suddenly metamorphosed into a spider, I wasn't going to be shooting up these walls anytime soon.

I puffed uncomfortably, but didn't feel like I could really stop and take a break, not with Evil hostage somewhere. The image of myself shot dead by the side of the highway may have helped encourage me.

Cars passed, and I tried not to look at them. No one stopped, and no one shot me.

At the top of the canyon was a grassy meadow speckled with stands of aspen trees. They rippled in a slight morning breeze as if they were waving at me, but I didn't feel welcomed or comforted. At the far end of the field, the Ups rose again and another canyon cut into them, leading higher up and further back into the mountains. Another couple of little rises like this one and the road would hit the Millard Fillmore Dam and Reservoir, the big gift of the Roosevelt Administration and the WPA to Howard County. From there the road wound around the Reservoir, launching smaller paved roads up into the mountains every couple of miles. Those mountain tracks mostly just led to ranches, though a few of them went to fishing holes or backpacking trailheads, and one or two, if you followed them doggedly enough, would carry you all the way through the Rocky Mountains.

My phone buzzed. Three bars.

Evil (only it wasn't Evil, and at the sight of his name a shiver ran down my back): *Turn right here. Follow that dirt road.*

I looked right and had to squint to find the dirt road he was talking about. It was a track left by four wheelers, maybe, and from the edge of Reservoir Road it cut out at a right angle and ran straight until it disappeared into the trees.

Something bothered me, some connection in the back of my head that wouldn't quite come up into my conscious mind. I grabbed for it but missed, and then it was gone.

The person using Evil's phone didn't have to be a man. It could be a woman. Evil was a pretty strong guy, so whoever had tied him up had probably had the drop on him with a gun, and hadn't just pounded him into submission. A woman could do that as easily as a man. I looked at the photo again—no obvious bruises or cuts on Evil's face.

So my...enemy, for lack of a better word, my tormentor, my *foe*, could be a man or a woman. Or both. Or, heck, an artificial intelligence, a sapient pumpkin, or a flesh-eating unicorn. I had nothing to go on—

Stop! I told myself, reeling my brain in. Anything was *possible*, but only some things were *likely*. I had seen two men—and they had both been men, I was pretty sure of it—at Dad's office the night before. Most likely one of those men, or maybe both of them together, had Evil prisoner.

I flinched as I entered the trees, half-expecting someone to jump out and grab me. No one did, and I followed the track up around a shoulder of the hill, eventually breaking out of the forest again. Over a crested hump of earth to my right I could see Howard, and the

Flats. Out in the distance, more ridges of rock and earth snaggled up out of the high desert plain, hiding the Columbia River that I knew was somewhere out there.

The road turned left, away from the view, and suddenly I realized what had been niggling at my mind. Aaron Wilding. I had never been, but Dad had, and everyone knew that Wilding's ranch was the first right turn after the Dam. Everyone knew because the hunters always complained about it. I knew because Evil and Dad were both hunters.

And then I hit the fence.

The Ups are full of ranchers, and the Flats are farm country, so I was no stranger to fences. This was a serious one. Its poles were metal and its wires were barbed and taut, and right in front of me were three signs stacked one on top of the other. The signs read PRIVATE PROPERTY NO TRESPASSING, HUNTING NOT ALLOWED, and THIS PROPERTY PROTECTED BY SMITH & WESSON.

But the signs hung on a gate.

I stared.

I shouldn't be shocked, I told myself. The dead man had been Wilding's employee. I had no idea why he had been trying to talk to me, or why he might have been in Dad's office, but the fact that whoever had killed him now wanted me to come back to Wilding's ranch...

Well, I couldn't explain it. But somehow, it fit together.

Maybe the killer wanted something of Charlie Herbert's, and thought I had it.

Maybe the killer wanted information Charlie had had, and figured he'd talked to me before he died.

But why lead me back here?

I screwed up my mind and struggled with the problem. There was something here, and the killer thought I knew how to find it? Thought Charlie had told me where something was, or given me a map?

I don't know how long I'd been standing there, but I was snapped out of my train of thought by the buzzing of my phone.

Get moving.

I looked around. The ridge rose above me into another stand of trees, and below me dropped off until it fell down to Howard and the Flats. I saw no one. I even scanned the sky with one hand over my eyes, and saw nothing but a single hawk circling out over the valley. Where was the man hiding?

Buzz. *Get moving NOW.*

Who are you? I typed. My legs hurt and I didn't want to go any farther. I felt spooked by the fact that this guy seemed to be able to see me but I couldn't see him. And I was worried that if I walked into the next stand of trees I might get shot. *Tell me what you want. Maybe we can work together.*

The last one in particular was a bit ridiculous, but I felt trapped.

The next buzz dropped another picture into my stream of texts.

Evil. Sitting in the same bathtub. Only this time whoever was taking the picture was also pointing a gun at Evil's forehead.

My heart boomed like a cannon, but I forced myself to focus. I couldn't identify the pistol for sure, but I saw that it was a black semi-automatic, not a revolver. I saw that the hand belonged to a man. And I saw a look of angry defiance in Evil's eyes.

Angry defiance mixed with a little fear.

Here's how we're going to work together. Go to the damn house, knock on the door, and repeat the message I tell you. Anything else, and I shoot Mr. Patten. Or should I just go ahead and shoot him now?

I pushed the gate open and stumbled through.

I'm going.

No answer.

I was braced for it, but no one jumped me in the trees. Beyond them was a vale, a shallow bowl of earth with a building in the center. The building was semi-circular. Its curve faced south and showed ceiling-high windows with floors of poured concrete behind them. I could see through the windows that the entire thing was built with an envelope of space all around, like a house inside a house. The dead air in between the two parts of the house would act as insulation, I knew. This was a total hippie house, energy-conscious and environmentally impeccable. Rich hippie house, not the only one in Howard County, but a nice one. House like that, I would have guessed it had its own well and geothermal power even if Dad hadn't already told me it did.

The Wildings had probably had their house featured in *New Earth Monthly*.

In the driveway next to the house were parked Mrs. Wilding's canary yellow H3 and an unremarkable white sedan. The H3 at least was a strange fit with the house, a gas guzzler and chewer-up of the atmosphere and not the usual first choice of hippie software gurus, I imagined. Not that I actually knew any.

I walked toward the front door and my phone buzzed.

Ready for the message? Word for word.

Ready, I texted back.

The next text message came all in capital letters. *MY BOSS HAS WHAT YOU'RE LOOKING FOR. IT WILL COST YOU $50K.*

CHAPTER
9

I stared at the screen. This was crazy. I couldn't ask Mrs. Wilding for fifty thousand dollars.

My boss? I typed.

Get the cash or not, either way, you retrace your steps. Got it?

I was at the door, which was totally glass. *Yes.*

I pressed the doorbell.

There was no immediate answer and I shivered, even though the day was shaping up to be a warm one and the bowl of earth the house sat in shielded me from any breeze. I realized as I stood waiting for the door to be answered that when I'd seen Marilyn Wilding's canary yellow H3 before, it had also been with a white sedan. Or at least, parked near a sedan.

It had only been the day before, but it seemed years earlier. I focused on remembering. Mrs. Wilding had parked her H3 and come into the Fun Lanes door; a Greek-looking guy in a turtleneck and sunglasses had parked a white sedan and gone into the door to McCrae's. He'd drunk a bottle or two and left, I hadn't seen him again.

Probably coincidence. There were a lot of white sedans on the road. Still, I wished I'd noticed the make and model of the Greek guy's sedan.

I punched the doorbell again and as I did I also pressed my ear against the glass to be sure a bell actually rang. The opening chords of Deep Purple's "Smoke on the Water"—the famous ones, *duh duh duh, duh duh DUH duh,* and before you ask, I know them because that's the kind of thing Dad listens to—rang inside the house.

I almost laughed.

I saw Marilyn coming because of the house-within-a-house design. She came through a big open kitchen space wrapping herself in a kimono. I smiled and stepped back from the door a respectful distance. This was a client, after all.

She opened the door and frowned. Her hair was tousled and makeup smeared—she looked as if she'd gotten ready for the day and then had a pillow fight. "Did your father send you with the will?" she asked. "That was fast."

Dad had been here. That was good. He was easily distracted, but if he was out shaking a leg this morning without me reminding him, he was off to a good start. Only he hadn't brought Mrs. Wilding her husband's will.

"No. I mean...didn't he have it with him?"

Marilyn Wilding squinted at me through smudged mascara. "What do you mean?"

The question knocked me off balance a little. "Uh...Mr. Wilding's will. I guess Dad didn't have it."

She pursed her lips into a pouty you-are-a-strange-child-and-I-don't-know-what-to-make-of-you look. I get that sometimes.

"Then what are you doing here?" she asked.

Oh. Right. I looked down at the phone. I felt a cold hard ball in the pit of my stomach; this was not going to go over well. "My boss has what you're looking for. It will cost you fifty thousand dollars."

Marilyn Wilding should have looked confused, and she did, alright. But she also looked like I'd punched her in the gut. "What did you say?" she hissed, all the air rushing out of her around her words. "Your father has...what does your father have?"

Oh no. "Not my father," I said. "*Not* my father. Someone else." I looked at the phone again. "My boss has what you're looking for. It will cost you fifty thousand dollars."

"Am I supposed to give you fifty thousand dollars?" Her expression changed as she spoke. Now she looked at me like I was a cockroach, or a coiled snake. I hoped she didn't have a taser in her kimono pocket. "Is this some kind of shakedown?"

"Or not." I waved my phone, as if that would explain anything. "I have to deliver the message. I'm sorry. I have to deliver it. I—" I was about to spill the beans completely, babble about Evil and Charlie Herbert and everything I knew, just to get out of this situation, but she cut me off by turning away.

"Wait here!" she called over her shoulder. She left the door open, and the kitchen door within, and moved quickly back into the house. So quickly she was almost running, and the kimono bounced and flapped around enough for me to realize she wasn't wearing anything else underneath it. "Nick!"

Done, I texted.

Who did you talk to?

Mrs. Wilding. She went back in the house. I poked my head in through the door and looked, but didn't see any sign of her coming back.

There was a brief pause. *Start walking back,* my unknown enemy finally messaged me. *Not too fast, and I recommend you keep an eye over your shoulder.*

I did as he suggested. I walked at a calm pace, and I looked back constantly, and that was why, when I was about thirty yards from the house I saw the Greek-looking guy come hopping out. He wore jeans and a blue Jack White t-shirt but had bare feet, and he held a long shotgun.

I ran.

"Hey!" he shouted.

I ducked my head and sprinted for the trees.

I left the path. It wasn't what I'd been told to do by Evil's captor, but I wanted to get something between the shotgun and my shoulder blades sooner rather than later. Also, I figured his bare feet might be an advantage over my hiking boots on a smooth dirt path; if I could get into the pine trees, with little sticks and pebbles and needles all over, I might be able to flip that calculus around the other way.

Boom!

The shot missed, probably on purpose, but it bit a chunk out of a bluish spruce tree just ahead of me.

"Stop!" the Greek guy yelled again, but I was in no mood. It was one thing to cooperate when a bad guy had Evil hostage, but something else entirely to chicken out just because some loser had a gun.

I burst into the trees kicking up needles like water from a puddle.

Zigging and zagging, I tried to put more trees between me and the man chasing me. As I ran, I reviewed the trail ahead in my mind. On the other side of the fence I'd be a sitting duck on an open hillside for a good long while. To heck with that.

I turned left in the band of trees, totally off the track. I felt my phone buzz in my hand. I hoped it was someone else besides Evil's captor, anybody else, but even if it was him, I had no choice. I ignored the phone and ran.

My breath and my heart pounded inside my chest like two fists. I couldn't stop to wonder why the Greek guy was chasing me, or what it was that my faceless enemy had and had offered to Mrs. Wilding for fifty thousand dollars, or who that enemy was. Dimly the uncertainties spun around my mind like the rocking landscape of yellow mountain grass, green and blue evergreens, and faded sky. I couldn't focus on any of it.

Instead I focused on my feet, and on putting things behind my shoulder blades, as fast as I possibly could.

I hit a patch of the grove in which the trees crept up the side of the bowl. I had no idea what was on the other side; it could have been a bare coverless field, or a thicket of barbed wire, or a sheer drop. But I didn't have the luxury of picking the terrain. If I stopped, I was sure I'd be shot, so I had to stay undercover as long as I could. I bolted up the slope and over the lip of earth at the top.

The other side was a steep slope of dirt and pebbles. At the top I snagged a toe on the root of the grove's last tree and tumbled forward, bouncing down the slope like so much denim in the spin cycle, over and over, and then I was up on toes and knuckles and hurling myself into scrubby little trees at the bottom of a narrow defile and—

Boom!

I heard the shotgun slug pop through the air over my head. It might have hit me in the back except that I was tripping again, and when I hit the ground it was in cold, shallow water. I rolled and splashed back onto my feet, crouching, shaking water off my phone.

The trees momentarily hid me, but I could hear grunting and cursing as my attacker chugged after me down into the defile. I rose to run again and my eye caught on the thing that had tripped me and saved my life.

It was a deer. A dead deer. It lay on the edge of the stream, face in the water and hindquarters ramped up awkwardly on the bank, as if it had dropped dead in mid-drink, with not a mark on its body.

I ran.

The trees around me grew closer together and thicker, and for a moment I imagined that I was about to disappear into a dense jungle (as if any such thing existed in the Ups, or could exist there) and get away. The Greek guy had to be someone associated with the Wildings. Family of one of them. He was too old to be Mrs. Wilding's son—might he be a son of Aaron Wilding, by an earlier marriage? Would that make him the son Dad had been talking about the night before, the one who went off to military school?

Or, given her state of undress when she'd answered the door, might he be Mrs. Wilding's...boyfriend? I tripped over a second deer.

It lay dead, right across the middle of the stream.

I couldn't even look at it. I picked myself up out of the water and staggered on. I could hear Greek Guy behind me, huffing and puffing. He was thin enough, but the running was giving him trouble, so maybe he wasn't all that fit. Or maybe the altitude was getting to him. For that matter, the altitude was starting to get to me. I felt light-headed and my legs and feet ached.

The trees ended. Ahead of me the defile stretched downward in a straight shot, the stream rushing merrily at the bottom of it, and not a scrap of a tree to hide behind. Out of sheer disappointment, I suppose, I tripped and fell a third time.

Before I could stand, something hard and heavy smacked me across the back of the skull. I fell gasping into the cold water of the stream and stars raced across my vision.

"Talk, bitch!"

I hurt too much to be angry. My vision spun and I wanted to throw up. I realized I still had my phone in my hand, but I couldn't think how that was any advantage to me. "I don't know anything!" I yelled, holding my hands over my head.

"You're the lawyer's kid!" the Greek guy snapped. "What's your angle? You trying to blackmail Marilyn, you made a dumb mistake!"

He had followed Marilyn into McCrae's the day before. Why? Had he just hung back to give her room to talk to her lawyer, or had he been along for something else? Had he come to case the joint? Could he have been one of the two men in Dad's office?

I saw bright flashes of light and couldn't really focus on Greek Guy. Nick, that was what Marilyn had called him.

Nick was going to kill me.

Then I realized what I ought to be doing with my phone. "Look," I said, and I pointed at the phone. I climbed slowly to my feet and turned, careful not to show any sign of making a break for it. Nick pointed the shotgun right at the center of my chest—it was a Remington 870, a go-to gun for police forces everywhere, and poncho or no poncho, at this range it would punch a hole right through me. I would have tried to fake fear, except that I was so afraid and tired from running that I was shaking like a Quaking Aspen in a thunderstorm anyway. "It isn't me. I don't know anything, this guy is sending me texts!"

It had the virtue of being true. Also, since I was pointing at and fumbling with my phone, it had the virtue of letting me click on the video camera. I didn't dare point the camera directly at Nick, but I tried to aim it in his general direction. At least it would capture sound, and if I was lucky it might even get his face.

That way, I thought as I took a deep breath to steady myself, they'd have a video to play at Nick's trial for my murder.

Nick looked suspicious. "What is it you have?" he asked, sniffing the air. "What are you offering? You making some kind of threat?"

"I told you," I repeated, "I don't know anything."

Nick snorted, pumped the shotgun to chamber a shell, and pointed it at me.

Bang!

With a look of surprise on his face and a chunk of his skull missing, Nick fell forward into the stream.

CHAPTER
10

I jumped back, shaking. I'd been prepared for a bang from Nick's gun, but not a blast out of nowhere. Also, I'd never seen anyone shot in the head before. Howard County had the occasional gun accident, because it had more than its share of hunters, but it had never happened in front of me. One moment, Nick was scowling at me, his face flushed and angry and disbelieving.

The next, he collapsed to the ground like so much meat.

There was a lot of blood. I don't know what I'd imagined, but those veins in the head carry a lot of fluid, and it flooded out in a wash that darkened the grass and the water of the stream.

I stumbled but managed not to fall. As I turned to look for the source of the shot I heard the *snicker-snack* of a bolt-action rifle ejecting a spent cartridge and snapping a fresh round into the chamber.

A tall, thin man stood at the top of the defile. He wore a tight, high-end black fleece jacket and slim gloves, and he had a black ski mask pulled down over his face. The drop beneath him was steep enough that there was no way I was going to charge up to the top and get the gun out of his hands. Not before he'd shot me half a dozen times.

Nick's body lay crumpled on top of the shotgun, and he was several steps away, too. I'd never make it.

Ski Mask raised the rifle to his shoulder, pointing the gun straight at me—a body slammed into Ski Mask from behind.

Bang! The rifle went off and the shot missed me, thumping into the dirt at my feet.

Ski Mask and his attacker went down in a tumbling whirl of long limbs, fleece, rifle, and—I now saw—Evil Patten. They spun over and over each other, yowling like cats, and crashed into a pile on top of Nick.

"Evil!" I yelled.

He was on top of the heap of elbows, but there was something awkward about his stance. It wasn't until he reared back onto his knees that I realized that both his hands were behind his back. Also, he had a cloth gag wrapped through his mouth.

I rushed to him.

Ski Mask tried to roll away sideways, clutching at the rifle under his body. Evil fell on him like a Legion Hall semi-pro wrestler, face first, and he smashed Ski Mask in the temple with a head butt that was as loud as the crack of the rifle. Ski Mask collapsed.

I grabbed Evil by the elbow and dragged him to his feet. His hands were tied together at the wrists. That fixed his arms in a single position, and helped me lever him up.

He made choking noises around his gag, and we ran.

Maybe I should have grabbed the rifle first, or the shotgun, but Ski Mask was on top of both of them, and since he still had the guns, more or less, I couldn't really take him prisoner. Even with Evil, I felt very alone; what allies might Ski Mask have hiding in the trees? Also, cut me some slack—I was sixteen years old, exhausted, and scared.

We followed the stream down. The arroyo walls got steeper; they felt like a blanket being pulled over my head, which is fine when it's because you want to snuggle with someone special, but terrifying when the blanket is in the hand of someone who hates you, and in the other hand he holds a hammer.

I felt a little better when the canyon took a sharp right turn, toward the Flats. Good enough that I stopped Evil. With the tiny pocket knife on my car keys I gouged through the plastic that wrapped his wrists together—they were really thick zip ties, but they gave way after a little bit of persuasion and fell off. He tore off his own gag, then grabbed my hand and we ran again. I didn't dare peek around the corner to see how far behind us Ski Mask was.

"Who is he?" I puffed.

"He didn't exactly show me ID," Evil snapped. As snapping went, though, it was pretty good-natured, just a joke with a slight edge to it. For a guy who had just pounded his own forehead into his captor's skull, Evil was impressively gentle.

The stream passed under the barbed wire again, which I guessed meant we were at the edge of the Wilding property. There was no gate, but the stream created enough of a depression that we could both lie on our bellies and slip under the wire. The stream dropped down a steep bank of stone and we rattled along its edge. I really needed to stop running; my feet felt as if someone had held me upside down in vise grips and pounded on my soles with a mallet for two hours. I was also weak from lack of sleep and food and shaking from effort. My poncho was beginning to feel really heavy. On top of everything else, I looked like I'd been rolling around in the mud.

"There's no cover," I said. The stream splashed down into another canyon, bare of trees or decent-sized rocks. We ran on stony ground, and my ankles felt as if they might give way. "He'll catch us."

"Maybe he won't follow us." Evil shot a look over his shoulder as he ran.

"We're witnesses," I pointed out. "We saw him kill that man."

"And kidnap me," Evil pointed out. "I'm not a lawyer, but I'm pretty sure that's also a no-no."

"Did he...hurt you?" I asked, breathing hard. I risked a look back —I could see the water of the stream splashing down over rock from the defile, but no sign of Ski Mask. I felt a little bud of something in my heart that might have been hope.

Evil shook his head. He had more control over his breath than I did over mine. "Scared the pants off me. Shook me up."

"How did you escape?" My steps were beginning to falter. I wasn't running anymore so much as speed-plodding.

Evil laughed. "When he took the rifle and left, I figured it was my best chance. He'd tied my ankles, but it was just with zip ties, you know, those big ones they sell in truck stops. The faucet of the tub I was in was old and a little jagged. I used it like a saw, rubbed the ties against the faucet until they broke. My ankles are cut up some, and I've totally shot a good pair of socks. I would have freed my hands too, except I was afraid he'd come back."

"You came to rescue me with your hands tied." I was a little astonished Evil could be so brave.

"Nope." He laughed raggedly. "I just ran. But then I saw him shooting down into the draw, and I figured I had to stop him."

"You didn't know he was shooting at me?"

"Nope. But I knew he wasn't shooting deer, and...well, I owed him one."

Deer. "Evil," I said, "the canyon behind the house up there is full of dead deer."

"Wasn't hunters," Evil said defensively. "We don't trespass."

"No, they weren't marked, just dead." The stitch in my side cut like a knife, and I shuffled at a speed barely faster than a walk.

"Disease, maybe. It happens." Evil looked back. "We gotta get out of here. Around the bend is that little picnic area and campground, but there won't be anybody there to help us on a weekday morning."

"Any good place to hide?" I stopped running, trying to catch my breath and willing the sharp pain in my side to go away. Evil knew the Ups a lot better than I did, from hunting, fishing, and backpacking.

Evil stopped with me, watching the valley behind us. He shrugged. "Under a picnic table, I guess. You won't stay hidden long."

A thought struck me. "So he was with you the whole time?"

Evil nodded. "From when he jumped me in the Fun Lanes until I escaped. He had me tied up in a car, and then a cabin." He pointed. "Up there on the Wilding place. Old hunting cabin, I guess, or a place for ranch hands to sleep, back when they ran cattle in these valleys."

"Then how did he see me?"

Evil took my hand and pulled me along. "He didn't. He took my wallet and made a stop in the Dog Ears, and then he sat on the toilet watching me and playing with my phone."

With Evil's phone. "Oh no," I said. I pushed my wooden legs to swing faster, and focused on my phone, scrolling sideways through pages of apps to find the one I was looking for.

"What is it?"

I looked over my shoulder as I found the app. We were nearing the bend of the canyon, and I could see a smudge of black behind us, where the stream poured into the valley.

And sure enough, when I pulled up FindMe, I tapped on *Evil Patten* in the *Friends* menu and saw the pulsing red dot right on the GPS map image of the canyon. "Remember that FindMe app that seemed so useful when we were lab partners?" I asked. We passed the bend of the canyon, but the Flats were still a long way away, and I felt, if anything, less safe.

"Yeah," Evil said. "Also, it was a good way for me to be sure you weren't out at the movies with other guys while I was working."

Maybe I should have been offended, or maybe I should have laughed. I couldn't do either. "He used it to follow me all morning. He's following us with it now."

Evil cursed.

I had an idea. "Look for a piece of wood." I scanned the ground as I stumbled along, looking for anything big enough to float and carry a little extra weight with it. All I saw was dried yellow grass, gray rock, and patches of bare earth.

We hit the campground. It was empty, three dry sandy circles of pale earth around three picnic tables. I looked into the fire pit of each. The pits were full of ash and dead coals, but no sizable wood.

"What do people burn in their fires up here?" I snapped, exasperated.

"When you pack in your own firewood, you pack out what's left." Evil looked with me, kicking around in the ashes with his Redwings. "What are you thinking, Bucky?"

I waved my phone at him. "I'm thinking we send this phone on down the stream and him after it."

"Still no place to hide," Evil pointed out.

"If he's staring down at your phone, we might not have to hide very well."

Evil nodded, catching on. "In that case," he said, pulling something out of his back pocket, "what about this?"

I stared at the thing in his hand. "That's a condom. And if you think that now is the right time to suggest this to me, your head is flatter than I ever realized."

"Yeah." Evil tore off the wrapper with his teeth. I couldn't imagine what he was doing and I couldn't bear to look at his hands, so I watched the intent expression on his face. He puffed once into the condom, inflating the tip of it like a balloon. "And if I tie a knot in the end, it should float."

I felt a little stupid. "Thanks." I checked FindMe one last time, then took the condom and shoved my phone in. It went in awkwardly, with lots of tugging, and I couldn't help but giggle. "This isn't quite like health class," I said.

"Yeah, the banana was closer to the...you know."

I was glad my face was flushed already. "Shush."

He took the phone and started blowing into the prophylactic. "Good thing I got a big—"

"Evil!"

"What? *Condom*, I got a big condom was what I was going to say." He blew in one last lungful of air and tied the condom off at the end. It held, a dull white latex bubble with a little brick of a phone inside.

"Good job," I said.

"No problem."

I trotted over to the stream. The flow was wide and calm as it passed the campground, which was perfect. I laid my phone into the water in its prophylactic vessel and it quickly bobbed away. Hopefully it could get far enough down the canyon to be around the next bend before Ski Mask showed up. Hopefully it wouldn't get caught on a rock.

"Now what?" Evil asked. "Squat down behind the tables and hope?"

"We can do better than that," I said, and I shrugged out of my poncho. "Find a big patch of dirt where we can lay this down and lie under it."

"Bucky." Evil grinned. "You're so romantic."

"Shut up and do what I tell you," I told him. "He'll be here any minute, and he has all the guns."

CHAPTER
11

The first thing I realized when we were both underneath the poncho was that I smelled bad. Evil smelled worse, but that didn't make it any better for me. We both needed showers and fresh clothing. For that matter, he probably needed a tetanus shot. Fortunately, I had my face pressed against the neck hole of the poncho. I did that so I could see better, but it also gave me more than my share of fresh air.

"This is snug." Evil's face was pressed against my shoulder and his knees crunched into my hip.

It was the worst cuddle ever.

"Shh." I watched the canyon. We lay under the wool several hundred feet from the stream and the canyon center. The dry dirt beneath us was nearly the same color as the poncho, and the grass was tall enough to hide us. Well, not really to hide us. But we were inconspicuous, and if Ski Mask jogged fast enough, he just might miss us and trot on past.

He appeared upstream, and he was running fast.

He stared at the ground under his feet or at his hand. He had to be holding Evil's phone and watching FindMe's tracker screen, because he also occasionally shot glances ahead of him, down the canyon, where my phone was hopefully drifting along in its condom balloon boat.

The ski mask was peeled up now so that it just covered the top of his head, like a stocking cap, and I could see his face. Ski Mask, the man who had taken Evil prisoner and forced me to carry his message to Marilyn Wilding, was Michael Fellows, the guy who'd left his resume with Gladys and said he was looking for a job.

I slapped at my flannel shirt pocket out of reflex. I wanted to send Dad a message, warn him, but of course I didn't have my phone.

"What's going on?" Evil whispered.

"Shh. Nothing," I lied.

In his left hand, Fellows held the long rifle. I was pretty sure Eddie Eagle wouldn't approve of the way Fellows held the gun, but Eddie Eagle wouldn't approve of running with a loaded weapon, either. Or taking potshots at innocent people, which is to say, me. Not to mention the Greek guy, Nick—he might not fit the ordinary definition of *innocent*, but Fellows had shot him in the head without so much as a warning.

Fellows looked around him again just before he drew level with us, and I had the terrible sinking feeling that I was meeting his gaze and he noticed me. His face was hard, fixed, and cruel, with none of the boyish handsomeness I had seen in it the day before. This Michael Fellows wasn't a guy who would stand up and win cases in court; he was a man who would shoot you in the back.

Kings County District Attorney, my eye. I wondered who he worked for, and what he wanted. Had my encounter with Nick at the Wilding house gone according to his plan, had he intended to kill Nick? Or was killing Nick damage control, and was his plan something else? Was I supposed to come away with fifty thousand dollars? It didn't seem likely, since Fellows had warned me to walk away from the house and be ready to run.

What was his connection with Nick, that he would want to kill him? Was one of them the man who killed Charlie Herbert? What was going on at the Wilding house that had so far resulted in two deaths? My head spun from the centrifuge of questions rattling around inside it, and I was glad I was lying down to start with. Otherwise, I might have fallen over.

And then I realized the dumb thing I'd done; I'd given my phone to a man I knew was a murderer. A man who had used Evil's phone to trick me into thinking he was Evil, and forced me to do his will.

Once he had my phone, what might he do?

The device had a password, of course, and the screen saver would certainly have kicked in and locked the phone by now. Still, the password was a simple four-digit PIN and not particularly creative, just the street number of the Fun Lanes. He might figure that one out. Or maybe he had a device that would trick my phone—he was some kind of professional killer, after all, like a secret agent or an assassin. If that kind of technology really existed, he would be the guy who had it, wouldn't he?

What if he texted Dad, claimed to be me, and told Dad to come out to some remote spot?

But why would he even do that? I tried to reassure myself.

It didn't work. The fact was, Fellows had been one of the men who had broken into Dad's office. Not the one who had shot Charlie Herbert, apparently, but he'd proved himself a killer since, and he was a kidnapper and a liar to boot. He wanted something from Dad, or Dad's office, and if he had my phone he might use it to get what he was after.

Fellows jogged out of sight downstream.

I dragged off the poncho and took deep breaths. "We have to go back up to the house."

"Is that safe?" he asked. We both climbed to our feet, and I left the poncho where it lay. It was dirty from the ground, but so was I, and I knew if I ended up out of doors after the sun went down, I'd be glad to have lugged it around all day. On the other hand, I was really tired.

Tired won.

"No," I said, remembering that Marilyn Wilding had sicced Nick on me. "But I have to warn Dad." And Sheriff Sutherland? But no, I still had no idea which of his deputies was dirty. Or if *he* was dirty. "We can't follow him down, he's got a gun. Maybe we can loop up around and borrow one of the Wildings' cars. Or hike down the other side of the mountain."

"*A gun?*" Evil looked at me funny. "Which gun did he have?"

A light went on in my head. "The rifle," I told him. "Which means he left the shotgun behind."

"We could use that, you bet," Evil said. "And there's a phone in that cabin I was tied up in. I don't know for sure that it works, but if it does you can call your dad from there."

I didn't wait for any more encouragement. Looking over my shoulder to make sure Fellows hadn't found my phone and turned back, I jogged upstream. Well, stumbled is more like it. I must have looked like one of the walking dead, shuffling raggedly along the side of the water and cursing under my breath.

Evil followed.

"You know, there's a reason I carry a condom in my pocket all the time," he grunted.

My legs ached; the few minutes of lying down had made all my muscles knot up, and now they rebelled. I forced them to do my will by sheer whip-cracking effort. I reminded myself that my life might depend on my ability to move as fast as possible; that helped.

"Is now the right time for this?" I asked.

"It isn't what you think."

"Okay." I looked over my shoulder. "I owe you my life. I guess you can tell me why you carry a rubber in your pocket."

"Water," he said.

That surprised me so much it took me almost a minute to organize a response. When I finally collected my thoughts, though, at least the first words out of my mouth were clever and sophisticated. "What the crap are you talking about, Evil?"

"Water," he repeated. "Look, it's a wilderness survival thing, same reason I always carry a pocket knife. You can fill a big condom with enough water to last you a day, maybe. So I never go anywhere without one."

"Are you pulling my leg?" Even the act of saying the word *leg* reminded me of how stiff and sore my own legs were, and I winced.

"Nope. Also, you can start a fire with them."

I tried to imagine what he was talking about, and couldn't. "Okay," I finally said. "I'll bite. What do you mean?"

"A condom full of water refracts light, just like a magnifying glass. You remember burning ants with a magnifying glass when you were a kid?"

"I never did that. It's more of a boy thing."

"Yeah, well, *I* did. You can start a fire that way, if you fix that little white light on a dry piece of tinder, or leaves. And it turns out you can do it with a condom, too. After a pocket knife and a blanket, a condom's just about the most useful survival tool a guy can have in the mountains."

"I'm surprised they don't sell them at REI."

Evil laughed. "Nope. The wilderness survival condom is pretty much strictly the secret of us non-REI shoppers. Along with the aspirin bottle survival kit and the garbage bag rain slicker."

"Those don't have the same romantic applications though, I suppose." We were in sight of the rock drop and the barbed wire again. I really wished I had my phone back and was watching Fellows's location on FindMe. I felt an itch between my shoulder blades as if he were right behind me with the rifle at every step.

Evil shrugged. "Hey, you want to be prepared if you meet a girl."

I bent to use my hands as well as my feet as I started scrambling up the slope. Cold water splashed against my forearms and ankles, startling me and perking me up. "If you meet *a* girl, huh? Flattering. I guess just any one would do. I suppose I should be glad you don't see me as interchangeable with a farm animal."

Evil grabbed my ankle and stopped my forward climb.

"Hey," he said. "It was a joke. You know I'm not like that, and if I ever wanted to be with a girl... I mean, when I want to be with a girl... well, you know I'm sweet on you, Bucky...I mean, *Becky* McCrae."

"Woman," I corrected him, and kept climbing. "Get moving."

He splashed up the stream behind me. "Besides," he added, "just 'cause I'm a sagebilly doesn't mean I'm a deviant."

"No," I agreed, squishing underneath the barbed wire and smearing more mud on my jeans. "You come by deviancy more as a matter of personal choice."

"I'm glad of one thing, though," he said, following me.

"What's that?" I scanned the valley below. The sun was crossing noon above us and descending into afternoon, and the valley was a warm, dry yellow. Fellows wasn't in sight, but in my mind's eye I saw him just around the bend and coming my direction. I turned and climbed up into the defile that led to the Wildings' house.

"I'm glad I didn't get the lubricated condoms."

I squinted over my shoulder, and the screwed-tight expression of mock disgust on Evil's face made me laugh. "Ronald E. Patten," I puffed. "You're alright."

"Please," he said. "Call me Evil."

We chugged up the defile like a two-car creeper train, putting one boot in front of the other and ignoring the pain.

"Wait," I said, just as I thought Nick's body—and the dead deer—should have been about to come into view. I was whispering. "What about Marilyn Wilding?"

Evil chewed his lip. He whispered back. "What about her?"

"She sent Nick after me with a gun. She heard shots. What did she do then?"

Evil considered. "Called the cops?"

"Maybe." I hoped not. I was already nervous enough about the Howard County Sheriff Department. And assuming Sheriff Sutherland wasn't involved in the burglary and shooting in Dad's office, it would still look really bad for me to be caught on the scene of a second felony in twelve hours. "Or did she get another gun and come out after him?"

Evil looked around us, tilting his head back and forth as he examined the ridge behind us and the sun sloping off toward the Flats.

"What are you thinking?" I asked.

"I'm thinking we leave the shotgun. If we cut across that way"—he gestured—"we ought to hit that little cabin he had me tied up in. There's a phone. We can call Jim, or the sheriff, or the FBI, or whoever you want. Heck, maybe we ought to call 911 and tell 'em we need to be life-flighted down to the hospital in Boise or Spokane."

It wasn't a bad idea, actually. Except that Michael Fellows had my phone. "I have to warn Dad," I said, and I started crawling out of the defile in the direction Evil had pointed.

"Shoot." Evil followed me. "It'd be kind of fun to lie down on the landing skids of a helicopter and watch Hells Canyon zip past underneath, don't you think?"

"I think I'd vomit," I said. "And I don't know if they're called *landing skids.*"

"In matters of combustion engines and bitchin' modes of transportation," Evil advised, "never, ever go up against a sagebilly."

CHAPTER
12

I kept my head down and scooted up the slope. It crested in a warty knob of rock, mottled with lichen on one side, and I paused to let Evil catch up. I wished he'd been further behind, so I could have rested.

"How far do you think we are from the body?" I whispered.

He crouched beside the rock with me and pointed. "Right over there's where the guy was standing when he pulled the trigger."

That put us within a stone's throw. I had to look. "The guy uses the name Fellows, by the way." I dropped to hands and knees and crawled forward, keeping low in the grass and moving slowly. In this warm weather, the lower canyons and foothills of the Ups become rattlesnake country, and the last thing I needed was to put my hand into a nest of baby rattlers.

"You know him?" Evil followed.

"He's the guy who came to my office. To Dad's office." Grass poked me in the face and the warm vegetable smell of it filled my nose and throat. Good thing I've never suffered from hay fever.

Evil grabbed my ankle again. I yanked it away, not in an irritated way, but out of principle.

"Is all this about you, somehow?" he asked. "Or Jim? Your dad?"

"Not unless we're the last of the Romanovs and don't know about it," I said. "We've got nothing to take except the mortgage on the house and the Fun Lanes."

"They *are* Howard County's only bowling lanes that are also a law office," Evil said.

"Don't forget the bar." I crawled forward on my belly.

Nick lay dead on the bottom of the defile below me, not far from the second of the two dead deer. His shotgun still lay under him, and I saw no sign of anyone else.

Evil crunched onto his elbows beside me, scattering a beetle that ran across the back of my hand. "I could go get the gun," he whispered.

I grabbed his wrist. "No." I wished I could see the Wilding house and the vale it sat in, rather than just the slope leading up to it and the pine woods on the slope. "No one's moved the body, which means... I don't know what it means."

"Mrs. Wilding probably didn't call the sheriff, for one thing," Evil suggested.

"But why?"

"She's in on it," Evil suggested. "Fellows is her accomplice, and together they lured the other guy out of the building to kill him."

The suggestion rang hollow to me. "That's an awful lot of work to kill a guy. I can't be sure, but I think Marilyn Wilding might have been sleeping with that guy Nick. Or maybe he was her son. Stepson."

"There's a big difference between a lover and a stepson. Usually."

"She was hanging around him...pretty undressed."

"So, lover."

"Yeah," I agreed. "So if she wanted him dead for some reason, it should have been as easy as shooting him in the back."

"She didn't want blood on her own hands."

"Well then she could have sent him out for a donut and had Fellows shoot him in the back. Involving me doesn't make any sense."

"So...Marilyn Wilding and Nick somebody on one side, and Fellows somebody on the other." Evil held up fingers as he talked. "What's going on? And who else is in on this?"

"Michael Fellows. But that's got to be a fake name. Someone in the sheriff department," I said, feeling miserable. "Maybe the sheriff, maybe just a deputy."

"For what? This has to be about the Wildings somehow, doesn't it?"

"Sure seems like it. He had a lot of money, I guess, but this isn't the wild west. You can't just shoot people and take their cash."

"The wild west was never like that," Evil said. "You're thinking of Detroit."

I chuckled, but I was perplexed.

"Come on." Evil tapped me gently on the shoulder. "This is bigger than us, whatever it is. Let's get to the cabin and call your dad."

I followed him. We ran hunched over, which might have been pointless and certainly looked silly, but it made me feel better to at least *try* to stay hidden. I felt better still when we dropped down a slope and into another shallow depression with a house in it. This house was a ragged little A-framed cabin, it was surrounded by trees, and in the gravel strip beside it was parked a car I knew: a blue Corolla. Michael Fellows's California rental.

Evil turned back to hiss at me, and I realized I'd stopped. "Stay focused, Bucky!"

I straightened up and ran through the trees. I ran faster than Evil or he let me catch up, because I beat him to the door and tried the handle.

"Locked," I said. "I guess it locked behind you."

"Don't you know any law at all, Becky McCrae?" Evil said. "This is an emergency, and I'm making a citizen's arrest on this door." He raised one Redwing-clad foot and smashed the door open in a single kick, ripping the deadbolt right through the wood.

"You may not have the law quite right," I told him, "but thank you."

The A-frame was tiny. Immediately behind the door there was a kitchen, with a table and two chairs. In the other wall opened a passage with a sleeping cubby on either side of it, ending in a warped white door. The door was open and I saw the tile of the bathroom.

Just this side of the door was a ladder set into the wall leading up, so there must be a small loft above us—maybe a third sleeping space.

"Phone's on the counter," Evil said, and he turned the knobs on the kitchen sink. The pipes groaned; brown water spat and bubbled from the faucet. The place had an odor of dust, old-and-mostly-faded body odor, and disintegrating pine that filled my head with visions of swarming spiders.

"Yuck."

I picked up the phone, a flat, angular model the color of an old coffee drinker's teeth. At least it got a dial tone. I noticed a big duffel bag on the table as I punched in Dad's cell phone number. Its zipper was open, so I started poking through it.

Dad picked up immediately. "James McCrae."

"Dad, it's me."

"Where are you, kiddo?"

I didn't cry, because I wasn't a little kid and I wasn't hurt. But I'll admit the sound of Dad's voice made me feel a little misty. I opened the duffel wider and shoved my hands inside to distract myself. There was a semi-automatic pistol, a black Glock—probably the gun I'd seen Fellows carrying the day before in Dad's office—and its shoulder holster. There were two more full magazines for the pistol; I could tell because Glock magazines have holes in the rear-facing surface, so you can see how many rounds they're holding.

Under the Glock and its magazines lay a big manila envelope.

"I'm at Marilyn Wilding's place," I said.

"Thank heaven," he breathed. "How did you get there? Are you hurt? Thank her for me. Jeez, I'm going to have to give her some free labor for—"

"Dad!" I cut him off. "I'm not in her house. I'm in...I don't know, maybe an old hunting cabin on her property."

"I'll call her," he volunteered.

"No, I don't think we can trust her. Anyway, I'm not sure."

Silence for several long seconds. "What's going on, Bucky?"

Evil set a bottle of water in front of me. "Found these in the cupboard," he whispered.

Idly I opened the envelope, which was held closed only by a length of red string. I didn't want to make Dad nervous, but I didn't want to hide anything from him, either. "Dad, another man got shot." Should I tell him that the shooter was Michael Fellows, the man he'd let into his office to be interviewed by his daughter? Better not, I decided. "Killed, on the Wilding place. I'm not sure what's going on, and I don't know whether Marilyn is involved."

"Becky," he asked, "are you safe?"

"No," I laughed to try to make a joke of it, and my laugh surprised me by almost turning into a sob. Almost, but not quite. "But Evil's here." I grabbed the pistol from the duffel bag and felt more reassured than I'd imagined I would. "We'll be okay."

"I'll tell Sheriff Sutherland."

I sniffed the water and it smelled fine, so I took a sip. I hadn't realized how thirsty I really was until suddenly I'd gulped the entire bottle. "No, Dad."

"Him too?"

I set down the pistol and opened the envelope. Papers fell out, and the words at the top of the first page bellowed at me like a screamo front man:

LAST WILL AND TESTAMENT

Under the title, the text started *I, Aaron Wilding, being of sound mind and body...* *Aaron Wilding* was written in by hand in shaky blue ink.

"I'm not sure, Dad," I said. "I have stuff I have to tell you, but I don't know what's going on yet." My hands shook holding the will. "I think this has something to do with Aaron Wilding's death. Or his property." My breath came fast and shallow. I shoved the will back into the envelope, tucked it under my arm, and picked up the pistol again. "Right now, I need to get out of here."

Evil moved to the cabin door and stood pressed against the wall to keep out of view, peering outside.

"Got it." He considered. "Maybe I can drive into Marilyn's driveway and make up a reason to talk to her...about the court filing. You can sneak into the car."

"Dad," I said. "I have the will."

"What? Bucky, are you saying you took it from the office? What's going on?"

"No. I..." It was too complicated to try to explain, and I only had guesses. I didn't know whether the copy of the will Michael Fellows had was the one Dad apparently hadn't been able to find in his files. It might be a different will entirely. It might be older, or more recent. And anyway, I imagined Dad stepping out of his Taurus in Marilyn's driveway and getting shot by Michael Fellows. "It's too much to try to explain. And I have a better idea. You go park at the marina, and we'll come find you."

"That's a bit of a hike."

"Yeah, it is." My feet ached at the thought. "And Dad, you better drive the long way around. And be sure no one's following you."

"Got you. It'll be an hour and a half, then."

"Yep. And Dad, do you have FindMe?"

"What?"

"Never mind. I'll see you in an hour and a half."

"Rebecca?"

"Yeah, Dad?"

"I'm proud of you. You can do this. You're going to be fine."

"Thanks, Dad." I laughed a little, and felt lighter. "You too."

I hung up the phone.

"Psst!" Evil hissed, stepping back from the door.

"What is it?"

"The shooter is back. He's coming this way."

I cursed mentally. "We can kill him when he comes in the door."

Evil raised one eyebrow at me. "Are you ready to do that?"

"No," I admitted. "But if it's necessary—"

"If it's necessary," Evil cut in, "*I'll* shoot the son of a bitch. Killing a man's gonna look funny on your law school applications, even if it is justifiable homicide." He held out his hand and I gave him the pistol. He was right. He was probably a better shot than me, too, and frankly, I wasn't sure I could trust myself to pull the trigger.

"The loft," I said, and pointed. Before Evil could say anything else, I scooted up the slats of the built-in ladder. The sleeping cubbies were useless as hiding places, just bare flat holes a hunter could throw a sleeping bag into, and the bathroom was no better. At least from the top we could get the drop on him if we had to.

Of course, we'd have to. We had his gun, and Evil had smashed the door open. He'd know we were here.

"The gun," I whispered. "Put it back."

The loft was formed by two-by-eights nailed as planks across more two-by-eights as rafters. I stretched flat on it, sending up billows of dust.

"Too late," Evil hissed, lying down next to me with both hands on the pistol grip. "Besides, he won't know when I took it exactly. I might have taken the pistol when I escaped from the bathtub."

That was when I realized I was still holding the will. I bit back a curse just as the door banged open.

I didn't dare peek, and I didn't dare move. I lay still and listened to the little cabin creak as Fellows stepped inside.

"Damn," he said.

The two bottles of water. I kicked myself mentally. He knew we'd been here.

I heard the soft click of icons being tapped on a phone, then a pause.

"You really should stay away," Fellows said. Talking to someone on his phone. "People are dropping dead around here, and the dying isn't finished. Not...quite yet."

CHAPTER
13

It seemed impossible that Michael Fellows couldn't hear my heart, it was pounding so loud. I breathed slowly through my mouth, to avoid any sniffing sound.

"I don't know how much they know," Fellows said into the phone, "but there are two witnesses. Loose ends, and I'll tie them up. Not that you care."

During a pause I looked at Evil. He lay flat on his belly with both hands on the stolen pistol. His eyes showed the tight focus of concentration. He looked as if he was lying in wait for a deer, and that made me feel a little better.

"It's better that I don't tell you who. But I'll take care of them. They have the old will, so I'll get that back from them."

What did Michael Fellows mean by *the old will?*

I looked at Evil and arched an eyebrow. I meant it to be quizzical, but he just winked at me.

"No, it's not her problem. I keep telling you to keep her out of this, keep her ignorant, don't bring her here. I'll do what needs to be done."

It took a real effort not to gulp.

"If she keeps pushing, tell her bears in swimming suits want her to stay away."

Huh? I tried to remember...hadn't Charlie Herbert said a similar thing?

But no, Charlie had muttered something about bears and balloons. If I'd even heard him right in the first place. Maybe bears in pantaloons? But swimming suits weren't pantaloons, either.

"Just stay away. I'll call you."

Fellows knew we had the will. That meant he had looked inside his duffel, which meant he also knew we had taken his pistol. I imagined him pointing the rifle at me through the cheap plywood of the loft, and it took a real effort not to raise my head and peek.

Instead, I turned and looked at Evil again. He still looked cool and focused.

I took a slow, deep, silent breath.

I heard the soft *bang* of a shutting door. I was about to sit up, but Evil grabbed my wrist, then motioned me with a finger to wait a minute.

I waited at least a minute, but it seemed like ten. I just watched Evil and waited, and then he lurched forward to the edge of the loft, pistol first.

"He's gone."

My soft, controlled breathing exploded into a noisy *puff*.

"Did you hear all that?" I asked.

Evil nodded. "That guy wants us dead."

"There was more to what he said than that," I objected.

"Yeah, but that's the piece I cared about." Evil crept down the ladder and peered out the windows. "His car's gone."

"We have to find out what's going on. And we have to warn... people, I don't know. Dad."

"We have to get to safety. And right now, that means the marina. Which is a long hike, and we just lost ten minutes to playing hide and seek with a hitman, so we'd better get started."

Evil was right. I folded up the will and shoved it in my jeans pocket. Which will was it? Was it, after all, the will Dad had on file in his office? Or some other will?

Had the men who had broken into Dad's office—Michael Fellows and the other one, who was still a mystery—been after the will? And had Michael beat the other fellow to it, or were they in cahoots? And what had Charlie Herbert been doing there? And who was Michael Fellows working for?

Evil snapped his fingers in front of my eyes. "You've got your thinking face on," he said. "Ordinarily, I don't object. But right now, we need to have our running and hiding faces."

"Yep," I agreed. "Let's go."

Evil led the way, and we headed north. The marina was a collection of docks on the Millard J. Fillmore Reservoir, where a few people kept boats and more people dragged boats up behind their trucks, to go fishing, waterskiing, or just boating. It was several miles' hike, and not on level ground.

We'd meet Dad, I'd tell him what happened, and we'd plan.

Just as I was telling myself that, we crossed an asphalt drive. I stopped.

"Evil," I said, "aren't we still on the Wilding property?"

"Yep." He nodded, but his eyes moved constantly in a circle around us, watching. "We haven't hit the barbed wire on the other side yet."

"The driveway must go out the other side of the property, right?" I pointed. "West? So what's this?"

Evil shrugged. "A private road. It ain't illegal to put in your own road on your own property."

"Aren't you curious?"

"Sure. I also want to avoid getting shot."

"This kind of heads our direction." I turned right and walked along the asphalt. "Let's just see where it goes."

"Bucky," Evil snorted, following. "This may not be the right time."

He was right, of course. But I was sick of running away, and sick of having my hand forced. I wanted to be the hunter for once, not the prey. "Something's going on up here, and I want to find out what. Besides, Fellows went the other way, right? So unless he suddenly goes off-road with that Corolla of his, he's nowhere near us. Just keep an eye behind us in case he doubles back."

The thought of him doubling back made me uncomfortable, so I picked up the pace. That hurt, but I could survive an awful lot of bruised feet and strained ankles. The feeling of being on the chase was exhilarating.

"Doggone it, Bucky," Evil puffed on my heels, "you're not supposed to run *toward* danger."

The road didn't go far. It wound down a slope and then up a hill and stopped, in about ten minutes' walk, in front of a little house. One of those one-bedroom, pre-fab kind of houses, that you buy from the company and it just comes out and drops the house on your lot in an afternoon. A kit, and one that had been assembled here years ago, judging by the deep sag of the porch. The house was painted the same bleached shade of yellow as the tall autumn grass.

There was no car parked in front, no number on the door, no mailbox.

"Bucky—"

"Fellows isn't here." I stepped onto the porch.

"But you don't know who *is*." Evil quick-stepped to get in front of me, took one last look around from the porch, and then tried the door handle.

It turned, and he let himself in. I followed.

The interior smelled like stale sweat but it was neat, mostly because there wasn't much in there. A single ratty La-Z-Boy by one of the windows and two bookshelves built of cinder blocks and long planks made up the entire furniture of the front room. The shelves were packed with worn paperbacks. I didn't recognize all the titles, but the ones I knew were science fiction: *Dune*, *The Moon Is a Harsh Mistress*, *Empire of Silence*, and so on.

"A nerd lives here," I said. "And he lives alone."

"Could be a woman," Evil shot back. "Don't be sexist."

"Could be, but I'm just playing the odds." I picked up several of the books and looked inside them. They all had the same name penciled on the inside front cover in a ragged, loopy-looking hand. "And look at that, I win. This is Charlie Herbert's house."

"That's the guy who got shot in your Dad's office last night."

I nodded and kept looking around.

Two-thirds of the little house comprised a single space, shaped like an L. The front of that space was the Spartan living room, and the back was a kitchenette. The cupboards were full of beans and canned soup. A dish drainer on the countertop held a couple of bowls and some silverware.

In the window over the kitchen sink was a single plant. I stared at it.

"That," Evil said, "is marijuana. Skunk. Pot. Grass. Reefer. Burrito. Broccoli. Hash."

"Broccoli?" I asked. "Really?"

Evil nodded. "Mary Jane. Stinkweed. I'm sure you've heard of it."

"Well, yeah," I said. "I just haven't seen it in real life. In pictures...you know." Dad had represented plenty of kids, and adults too, busted for possession over the years. I'd been offered a joint once or twice, but I'd never taken it. I'd even seen marijuana as a processed product, ready to smoke but balled up in the sheriff's evidence bags, but I'd never seen an actual growing plant.

"Huh. Funny life you lead, Becky McCrae."

"Isn't that the truth?"

I poked around in the rest of the building, but there wasn't much else to see. A bedroom with a single, tiny, sagging bed, and a bathroom with a toilet and shower. All of it not particularly clean.

Out the window in the kitchen's back door, by accident, I caught a glimpse of something more interesting.

"What do you make of that?" I asked Evil, pointing.

He looked. "There's another road. And a truck."

"Yeah," I agreed. "*Another* road, not the same road. This house isn't on a single road, it has two roads that lead to it."

"Weird."

"Or one road that leads to it, and one that leads away." As I said it, I tried to digest what it might mean.

Evil stepped into the bedroom to look out the window there. "Want to hear something even weirder?"

"Why are you teasing me?" I joined him to look.

He pointed out the window. A fence ran from the side of the house out a hundred feet or more to a rock wall. "What do you make of that?" he asked.

I thought about it. "This house isn't *on* a road," I said. "This house *blocks* the road. It's like a gate. It stops you from going any further, unless you get out, and switch vehicles to that truck back there."

"There's something down that road," Evil suggested. He's not dumb, Evil Patten.

"And Charlie Herbert was the gatekeeper. Whatever's down that road, to get there you had to pass Charlie."

"Or maybe he was the only one who was supposed to go there. He wasn't all that scary, as guards go."

I nodded, trying to remember what Charlie had said, when I'd nearly shot him at the Fun Lanes. Something about trailers...he'd gone to the wrong trailer, he'd said.

"Would you call this building a trailer?" I asked Evil.

He stared at me. "Nope. This is a house."

"What about that cabin? The A-frame?"

"A cabin."

"Are you sure?"

"Trust me, I'm an expert in trailers, and this is not one. Why?"

"Charlie said, at Dad's office, when I was locking up and Charlie came up to me, he said he'd gone to the wrong trailer. I'm just thinking...maybe it has something to do with what's down that road."

"Maybe there's a trailer down the road. Maybe there's two, and Charlie went to the wrong one." Evil shrugged. "But why would Charlie come tell that to you? Or your dad?"

I shook my head, stumped. "Maybe it's irrelevant."

"But you're not thinking we're going to go down that road, right, Bucky?" Evil asked. "Because that road will keep taking us east, and we've come just about as far east as we need to come. If we don't go north now, we're going to leave Jim sitting around and twiddling his thumbs at the marina, wondering where we are."

"That wouldn't be good."

"Not with that guy on the loose with his rifle. And we still need to tell the sheriff about him. About all of it."

"The sheriff." I nodded. "Or somebody."

"Somebody," Evil agreed.

I went to where I'd dropped the science fiction novels and picked them off the floor. It's not that I'm a neat freak or anything, but I was imagining what future investigators might think if they came poking around, trying to find out who killed Charlie Herbert and why. I didn't want them to find Charlie's copy of *Empire of Silence* on the floor, and my fingerprints all over it.

So I wiped the books' covers with the edge of my flannel shirt, and put them back where I thought they'd come from.

"Right," I said. "Let's—"

Bang!

One of the house's two front windows shattered, and a bullet hit me.

CHAPTER
14

I fell.

Insanely, the thought that went through my head as I hit the floor was *I should be screaming. I'm not screaming. What's wrong with me?*

The bullet hit me in the upper arm, my right arm. I felt my flesh tearing, and I felt the crack as the bullet hit bone. Glass showered around me as I toppled backward.

Then I hit the floor, and didn't feel it at all.

"Evil," I said.

He threw himself to the floor and skidded to my side. "No exit wound," he said. "Bullet's still in there."

"Pretty sure my arm's broken."

He nodded. "The truck in the back. That's our best way out of here. We get to the truck and drive off, he's going to have a heck of a time getting that Corolla over the fence and into the backyard."

"Depends on how long that road is." I pointed.

"It's our best shot."

"No pun intended."

"Of course not."

"Thanks for not saying *I told you so.*"

Evil grinned. "I don't know what you're talking about." From where he lay on his belly, he looked out the shattered window. "Think you can stand?"

"Probably." I was feeling a little woozy, but I didn't tell Evil that.

"I'm going to give this guy something to think about, slow him down. The minute I start shooting, you get up and run for the truck out back."

"I don't have a key."

"Hey, sagebillies and internal combustion engines, remember? This is my field. I can hotwire it, you just need to get yourself behind the wheel with your head down."

Before he'd finished his instructions, Evil was crawling across the floor to the unbroken window. Raising himself on one elbow, he peeped out the window's corner into the front yard.

"I see him," Evil said. "You ready?"

I nodded.

"Now!"

Evil started firing. *Bang! Bang! Bang!*

The window's glass shattered and I heard cursing from the front yard, but as soon as the firing started I moved. I stumbled to my feet with my right arm hanging by my side. I shot a quick glance around the kitchen, looking for a peg with truck keys on it, just in case, but no such luck, and then I kicked open the back door and ran.

Bang! Bang! Bang!

The yard behind the house was a gnarled mountain hillside, spotted with clumps of tall grass. My ankles burned, but I staggered down to the truck and yanked on the door handle. Mercifully, it opened.

I peeked behind me as I fell into the front seat. Evil crashed out the back door of the house and raced my way full tilt. I slid behind the wheel and slumped low.

Ahead of me, a tongue of asphalt wound down and left, into a valley and out of sight.

"Brake!" Evil shouted. He yanked open the shotgun-side door and threw himself in onto the floor of the truck. He grabbed the casing around the base of the steering column and ripped it off, exposing a mass of wires.

I released the hand brake.

"Right," Evil said to himself, poking at the wires. "Now, which of these...?"

Just in case, I reached up and flipped down the sun visor. Tucked into an elastic band behind it was a key.

Bang!

The front and rear windshields of the truck shattered together, spraying cubes of safety glass all over me.

I grabbed the key. "Evil!"

He looked up. "What are you waiting for?" Sliding up beside me in the seat, he pointed the Glock out the back window and started firing again.

The truck coughed into life as I turned the key. I risked one quick glimpse ahead of me as I pushed the truck into drive, then ducked and let the vehicle roll.

"Is it Fellows?" I asked.

Bang! Bang!

"Are you saying there are people *besides* him who want to kill you?"

It hurt, but I laughed. Another shot from Fellows's rifle *whooshed* through the truck's cab.

"He's on foot, right?"

"Yeah, but he's gaining. You want to go a little faster?"

I felt the bump as the truck slipped off the shoulder and pulled the steering wheel left. My right arm wouldn't move, so I only had my left hand to do it with. Feeling exposed, fearing a bullet to the back of the head at any second, I peeked over the dash to see where I was going and stepped on the gas.

A final bullet whined and banged away off the side of the truck bed, and then I'd made the turn. We had to be out of sight.

I scooted up a little higher.

"Evil," I said, "I don't feel so good."

He set down the pistol. "Don't get funny about this, but I'm going to take your shirt off."

"I kind of feel like swooning, but I think that's just loss of blood."

"Could be just sight and smell of it, too. Most people aren't used to seeing blood, and when they do they feel faint."

"I feel faint."

"Breathe deep and keep us on the road." He held up a kitchen towel. It looked clean; he must have taken it from Charlie Herbert's kitchen. "I'm going to slip your arm out of your shirt and bandage you."

"Just the flannel," I warned him. "You try and take my t-shirt off, I'll wreck the truck. On purpose."

Evil grinned. "Might be worth it, though."

I grinned back and clutched the steering wheel for dear life with my left hand.

Evil was gentle. I'm not a hunter, but he is, and I hear from the kids who hunt that you have opportunities to administer first aid from time to time up in the hills, waiting behind blinds for deer to wander by. Whether it was because of practice or natural talent, Evil was patient and sure-handed. He eased my right arm out of its sleeve.

"Is there a lot of blood?" I didn't look. I wasn't afraid, but I was worried by how light-headed I felt. Fainting and crashing would be a bad way to die.

"Naw," he said, "it's nothing." Then he did his cheesiest Monty Python English accent. "It's only a flesh wound."

"I've had worse." My own bad English accent mostly sounded Australian, which sort of made it funnier. We both laughed, and Evil wrapped the towel around my arm.

"That'll do for now. But the bullet's in you, and you need your arm set, and frankly I wish I had something to clean the wound with. We need to get you to a doctor."

"Maybe this road will take us to the marina," I suggested.

"Yeah." He didn't sound convinced. "Maybe."

But to go back to the marina, the road would have to turn left— north. Instead, it weaved left and right, but continued basically straight—east.

The sunlight was bright in my eyes.

The end of the road was approaching. I could see it, with a tall stand of pine trees clumped around the edge of a hill. The hill was shaped funny—its side facing the trees was vertical. Like a cliff face.

I tingled.

"Evil." My own voice sounded far away.

"Yeah?" He was looking out the back window.

"I think I might be passing out."

The edges of my vision faded, and things in the center fell back. It was as if I was suddenly looking through the wrong end of binoculars. I felt my hand slip from the wheel.

Uh oh.

Then Evil was there. He grabbed the steering wheel, and threw his leg across mine. "Evil," I murmured, a sort of objection, but of course he was going for the brake pedal.

I couldn't see anything. I felt Evil nearly lying across me and squirming as he tried to control the truck, but it felt as if we were going faster. I sucked in a deep breath of air.

Evil cursed.

My vision came back, and I saw that we were barreling toward the pine trees. Evil was trying to step on the brake, but I was in the way, and he was instead forcing my foot down on the accelerator.

"Bucky!" he shouted.

I couldn't shout anything back. I didn't have enough breath.

Instead, I grabbed the handbrake and yanked it up.

The truck screamed in protest and drifted sideways, turning as if it wanted to begin a parking lot donut and at the same time shuddering as if it might fall apart. I was still on the edge of fainting, and I saw trees and hillside spin around in my vision, like a wilderness crown over Evil's head as he tried to control the wheel. We spun, rocked, bounced...

And stopped.

Evil banged into the steering wheel and then fell on top of me, squeezing the last air out of my lungs in a pathetic little *whoof.* Immediately, he jumped back, collapsing into his own seat.

"Bucky!" I couldn't see him, and he sounded a million miles

away.

"Present." I inhaled slowly, my head tingling. "Breathing."

Evil laughed. As my vision crept back I started laughing, too.

"Well," he said finally. "Let's get you inside. There's got to be some stuff in here we can use. Rubbing alcohol and a real bandage, for example. Some fluid for you to drink."

"Inside?"

Evil pointed. I looked and saw that the sheer cliff face I had noticed as I was blacking out was not natural. The front of the hillside had been carved away, and embedded in its face was a sliding metal door, like you'd find on a big self-storage unit.

"I don't get it," I said.

"Don't you?" Evil climbed out of the truck and walked over the door. He had the Glock in his hand, and he pointed it at the heavy padlock that hung on the door, closing it. "I think it's pretty obvious we'll find some useful things behind this door. And maybe even informative things. Maybe we'll learn what Charlie Herbert was up to."

"Like what?" I opened my door and stumbled out. I looked up the road behind us to be sure Michael Fellows wasn't in sight. We'd got a head start on the assassin, as I was coming to think of him, but he could catch up, especially if we stopped moving. "Charlie Herbert was a computer programmer." As I said it, repeating what Dad had told me, I realized it might not be true.

"Yeah? You see any books on computer programming in Charlie's house? You see any computers?"

I shook my head.

Bang! Evil shot the padlock, which jumped, and then fell to the ground.

Evil grimaced from pain and effort as he bent to grab the handle of the rolling door. With a grunt, he heaved the door up and shoved it into the ceiling.

Behind the door, and going deep back into the hill, stood row after row of marijuana plants.

CHAPTER
15

I stared. I saw drip pipes, fans, and misters. I saw thermometers and bags of soil mixes. I saw long white lights, softly shining. All over, I saw gloves and trowels and utility knives.

And row upon row of leafy green marijuana plant.

"How much do you think this is worth?" I asked.

Evil snorted, and then I realized he wasn't standing next to me anymore. He'd turned from my side and was rummaging through a standing rack of metal shelving. "What makes you think I know the street value of weed?"

I shrugged. "Fair enough. But you know some surprising and even useful things."

Evil shot a glance at the plants, sticking his tongue out of the corner of his mouth and squinting past his thumb. "Rough estimate?"

"Rough estimate," I agreed.

"A lot." He turned from the shelving with a first aid kid in his arms, the Glock tucked into his belt. "I'd say the street value of this weed is *a lot*. You want to get technical, I'd say it probably even amounts to a *shizload*. Even legal."

"It isn't exactly legal," I said. "It's still against federal law and the state laws in plenty of states. And I hear banks don't like it—they won't deposit your cash if you're selling marijuana to earn it."

"Yeah? That gives me an idea for a business."

"Marijuana farmer, like Charlie Herbert?"

Evil scratched his chin. "I don't want you to think I'm too much of an expert, but I think in marijuana terms, this is no farm."

"Looks like a lot to me."

"Yeah, but compared to what? I mean, I think a real professional outfit would have a bunch of these sheds. Or a canyon full of Stinkweed. This is to real marijuana farming what raised beds in the backyard are to Monsanto. This is just a small business, or for personal use."

"That was well put," I said. "Color me impressed. So, big-time weed farming for you, then."

"Nope." Evil grinned. "Marijuana banker. Could you see yourself married someday to a big city marijuana banker? Or maybe a marijuana banker in a small city, like, say, Boise."

"It wasn't really what I had in mind."

"What did you have in mind, then?"

"I hadn't planned that far."

"So you're not saying *no*. Hold still."

I leaned against a heavy table stacked deep with weed. From the first aid kit, Evil dug out a tube of betadine. Then he pulled off the kitchen towel and smeared the antiseptic on my wound, which stung, and turned my arm red where it wasn't already.

"That probably hurt a bit," Evil said.

"You're supposed to tell me in advance."

"I'm just a poor sagebilly," he clucked, "doing the best I can."

"Man, you so want to be one of the Dukes of Hazzard," I said.

"I want both of us to be the Dukes of Hazzard. I'm generous that way."

"You think it's generous to imagine me wearing a pair of Daisy Dukes?"

Evil snorted. "What are you talking about? I had you cast as Uncle Jesse."

"I do look pretty fetching in overalls."

From the kit he also took gauze and tape. "I don't suppose you're carrying a tampon?"

If I hadn't been in so much pain, I might have slapped him. "Really, Evil? That's what you're thinking about right now?"

He shrugged. "Absorbs blood. That's what they made them for in the first place, didn't you know that? Plugging bullet holes on the battlefield."

I felt dumb. "No, I didn't know that," I admitted. "I guess maybe I ought to start carrying one around, in case I get shot."

"Or I could," Evil said. "I got a big wallet. A tampon would kind of be a matching set, you know, with the condom?"

"Kind of," I said. "But not really."

Evil rewrapped my wound.

"This is only temporary," he said. "The bullet's still in there. How you feeling? Lightheaded? Cold?" He touched my forehead. Checking me for symptoms of shock.

"I need water."

"I've got something better." Evil jumped back to the shelving and brought me two bottles of Gatorade. "Warm," he warned me, "but I'm pretty sure they haven't been opened."

"Perfect." I gulped half a bottle of orange Gatorade before coming up for breath. The effort left me gasping, and my mouth tasting like salt. "Now let's get out of here before Fellows catches us."

I took a step toward the door and fainted.

When I came to, Evil was hauling me to my feet again and leaning me against the table.

"Come on, sailor," he said. "I've got a better idea."

He disappeared down among the weed for a moment, and when he came back he had a wheelbarrow. "It isn't clean, but it's got wheels."

I looked at the wheelbarrow, big and black and rusting. It held a thin layer of soil in its bottom. "Correction: it's got *a* wheel."

"Fair enough," Evil agreed. "Pretty sure it still qualifies as a bitchin' mode of transportation. Now sit your butt down before you fall...again. And stay awake, Uncle Jesse."

"In a wheelbarrow?"

"We have to go off road from here. I don't think it's too far, but we're talking about little trails, not roads that will fit a truck. Maybe something with a higher suspension and bigger wheels would work, anyway, but not the truck we have."

"You're going to push me?" But I sat down.

"And take this stuff." Without waiting for my agreement, Evil dropped into my lap the Gatorade, a lighter, a rolled cigarette, and the pistol. Then he grabbed the wheelbarrow handles and pushed me toward the door.

The lightheadedness I felt made the cigarette seem all the stranger. I held it up and looked at it. "This has to be a joint, right?" I sniffed it; it smelled like pot. "Tell me it's not yours."

Evil shook his head. I had to hand it to him, if our roles had been reversed and I'd been trying to schlep him around in a wheelbarrow, I'd have been grunting and sweating by the third step. He seemed nonchalant. "I figure it's Charlie Herbert's."

"What am I going to do with it?"

At the door, Evil stopped to grab a fire blanket. He threw it over my legs and kept going.

"How bad's the pain?"

"Pretty bad."

"Smoke it." He shrugged. "If you want. That's what medical marijuana does, isn't it? Ease pain?"

I looked at the stubby little joint and laughed. "Evil Patten, we're alone in the woods and you're trying to get me high."

He chuckled, pushing the wheelbarrow onto a path between pine trees. "Can't blame a guy for trying."

"And the Glock?"

"Both my hands are engaged." Now he *was* grunting as he rolled me uphill. "If anyone needs shooting before we get to the marina, it's your turn."

I took the gun in my left hand and rested it on my right thigh.

That was the only convenient way not to have it pointing at either me or Evil, since I sat facing him in the wheelbarrow and my right arm was still useless. My flannel shirt had entirely disappeared, though in my hazy state I wasn't sure exactly when that had happened, so I had no pocket to put the joint into. Instead, I let it sit with the lighter in a depression left in the fire blanket where it stretched across my knees.

"Will it disappoint you that I'm not going to smoke it?" I asked Evil.

"A little bit." Sweat trickled down Evil's face and darkened his shirt under his arms.

"Tell you what," I offered. "I'll keep it. You and I can smoke it later."

"Unless it's evidence," Evil said.

"Evidence of what? That Charlie Herbert smoked marijuana? You can't prosecute a dead man. And anyway, there's a whole bunker full of pot, if anyone's wondering what Charlie's job was."

"Just trying to sound sophisticated." Evil grinned. "Like a good pot banker does."

"Pot bankers can probably afford lawyers to do the sophisticated thinking for them. Just no smoking at the Fun Lanes," I said. "We have enough rogue smells to try to control as it is."

"Well, if we smoke at my house, someone will tell us we have to pass it around."

"I guess that just leaves school. We'll be busted for sure."

"You'll have to be my lawyer."

"I'm not qualified."

"Pretty sure the court will let you make a motion. You can appear *pro hunk*."

I stared at Evil for several long seconds before giggling. Yeah, I was light-headed and profoundly relieved, and I actually giggled. "Evil Patten, did you just make a Latin joke?"

"Thanks for laughing," Evil said. "I've been saving that one up for a long time."

"I will appear *pro hunk* if necessary," I agreed. "But I'd rather smoke it somewhere where we won't get busted."

Evil shrugged and grinned. "Howard County's a big place. I'm sure we'll think of a good spot."

A turn and slight depression in the trail gave me a clear look at the climb behind us. Evil had understated how rough the trail was, I could see. I didn't think I could have pushed the wheelbarrow up this hill, even if it were *empty*.

"Evil Patten," I said. "This may be the pot speaking, but you're a good man."

"It ain't the pot," Evil shot back. "It's the blood loss."

"It's true I haven't smoked the pot yet. But maybe it's like a flashback. I'm having a flashforward, to when I will have smoked it." I wasn't sure I really wanted to smoke the joint, but the more I talked about it, the more normal it seemed for me and Evil to really light up a doobie and pass it back and forth. "The pot I will smoke in the future is coming back to the present to make me say dopey things. Kill brain cells, you know? I'll probably never be able to graduate college now."

"Pretty sure it's the blood loss. Try drinking a little more Gatorade."

I let go of the Glock long enough to finish the first bottle of Gatorade. Then I tucked the empty plastic down beside my leg where it couldn't get knocked out of the wheelbarrow and took my grip on the pistol again.

I didn't doze, but my mind wandered, and I slipped in and out of focus. Every once in a while, when I felt most dopey, Evil would stop pushing the wheelbarrow and pinch my knee. When we passed through trees, as we did from time to time, I noticed the birdsong and sometimes even the rustle of animals moving in the woods. When Evil trundled me along bare ridges, the heat of the sun soaked into the fire blanket and my skin. I smelled grass and sweat. At some point, Evil made me drink more Gatorade, and not long after that I had to ask for a halt.

"Call of nature," I said.

He frowned and set down the wheelbarrow handles. I had never realized before how strong he was. He'd been hiding it from me, I guess, which seemed wrong. If you had a buff boyfriend, shouldn't he be showing off his strength?

Of course, Evil wasn't my boyfriend anymore. Really, he hadn't ever been my boyfriend.

"I'm not sure you have the strength to stand," Evil said. "Maybe you ought to just pee in the wheelbarrow."

"Well, that would put an end to you wanting to watch *The Last of the Mohicans* with me."

"Would it?" Evil shrugged. "Or I could just help you scoot forward and you could pee over the edge of the wheelbarrow."

"That's enough." Too many unsettling images of Evil trying to help me urinate flooded my mind. No pun intended. I inched forward. "Help me stand up here."

Evil shrugged himself under my shoulder—he's strong, but he's not much taller than I am—and easily hoisted me to my feet. "There are trees over there," he said.

"I can walk." I disentangled myself from his grasp and started limping in the direction he pointed, to a small stand of aspens. "Besides, you've been working like a dog. You need a rest."

"Like a mule." Evil grinned. "Dogs don't generally carry stuff."

I threw a faint nod in his direction and stumbled away. My ride in the wheelbarrow had let my legs lock up and my feet fill with blood, and the first few steps were excruciating. Halfway to the trees, I'd regained my land legs a bit, and by the time I left Evil's sight, my walk was dignified again.

I found a place I could sit. "Don't listen!"

"I'm not!"

"Yes, you are! You heard *that!*"

Evil hesitated a few seconds before answering. "Well, I *have to* listen. Otherwise, how will I know if you're in trouble and need help?"

"For the last time, Ronald Evil Patten, I do *not* need your help to pee!" I thought about it a bit. "Whistle! Whistle loud!"

He promptly whistled, but not a tune—he let out a wolf whistle.

"No! Something musical!"

"Oh, right." Evil was quiet for a while, then started to whistle the opening bars to Metallica's "Enter Sandman."

That would have to do. I set down the pistol and did my business.

With the distraction of Evil's whistling, my having only one good arm, the aching of all my muscles, and the continuing lightheadedness, it took a few minutes.

Just as I was finishing, I heard a loud *crack!*

Evil's whistling stopped.

I almost called out to him. I would have called out, except for the *crack*. But that sound struck cold fear into me. What if Evil had tripped and hit his head? What if Michael Fellows had caught up to us, and had hurt Evil?

I couldn't wait, and I couldn't be a delicate flower, however much I might want to.

I grabbed the pistol. Without pulling up my pants, I stood up and shuffled back through the trees. At least I was wearing a long t-shirt, I thought with relief.

Evil lay on the ground beside the wheelbarrow. He wasn't moving, and there was blood in his scalp. Leaning over him, with one hand checking Evil's pockets and the other holding his long rifle, was Michael Fellows.

"Get away from him!" I yelled. Working the slide once to chamber a round, I pointed the pistol right at the center of Fellows's· chest. Aiming for the center of mass, especially with me using my left hand.

Fellows looked up. At another time, I'd have enjoyed the expression of complete astonishment on his face. As it was, my heart pounded in my ears and my head swam.

"Where's the will?" Fellows stood and started walking toward me.

"Stand back," I warned him.

"I know you took it, and your buddy there doesn't have it. Where's the will?"

"Stop!"

Michael Fellows raised his rifle.

CHAPTER
16

Bang! Bang! Bang!

I'd shot at a few targets in my life. Not a lot, but a few. But shooting a beer bottle or a paper cutout of Osama Bin Laden is a really different thing from shooting a live human being.

Michael Fellows jerked as I shot him. His body bounced up and back a bit with each bullet that hit, like a little dance.

Some of my shots missed—I was shooting with my left hand, after all, and maybe I was in shock, though at least I hadn't lit up the joint —but several found their mark, and then Michael Fellows hit the ground.

"Evil!" I shouted.

No answer.

I would have tucked the Glock into my belt, but I was afraid if I tried I'd shoot myself. I was shaking like a freight train, and my thoughts were bolting in six directions at once, too. I forced myself to concentrate.

I knelt at Evil's side. "Evil." Setting the Glock down in a clump of grass, I felt under his nose; he was breathing. I prodded him. "Come on, Evil, wake up."

I could see the bright pink flesh under his hair. Fellows must have hit him with the butt of his rifle, and the blow had just about scalped Evil. The blood trickling down onto Evil's forehead was shockingly red.

I shook his shoulder. "Come on, Evil, it's time to watch Daniel Day-Lewis and his perfect hair. *The Last of the Mohicans.* Come on, wake up."

"Mrmerumph. Erumph," Evil muttered into the dirt.

My heart jumped in my chest. "What's that?"

Evil turned his head slightly, getting his mouth out of the dirt. "Now I know you're desperate. You hate *The Last of the Mohicans*."

"I don't *hate* it," I said.

"That's a good thing." Evil's eyelids fluttered as if he were fighting sleep. "I've been waiting a long time for you to get desperate."

"Your plan worked," I told him. "All you had to do was get me to witness a murder, and then get lost wandering around the Ups with a killer on my trail."

"Simple as pie. My *Evil* plan."

"I have to ask you something." In the heat of the moment, I'd forgotten. "And it's kind of embarrassing." I pushed Evil's shoulder again. Until his eyes opened all the way, I worried about concussion. A hit to the head is a serious thing.

"There's nothing wrong with a guy liking My Little Pony," Evil said.

I laughed sharply, then caught myself, unsure whether he was joking. "Not that. It's that...well, I may need help pulling up my pants."

Evil wedged an arm under his cheek and pushed his face off the ground. He chuckled. "Well, that doesn't embarrass me at all."

"That makes one of us."

"Tell you what. If it will help you be less embarrassed, I'll let you pull my pants down before we start." Evil pushed against the ground, and rolled slowly over onto his back. "Ow, ow, ow." He covered both eyes with his hand.

"I respect your willingness to have a level playing field, anyway."

"I'm all about fairness. For instance, you got shot, so I went and let an elephant run over my head."

"It was Fellows," I told him. "I guess he snuck up on you."

"Must have. I was minding my own business trying to think of what to whistle next, and all of the sudden I'm on the ground feeling like I need to scream, with you standing over me asking me to pull down your pants."

"Up," I said. "Pull *up* my pants."

"Right. That's an important difference. Can you help me sit up?"

Evil stretched out an arm. I shot another look at Michael Fellows to be sure he wasn't rising to his feet like a zombie to come take his revenge, and then I helped Evil. Me pulling a little and pushing some and then with him leaning on me like a ladder, and Evil was able to climb to his feet.

"Okay." His breath was fast and deep, panting. "Let's get those pants up."

For all his joking about it, Evil was a gentleman when I needed him to be. He looked the other way, hooked his thumbs into the waist of my jeans, and hoisted them into place.

"Thanks." I snapped and zipped up. Even that was awkward, with just the one hand.

"Missed opportunities," he said. "Story of my life."

"You've got a lot of story left to write."

"So what would have been the right answer?" Evil bent slowly and picked up the Glock. He winced and grimaced every time he moved. "About movies, I mean. So, I get that you don't love *The Last of the Mohicans*. You have explained that fact, and I have heard it. So what movie should I have picked?"

"Evil, it isn't about the movie. It's about..."

"Yeah?"

And I hesitated. It's not as if I was going to become his girlfriend, because we'd been shot at together, or even because he'd saved me. But I did feel a little bit like I owed him.

"You know," I said, "I like movies that are funny. *Groundhog Day*. I'd rather watch *Groundhog Day* with you than *The Last of the Mohicans*."

"See?" Evil said. "Was that so hard?"

"Kind of," I admitted. "And I'm really counting on you forgetting this whole conversation, what with the blow to the head and all."

"You're forgetting about my Evil plans." Evil limped over to Michael Fellows. He bent down and put two fingers on the killer's neck. "Shoot." He stood straight and pointed the Glock at Fellows's head.

"Wait!"

Evil cocked his head in my direction. "You're in bad shape, Bucky," he said. "And so am I. We can't let this guy follow us. So as far as I'm concerned, the first time you shot him was self-defense, and you...fired a couple more bullets than you realized."

"It *was* self-defense," I said. "Shooting him *now* would be *murder*."

"I dunno," Evil said. "I see it more as additional self-defense. Of the preemptive kind."

"Don't do it." In that moment, I saw Evil clearly. Not the physical Evil, but Evil's person, his soul. He was a good person, with humor and patience. I was afraid he'd spoil all that if he killed someone. But that couldn't be the reason I gave Evil himself. "This guy's a witness. Remember, he's not the only one involved. The cops are going to want to talk to him, find out who he's working for."

Evil sighed. His hand shook a little, and I thought maybe he felt relief that I had taken the option and the responsibility away from him. "Then you gotta take his rifle."

I limped over to Michael Fellows and took the weapon. It was a bolt-action Remington Model 700, a hunter's gun. I worked the bolt, which was awkward with only one arm working properly, to make sure there wasn't a round in the chamber. Then I cradled the rifle in my arms and stepped back.

I breathed deeply to keep from feeling giddy. "Let's go," I said. "Dad's been at the marina for a while."

"Hold on." Wincing again as he bent down, Evil rummaged through Michael Fellows's pockets. He came out with keys, a wallet, and two cell phones, one of which was Evil's own. Evil tapped open some app and started typing.

"Email?" I asked. "Are you getting reception all the way up here?"

"Nope, just taking down a note." He turned his phone and showed it to me. *Groundhog Day*, he'd typed into a text file. "See? Now it doesn't matter even if I get hit on the head again."

Michael Fellows mumbled something and twitched. His eyes were closed. Close up, I could see that I'd hit him at least three times, once in the ribs and twice in the shoulder. He wasn't bleeding as much as I'd expected.

"I hope this guy lives long enough for Sheriff Sutherland or the FBI to talk to him."

"Really?" Evil asked. "Me, I kind of hope he dies. But I wish I had something to tie him up with in the meantime. Like those elephant-sized zip ties he used on me."

"He won't be coming after us." I nodded northward, toward the Reservoir. "Sorry I don't have a tampon to tape to your head. Let's go."

I walked right past the wheelbarrow without mentioning it, and Evil didn't say anything. He was in no shape to be pushing me anymore, he just held his own shirt to his scalp in one hand and the pistol in the other and walked. We limped north. The good news was that once we got along one more ridge, it was basically downhill all the way to the marina. Also, we had Evil's phone, so every fifteen minutes or so we stopped and looked to see if we had reception.

We looked over our shoulders, to see if Michael Fellows was coming after us, much more frequently.

Evil's phone connected with the network just as we crested the last hill and came in sight of the water. And before we could text or call anybody, Dad saw us. He sat leaning against his Taurus and scanning the hills, but the moment he spotted us he came charging across the two-lane highway and up the slope.

Just behind him came Sheriff Sutherland.

I sort of lost it at that point, to tell the truth. I don't remember much, except that I tried to tell the sheriff what had happened and it all came out in incoherent gobs, just like my story had the night before at his house. No, worse. I'm pretty sure in those two short conversations I managed to convince Sheriff Doug Sutherland that I'm the world's worst storyteller.

Evil said less than I did, and mostly to agree with me, and pretty quickly Sheriff Sutherland had him sitting on the bumper of his pickup truck while the sheriff looked to his scalp with a first aid kit.

We handed over both guns, and I told the sheriff I'd shot Michael Fellows. I skipped the detail about me being in the trees to urinate at the time Fellows attacked Evil, but otherwise I left nothing out. Sheriff Sutherland nodded and patted me on the back, and then he sent a couple of his deputies up into the hills the way we'd come.

Evil also gave the sheriff Michael Fellows's phone and I handed over the will. Dad saw the will and swore. He's no nun, but he's not a big one for blue streaks, either, so as soon as he'd cursed he looked at me and tried to explain himself.

"I think that was stolen from our office," he said.

Our office. For no particular reason, I liked that a lot.

Dad hugged me many times. He smelled like he hadn't showered, but I knew I smelled worse.

"Well, you both need to get to the Urgent Care," the sheriff finally said. It felt like hours had passed since we'd come over the hill, but I'm sure it had only been minutes.

"I'll drive them," Dad offered.

"I'll lead out," the sheriff said. "And I'll throw on the flashing lights so we can really kick some ass."

"Don't you want to go catch Fellows?" I asked.

Sutherland nodded in the direction of his men, disappearing over the ridge. "That's my responsibility and I'll take care of it. I owe a duty to you, too." Then he reached inside his truck and hit the flashing lights.

Evil practically fell into the back seat of the Taurus. I backed into the shotgun seat, feeling my entire body stiffen as I swung my feet into the car.

"You did great, Bucky," Dad said, as we followed Sheriff Sutherland's flashing lights past the Stub and into town. "Only you could have called me last night, you know."

"Dad." I didn't really have a sentence to follow it, so the word just dropped into the hum of the car.

"My guess is you were trying to protect me. But you could have called."

"Yeah," I said.

We passed the Law Offices of James F. McCrae and the Fun Lanes as I said it, and the parking lot caught my eye. It was full of cars.

Three black SUVs. On the small side for SUVs, kind of sporty-looking.

"What do you think?" I asked, pointing. "The feds?"

"We'll find out," Dad said. "First things first."

CHAPTER
17

Howard doesn't have a hospital. You need a real hospital, you have to get down to Boise or over to Yakima, and for specialties you might need to go as far as Salt Lake or even Seattle. Howard has a couple of doctors, and it has the Urgent Care.

The Urgent Care is owned by one of the big healthcare conglomerates that are eating up all the hospitals in this country, but since the sign on the front says *Urgent Care* in big red letters that glow at night, that's what everyone calls it.

In the lobby there was one guy with a bandage around his head and another fellow leaning over a wastebasket like he was going to throw up, both of them waiting for attention. But Sheriff Sutherland beat me, Evil, and Dad to the front desk by a minute or so, and when I limped up behind him he was saying, "Front of the line, Ginger. She's been shot, and he got whacked upside the head."

I didn't know the receptionist, but I guess her name was Ginger. I smiled at her, and she flashed me a grin full of snaggles. "Then they're next."

It's a small town. The sheriff asks you to do something, it's a good idea to do it.

Two hours later, I was sitting on the edge of a bed in one of the treatment rooms, my arm in a cast and the Percocet starting to kick in, when the door opened. Evil came in, and the sheriff followed. Evil had a bandage wrapped around the top of his head, neat enough it almost looked like a cap. His ankles were wrapped in bandages, too.

"Where's Dad?" I asked. "Dealing with the feds?"

"What feds?" The sheriff's face could jump from a grin to a scowl in nothing flat, and it did so now.

"I don't really know if they're feds," I said. "There were trucks at the Fun Lanes when we passed."

Sheriff Sutherland shook his head and clucked his tongue. "I'm afraid you just failed the job interview, Miss McCrae. A trained officer would have looked at the license plate while she was passing and would have known that those vehicles did *not* belong to the federal government."

"Yeah," I shot back, "but I'm not a trained officer. I'm just a job applicant, so you should hire me and train me to look at license plates."

The sheriff looked at Evil and bobbed his head back and forth, as if he were weighing the possibilities and looking for a second opinion. "It's true you preserved the life of a suspect in an ongoing murder investigation."

Evil blushed. "Hey..."

The sheriff laughed and clapped Evil lightly on the shoulder. "Truth is, if I'd been in your shoes, I might have shot the bastard. And if you'd done it, given all the circumstances...well, let's just say that my office would not have investigated you for anything."

"Thanks," Evil said.

"Which doesn't mean you got a license to go shooting people, kid. And which also doesn't change the fact that it is slightly problematic that our suspect is not where you left him."

I felt a cold hand close around my heart. "Can you track him?"

"We're working on it. Got a good old-fashioned manhunt going on, all my deputies and highway patrol helping out, cars watching all the major intersections."

"There just aren't that many roads," Evil said.

Sheriff Sutherland nodded. "But there's a lot of back country. If this guy's comfortable in the woods, and he's not hurt too bad, he might just hike out of state without ever being seen by anybody. And of course, if he's *not* comfortable in the woods, he might freeze to death in some canyon and never get found." He squinted at me. "What's your sense?"

I ignored the rushing sound of my own blood in my ears and tried to think. "His resume said he was from New York City, but that must have been fake."

Sheriff Sutherland nodded. "I called the New York State Bar. They don't know a Michael Fellows."

"Cell phone number?" I asked. There must be some way to identify this guy.

"Prepaid phone. Burner."

I thought about the sheriff's question. "The impression I mostly got was competence," I said finally. "I'd say this little trip to Howard isn't his first rodeo."

"Green Beret, Ranger, something like that," Evil threw in. "He was pretty comfortable shooting at people and tying them up." I thought Evil seemed excited to imagine that he had gone up against a Green Beret and won...but I didn't say anything.

Sheriff Sutherland took off his big hat and spun it around one fist. "Any reason you can think of he might want to come after either of you?"

"He wanted the will," I said.

"I think your dad's gone off to file that with the court. Or at least a certified copy, since the original is in my evidence room. Curious he was so interested, isn't it?"

"We're witnesses," Evil pointed out.

"Yeah." Sutherland sighed. "There is that."

"Who do you think he was working for?" I asked.

"Somebody interested in the will," the sheriff said. "Which in itself is kind of odd, don't you think?"

"Yeah? What's so odd?"

"I read the will before I filed it away as evidence. It just gives everything to the wife."

"Marilyn," I said.

"Yep. And under state law, Marilyn probably gets everything, anyway. I suppose Aaron had wealth from before their marriage that you could isolate, but...community property, and they've been married a long time."

"So someone has gone to a lot of trouble over a will that doesn't really matter," I said. "That tells the court to do exactly what it would have done if there hadn't been a will at all."

I thought about that.

Evil grimaced as if he was thinking about it too, and the sheriff put his hat back on.

"You'll be glad to know this, though," Sheriff Sutherland said.

"Tell me."

"We did a uniform audit down at the station. A uniform's missing. Stolen."

"So whoever killed Charlie Herbert, it wasn't one of your deputies." That took one worry off my mind, but of course it only created another mystery. Why would anyone steal a uniform and pose as a deputy in the first place?

"Probably wasn't a deputy." Sheriff Sutherland stepped into the door. "Now, as it turns out, I'm your ride. Where do you two want to go?"

"The office." I was tired, but if Dad was making court filings, I should be involved.

"Home." Evil grinned at me. "I could use the sleep."

We dropped Evil off first. The Pattens are sagebillies, but they live close to town, so it was only a couple of miles out into the Flats before the sheriff pulled over and Evil tumbled out. His parents hadn't come to the Urgent Care and they weren't at the trailer to meet him, either, but neither fact surprised me; Evil's dad was a long-haul trucker who was more often than not out of state, and his mom worked at a rest home in Yakima, three days on and two off. During her work days, she just stayed in Yakima with her sister, which meant that Evil was frequently the closest thing there was to an adult at his family home.

He waved at me as he loped through tall yellow grass toward the doublewide where he lived with his family. *"Groundhog Day!"* he called out.

So I was going to get another movie invitation. I could live with that. I smiled and waved back, and then Sheriff Sutherland took me to the Law Offices of James F. McCrae.

The canary yellow H3 was parked in front, right next to Dad's Taurus. At the sight of it I hesitated, not opening the door to let myself out of the sheriff's truck.

"Bucky?" the sheriff prompted me.

"Nothing," I said. "Just...last time I saw this car, it was right before Evil got tied up in a bathtub and then I witnessed a murder." I shuddered. "Two murders, actually, if you count the one I couldn't actually *see.*"

"I'll come in if you like." The sheriff turned off the truck.

That did it. "Nope." I opened the door and popped out. "Thanks. Dad's here. Besides, the H3 belongs to Marilyn Wilding. She's a client."

"You know," Sheriff Sutherland said, leaning across the shotgun seat and lowering his voice, "I understand clients are hard to come by around here, and rich ones are even harder. But if it turns out Marilyn Wilding had anything to do with, say, Charlie Herbert's death..."

"Dad might get conflicted out of a client."

"For starters." The sheriff looked me in the eye. His gaze was cold and clear, even though his face was warm. "I haven't had a chance to talk to her yet about what happened today. About Fellows and the strange things he had you say." He shrugged. "Maybe I should come in and talk to her in the presence of her lawyer."

This kind of stuff might not fly in the big city. It felt kind of incestuous. Conflict-prone. But in the big city, a woman like Marilyn might have five or six different lawyers. Here, there was Dad. His bad luck, or hers, that I happened to be his daughter.

And besides, there might not *actually* be a conflict. Marilyn might not have anything to do with the burglary and murder committed in the Fun Lanes.

I nodded and trundled slowly toward the door.

The sheriff caught up to me as I entered. We both waved to Gladys. She opened her mouth when she saw me, as if she wanted to say something, but then she saw Sheriff Sutherland and just waved back. We turned and headed for the office.

"You'd never believe it," Sheriff Sutherland muttered under the crashing of pins, "but that woman was hell on wheels once."

"I believe it."

"In some ways, she still is."

I kind of wanted to ask what that meant, but I was also a little afraid of the answer. I held my tongue.

The office door was shut, so I knocked. "Come in!" Dad called.

The last time I'd been in the office, there had been a corpse on the floor. I stepped inside, half-expecting to see Charlie Herbert still lying there, even half-expecting he'd sit up and crack a hobo grin at me and tell me I'd been punked on national television.

But I hadn't been pranked, and he was dead. At least his body had been removed from my Dad's floor. Someone had scrubbed out most of the blood, too, though the carpet still looked damp and a little dark.

Dad sat behind his desk, and Marilyn Wilding sat on the other side. On the desk between them rested a photocopy with a blue-inked notary's signature in the corner.

"Rebecca, isn't it?" Marilyn Wilding swooped down on me. "I'm so glad to see you're alright. Your father has explained about...about that man."

"Right." Sheriff Sutherland stepped forward. "This is a little messy, Ms. Wilding, and I regret that I haven't been able to speak to you earlier. But I gather you saw Bucky...that is, Rebecca, earlier today."

"This morning, yes, I did."

"And can you tell me what happened then?"

Marilyn seemed surprised to be asked the question. "Well, I had spoken to her yesterday about Aaron's will, and she explained...she explained to me a little about the process. Probate, you know. And her father was supposed to have come around with the will in the morning, to read it with me one last time before filing it with the court, only he hadn't."

"Just slept in, did he?"

"No, his office was broken into. And the will had been taken."

"Anybody you know who would want to take the will, Ms. Wilding?"

She shrugged. "I understand it's been found again. This man Fellows had it, though I have no idea why he'd want it."

"Do you know Michael Fellows?"

Marilyn Wilding only shook her head.

"Hmmm." Sheriff Sutherland took off his hat and carefully hung it on Dad's hat rack. "So Jim McCrae called to say he couldn't make it, and then what happened?"

"Then Rebecca showed up at my door. And she...forgive me for saying this, dear...she looked terrible. She looked like a mess. Like she'd been camping." She gestured at my jeans, which were still filthy. I nodded. "And she said something I didn't understand."

"Like, in Swahili?" Sheriff Sutherland didn't *actually* wink at me, but it felt like he did.

Marilyn shook her head. "I mean, she said her boss had the thing I wanted, and her boss wanted money. Oh, but she said her boss wasn't James."

All this, I had told the sheriff and Dad already.

"And could that thing, that Bucky was being made to offer...could it have been the stolen will?"

"I don't understand why. I don't think the will's remarkable at all."

The sheriff chewed on that thought a moment, nodding. "Then a man came out and chased Rebecca," he said.

"Yes." She looked at me with big, pleading eyes. "I'm really sorry about that. That was Nick. He didn't understand, he thought I'd been threatened, and he…I'm afraid he wanted to scare Rebecca off."

"How did he try to do that?"

"With a gun. A shotgun. He chased her, but then that…Michael Fellows…shot him." As she said these words, Marilyn's voice slowed down, and a tear formed in the corner of each eye.

"And who was Nick, exactly? Some kind of family?"

"Oh, no." Marilyn looked at the two men, and then at me. "This is awkward," she said. "You're going to think the wrong thing."

"I think that's a risk you'd better take," the sheriff suggested. "Don't you?"

"You're not going to like me." Marilyn Wilding nodded and took a deep breath. "Nick was my lover. But you don't understand."

"I think I understand," the sheriff said quietly. He avoided looking at Dad.

"No, you see—Aaron *knew*."

CHAPTER 18

I don't feel like I'm a sheltered person, and although I still can't buy beer or cigarettes in this state, I'm not a kid.

But I was pretty taken by surprise by what Marilyn Wilding had to say. I was surprised enough that I had to catch myself against the wall to avoid falling.

"Oh?" Sheriff Sutherland's voice showed no surprise at all. I guess he had years of experience taking things in stride. "Open marriage, was it? You both getting a little bit on the side?"

Now Marilyn looked away. "Not generally, no. But Aaron was ill for a while. And he...he wanted me to be happy."

I tried to set aside my personal shock and read Marilyn's face. She dared everyone in the room to judge her. I tried to imagine Dad saying anything similar to Mom, and it just didn't feel real.

"And you're sure you didn't know Michael Fellows? Or did Nick know him?" Sheriff Sutherland asked.

"No." She said it very quickly. "I mean, I don't think so. I don't know the name. Why?"

The sheriff shrugged. "Fellows shot Nick from behind. It wasn't self-defense, he didn't have to do it. In fact, it seems to me he probably lured Nick out into the open by sending Bucky here to offer to sell you something. One reason he might do that would be if Fellows had a grudge against Nick."

"Not that I know of."

"Well, the other possibilities are stranger. Because if he didn't have a grudge against Nick, then Fellows wanted Nick out of the way. That suggests that maybe he wanted something in your house. Any idea what that could be?"

"I...no."

"Or maybe he wanted Nick dead first, so he could get a clear shot at you. Only, no, you answered the door. If he'd wanted you dead, he could have shot you then. Or maybe Rebecca kept him from getting off a clean shot."

"Sheriff, this is...macabre."

"Yeah." The sheriff nodded, and showed no signs of stopping. "And it also suggests he knew he could get Nick out by claiming he had something to sell. Fellows thought you were in the market for something. You sure you have no idea what that could have been?"

"He had the will. Maybe he thought I wanted that so much I'd pay for it."

"Did you?"

"I already said no."

"Is this about the pot?"

"The marijuana?"

"Yeah, whatever you crazy kids are calling it these days. Maybe Fellows thought he could get to you and get his hands on the drugs. Or maybe he's an old drug-dealing acquaintance of Aaron's, and this is about revenge or turf or something."

"Sheriff, marijuana isn't as...illegal...as it used to be."

"Still drugs." Sheriff Sutherland shrugged. "Still attracts a rough crowd."

"No." Marilyn shook her head. "I have no idea who that man is, or what he wanted. And the pot...look, I knew about it. But it was Aaron's. Aaron's and Charlie's."

"Charlie Herbert, who tended Aaron's pot."

Marilyn nodded. "Charlie was an old friend of Aaron's. From his California days. And yes, he grew the weed."

"And why didn't you call the cops?"

"Over the pot?"

"Over the murder."

Marilyn ground her teeth. "One reason I didn't call your office immediately over the murder, Sheriff, is that I knew I was probably going to have to explain a whole bunch of marijuana in my backyard."

"Right." The sheriff took his hat back into his hands. "Local girl comes to the door, says something a little weird. Your boyfriend shoots at her, then gets shot in the back by a complete stranger. You don't understand any of it."

Marilyn shook her head.

"Not to be too hard about it, but you're saying it's just a crazy world, and weird stuff happens."

"Weird stuff happens," Marilyn agreed.

"So probably you wouldn't mind me coming up and looking around the house, huh? Try to figure out what it is Michael Fellows was after?"

Marilyn was pale, but held her chin high. "Of course, I don't mind. You won't mind if I invite my lawyer, just in case any legal questions arise." It wasn't a question.

"I wouldn't have it any other way," the sheriff said. "How about right now?"

"You have a right to refuse," Dad advised his client. "If you would prefer not to have your property searched, you can say no. Sheriff Sutherland would have to go before a judge and show probable cause that he could find evidence of a crime in order to get a warrant and come back. Or maybe you'd like to admit him later, after you've had a chance to sleep. You've had a rough few days."

Marilyn turned to Dad. "My husband died three days ago. Nick was really just a...a friend I had fun with."

Dad nodded. "Your call."

"I'd just as soon get this over with. Are you available now, Mr. McCrae?"

He nodded. "Rebecca," he said to me, "why don't you go home?"

I pointed at the copy of Aaron Wilding's will, which sat on his desk. "I thought I might finish up the filing, if you're not done."

"That's insane," he said. "It can wait."

"Yes," Marilyn agreed. "Please go home."

But I didn't want to go home. "I'll just stay here, and keep Gladys company a bit."

"You sure?" Dad looked me in the eye, and I knew he was remembering that Charlie Herbert had died in this room right in front of me less than twenty-four hours earlier. I hadn't forgotten it, either, but I wasn't about to show weakness, especially not in front of a client and the sheriff.

"You bet." The truth was, I didn't really want to be alone.

"That's nuts," Dad said. "We're dropping you off at home."

Being home alone didn't sound any better. Before I could object, though, Sheriff Sutherland put his hand on Dad's shoulder. "Tell you what," he said. "How about if Rebecca comes with us?"

So I got into the shotgun seat of Dad's Taurus and wrapped a wool car blanket around me, the kind you keep a few of in the trunk just in case you ever get snowed in somewhere. We hadn't pulled out of the Fun Lanes parking before the combination of sleeplessness, physical exhaustion, stress, shock, and Percocet knocked me out completely.

I DRIFTED in and out of sleep, waking up each time to find my forehead pressed against the cold window of the car. For a while, I saw the highway. Then there were flashing flights, and the jacket of one of Howard County's deputies, and Marilyn Wilding's half-moon house.

I shook myself and stepped out of the car. My mouth was really dry. The Percocet, probably.

"Hey, Miss McCrae," the deputy said. I didn't know him, but he wasn't too much older than I was.

"Call me Bucky," I told him. Evil calling me *Bucky* made me feel like he saw me as sexless, and a child. I didn't want the deputy thinking of me as a kid, but it wouldn't hurt if he thought of me a little less as a girl. His misplaced chivalry might make him try to keep me in the car.

"Bucky," he agreed. "Your dad said you were doped up pretty good."

"Yep," I said. "Got an anti-nausea pill and a stool softener in me too. Maybe we ought to start a pool on what happens first. Could be a real party."

I didn't wait for him to respond, and just walked forward.

I was back at the Wilding house, in the turf-built artificial bowl where Nick had shot at me. It was night again, and cold, so I was grateful for the car blanket. All the lights in the Wilding house seemed to be on, and since the building was mostly window, white beams shot out in all directions.

I heard the deputy's radio crackle behind me as he muttered into it. Probably asking for instructions about me.

Dad met me at the door. In the strong light, I could see dark pouchy flesh under his eyes.

"I gotta pee," I said. It was a pretext, but it was still true.

Marilyn Wilding stood behind Dad in the kitchen. Her arms were crossed and she glared at Sheriff Sutherland and one of his deputies, all of whom were methodically going through the kitchen's drawers and cabinets, looking behind flatware and picking up drawer organizer trays to see what might be beneath them.

She saw me come in, though, and nodded. She pointed down a short hall to a half-open door.

The floor was a beautiful stone tile, and I started to kneel down to unlace my boots with my one good arm.

"Stop," Marilyn said. "I'm not having the girl who got shot on my property fall down trying to untie bootlaces with her left arm. Just go ahead and track a little dirt, I'll live."

It wasn't that I had disliked her before, but I liked her a little better for that. "Thanks," I said.

She nodded. "You about done, Sheriff?"

Sutherland cocked his hat back on his head and scratched the short hair over his forehead. "Well, you never know where something might be hidden. Something this guy Fellows maybe knew about, and wanted to get his hands on. Heck, the fact that you don't know what it is only increases my suspicion that we're talking about something secret. Something taped to the underside of a table, or stuffed inside a mattress."

Marilyn Wilding harrumphed. "Plumbing isn't working too well," she said to me. "There's a pump bottle of sanitizer on the counter."

I nodded and passed them both, heading into the bathroom. I shut the door behind me.

"Just trying to avoid having to come back later, Mrs. Wilding," I heard the sheriff say before I shut out the sounds of the search completely.

Sheriff Sutherland had a folksy way about him, but I had to admire the fact that he'd talked Mrs. Wilding into letting him search her house immediately, without a warrant. If I were the sheriff, I'd want to do that, too. Search before any clues might disappear.

Of course, Mrs. Wilding might be innocent. *My client* might be innocent, that is. She had agreed to let the sheriff into her house quickly enough.

I felt torn. On the one hand, Marilyn Wilding was a client. To Dad, and to me, that meant we owed her professional behavior and courtesy and loyalty. On the other hand, her boyfriend had tried to shoot me.

Only maybe he hadn't. Maybe she was right, he had been trying to scare me off. Maybe he was frightened, maybe he knew something about Michael Fellows. I had, after all, said provocative things to Marilyn at the door. Maybe Fellows had made me say those things exactly because he knew Nick would come out and try to kill me.

It's too easy to believe in good guys and bad guys, this world just isn't that simple. But maybe Nick wasn't a murderer, or a thug. Maybe he thought he was defending his girlfriend.

And that memory, that Mrs. Wilding had a boyfriend, made me shudder and knocked me right off my train of thought.

I'm not a prude. I just, I don't know, my wounds from Mom leaving were still too raw, maybe.

I sighed. Maybe a career as a lawyer was not in my future. I wasn't hard-hearted enough.

Of course, Dad wasn't especially hard-hearted.

But then, he didn't have much of a career, either.

When I was done, I felt a little light-headed. Moving slowly, I turned on the faucet. Water splashed into the white basin and reminded me that Marilyn had said the sink wasn't working too well. I quickly shut off the tap, found the pump bottle, and sanitized my hands with the pungent alcohol gel.

I emerged from the bathroom with careful steps, trying to bluff my way through the woozy feeling with sheer determination. "Could I get a drink?"

The sheriff and his deputies had moved into other rooms. Dad had followed them, but Marilyn stood by the kitchen sink with her arms crossed, looking out the window into the darkness. She nodded and stooped to reach into the fridge. I saw several flatpacks of bottled water inside, and she passed me a bottle with a tired smile.

I took the water and headed out to Dad's car with short steps. The deputy opened the door and nodded, without saying a word.

I have no memory of getting myself into bed that night, or of anyone else helping me.

CHAPTER
19

In the morning, I woke up to the smell of bacon and the sizzling sound of frying fat.

I hurt, all over.

Squeezing out of the clothes I'd been wearing for three days, I found the joint in my pocket. At the sight of it, I kind of wanted to laugh, but I also kind of wanted to cry. In the end, I split the difference and did neither, just tucking the marijuana into my underwear drawer.

Then I managed to shower without help and get into jeans and a top mostly because the top was really baggy. It wasn't easy to do anything, with my right arm useless.

By the time I got downstairs, the sizzling had gone away and the smell of bacon had sunk deep into the wood and drywall bones of the house. Evil Patten sat at the table with Dad, stiffly picking at a couple of strips with a fork. They both moved slowly, and they had oversized mugs of coffee in front of them.

"You look like I feel," I said to Evil, sitting down in front of bacon and toast.

"You feel handsome?" He grinned.

I ate my bacon. It was a little crispier than I'd have liked it, but that's what I get for sleeping in.

"So," I said to Dad, washing down a mouthful of crunchy bacon with hot black coffee, "how's Marilyn this morning?"

"You mean, did Sheriff Sutherland find any reason to arrest her last night?" He waved his phone at me. "Not last night, and probably not this morning either, since I've already had two texts from her."

"Texts...shoot," I said. "I never got my phone back."

Dad shrugged. "A phone is easily replaced. I only have one daughter."

"What did Marilyn text for?"

"She wants to know what time I'm going to get the will filed with the court."

"I'll get right on it." I took another strip of bacon and started to stand.

Dad put his hand on my good arm and pushed me back into my seat. "Whoa, there. You're not coming into the office today."

"Who's going to put together the filing?"

Dad put on a fake hurt face. At least, I think it was fake, but I realized even as I said them that my words might be kind of insulting to him. "I think I can get a probate started." He looked at his phone. "I think I can even get it in by noon."

"All I mean is, you should be out drumming up business. You can do anything in the practice, so you should do the thing that brings the most value, and let me do paperwork. I think that's comparative advantage, or something. You know, economics." I was playing a little coy. I knew exactly what comparative advantage was, and if I'd been talking to, say, Evil, I'd never have downplayed my own knowledge.

But, you know, I only had the one dad.

"Right, comparative advantage, or something." Dad grinned, and even though he was sleep-deprived and probably stressed, and he hadn't tucked in his shirt or tightened his tie yet, in that flashed grin I saw the thing I knew Mom must have seen in him. Probably Marilyn Wilding saw it too, that boyish charm, confident, a little reckless, a guy you thought was willing to lose for the right cause, but was probably going to win. "You've been shot, Bucky. Take this as a message from the universe. You got the day off." He shrugged into his jacket. "Besides, I can't have you driving on Percocet."

"Evil can drive me." Then it occurred to me that Evil had been given big-time painkillers, too. I frowned at him. "Unless..."

"You don't have to worry about me," he said. "I already took the oxy they prescribed me down to the SuperMart parking lot and converted it into cash. You know us sagebillies."

"Liar," I said. His mention of SuperMart reminded me I'd left my car there, parked behind the building and next to the dumpster. "Just promise me you didn't drive here stoned."

"I didn't take any of that stuff this morning, Jim." Evil raised his arm to the square and crossed his heart with his other hand. "Promise. Made me feel kind of loopy yesterday, and today I don't hurt bad enough to need it."

I looked at the bandage wrapped around his head. "Really?"

"Hope to die. So I put all the pills in my first aid kit."

"Good man." Dad waved and was out the front door.

"In case someone gets shot while you're out hunting?"

"Wouldn't be the first time. But you know doctors. You tell them you need serious painkillers to take with you into the Ups in case someone gets hurt, they point you at the Advil. But if they give you ten days of oxycodone because you had a little minor surgery, they don't ask afterward what you did with it. Many a fine first aid kit has been built on past misadventures."

"You know, I think I probably owe you a thank you."

Evil snorted. "Shut up."

I sat back. "That's not a very graceful way to accept gratitude."

"Well, you could thank me for things. Like, I guess, tackling Fellows when he tried to shoot you. Or shooting him while you ran to the truck. Or wrapping up your wound. But then I'd have to thank you for things, too. Like shooting Fellows after he'd whacked me with a shovel. And driving the getaway truck. And letting me cart you around in a wheelbarrow."

I'm not really a giggler, but that one drew a snicker out of me.

"So forget it," he said. "Let's just skip to the part where we both put our feet up and say 'holy crap, that was quite an adventure we had.'"

"It was quite an adventure," I agreed.

"Good preparation for my marijuana banking business." Evil

grabbed a half empty bottle of water from the table and jiggled it. "This yours?"

I nodded. "From the Wilding house. Go ahead."

He drank the rest of the water. Some other guy might have been making a point by drinking out of the same bottle as me, or suggesting I was his girlfriend. With Evil Patten, I think it was more of a camping thing. He just had drunk so much water out of shared canteens and cups, he didn't think twice about it.

"Your dad told me you went back out there."

"With the sheriff," I said. "He looked through the house, and I don't think he found anything." Of course, I wasn't sure I would know if he had.

"Well, he was looking in the wrong place, wasn't he? All the really killer stuff wasn't in the house."

All the really killer stuff wasn't in the house.

Something niggled at the back of my brain.

"Say that again," I told Evil.

"Well, all the interesting stuff was out on the land," he explained. "The little cabin where I was tied up. The marijuana. Even the casings—all the shooting happened outside. I don't know what he thought he might find in the house."

"Evil," I said slowly. "How do you feel about driving me to the county records office?"

"I dunno." He tossed the empty plastic bottle into the kitchen garbage can. "How do you feel about watching *Groundhog Day* with me?"

"I feel good about that," I said. "If we can also somehow get my truck back."

"You mean the truck you left behind the SuperMart?"

"I only have the one."

Evil tossed something metallic onto the kitchen table. The object hit, spun, and slid my direction. When it came to a rest, I saw it was my keyring.

"I'm not your boyfriend," he said. "But I am the coolest guy you know."

I leaned over, gasping a little as my aching muscles stretched, to look out the kitchen window into the driveway. There sat my truck.

"Yes, you are," I said. "For that, I'll even watch *The Last of the Mohicans*. Maybe it won't be so bad if I can watch it slightly stoned."

"Just what I had in mind," Evil said. "But I'm still driving."

I hobbled back upstairs to take my meds. I took the antibiotic, because I'd been shot, and it'd be stupid to die of some infection after the danger had theoretically passed. But I passed on the oxycodone. It's not that I have anything against painkillers, and I don't have a hunting first aid kit to equip—I just wanted a clear head. I'd had an idea about the Wilding house, and I wanted to check something on the county records.

We took his car. Evil drives a 1971 Buick GSX, a dark red and black muscle car nearly as old as Dad. Evil will tell you all about if you let him, which I know, because I've accidentally hit that button once or twice and heard the whole spiel about how the hood-mounted tachometer is original and he rebuilt the big block 455 engine himself after he found the car in a junkyard over in Spokane and bought it dirt cheap. The paint job is his idea; I think the car was originally yellow.

Evil's Buick is not *a* bitchin' mode of transportation in his eyes.

It is *the* bitchin' mode.

I think he mostly likes to drive with the windows down and imagine he's fighting crime or bootlegging in some '80s TV show starring actors with big hair. But I don't tell him that, because it might start him off on his spiel.

"So, nobody's found your phone yet," Evil said.

"Not as far I know. You worried I'm missing all the action on Twitter?"

Evil shrugged. "What's in the records office that you want to see?"

"I want to look at the plans for the Wilding house. Aaron Wilding built that place, right?"

Evil shrugged. "I guess."

"So the county should have the plans."

Evil leaned into the open window. His hair would be ruffling in the wind, except that it was really short and now covered by his bandage. "You thinking about that grow building?"

"'Grow building'? Is that what you big city marijuana bankers call it?"

"Small city. I'm thinking Boise, remember?"

"No, I'm thinking about the water."

"What about it?"

"Well, you remember what a new age, ultra-efficient, hippy kind of house the Wildings live in?"

"*Lived*," Evil said. "At least, in the case of Mr. Wilding. I remember."

"Dad said a couple of times they have their own well. I want to confirm it, one way or the other."

"It wouldn't be too surprising." Evil scratched his chin, which was now sprouting a couple of days' worth of stubble. "Lots of houses in the Ups have wells. Geothermal heat pumps, even. Some of those places up in the canyons are on city water, though."

"That's why I want to check."

Evil looked as if he had more questions, but at that moment he was parking at county records. The records office was a brick building that had once been a bar and before that a bank. It's downtown, across a gravel parking lot from where Judge Ybarra holds her court in a trailer.

I knew Scott Brough, who ran the office. He was a sharp guy who used to work in health insurance down south somewhere before he came to Howard for the lifestyle. He collected model trains, and today must have been a slow day at the office, because he had a pot of fire engine red paint on the counter and was squinting down along a fine-tipped paintbrush at a locomotive he held in his hand, touching up a few spots where the paint had rubbed off. He was also wearing a navy and white striped train engineer's cap.

Welcome to Howard County.

"Bucky." He didn't look up. "Know what kind of train this is?"

"Uh...a toy one?"

"Pfff. Just because something is small doesn't mean it's a toy."

"Right. So it's a...locomotive, I guess. For a fairy train line."

"It's the locomotive Consolidation, two-eight-oh in the Whyte notation. Introduced in 1865, and by the mid-1870s, the standard freight locomotive on the Pennsylvania and Erie Railroads." Brough squinted past the pot of paint to glare at me. "A model, not a toy. This train will be *displayed*, not *played with*."

"I totally respect you," I said. "And I wish I had a train set as sick as yours."

"Hmm. So whatcha lookin' for?"

"Just some real estate records. Has to do with a client's will."

He dabbed paint. "Knock yourself out."

I know in a bigger town, there would be request forms and process and maybe permissions to ask and a wait. Not in Howard.

I'd looked up real property records before, so it didn't take me long to find the lot on the county maps, then locate the drawer where Aaron Wilding had filed his plans when he'd built his house. There was nothing on the plans about a grow building, as Evil had called it.

But there was a well.

"Huh," Evil said. He was looking over my shoulder as we hunkered together over a table in the reading room, which had once been the common room of the bar. "Look at that. Basement's the same half-circle shape as the above-ground floor."

"Yep." I was a bit distracted, focusing on the piece that interested me. "More space, though, because below ground you're not trying to build that envelope of dead air for insulation."

"You gonna explain your big idea now?"

"I think the well has been poisoned." I pointed at the well marked on the blueprints. "The poison must have got into the aquifer. That's what killed the deer. And Marilyn Wilding knows about it."

CHAPTER
20

"Pretty sure you're wrong about the aquifer being poisoned." This was the third time Evil had said these exact same words to me in fifteen minutes. "I don't think you're really grasping just how big the aquifer is."

"Maybe the poison's in the well. And just a bit leaked into the aquifer."

"Just a bit would disperse and not kill deer. Probably."

"Probably."

Evil sighed. "And you realize you're not a crime fighter, right?" This was the third time Evil had said this to me in fifteen minutes, too. "You're not a detective. You're not a cop."

He was driving into the Ups, toward the Wilding house.

"I know what I'm not," I said. "Thanks for the reminder. Let me remind you that you're not a hydraulics engineer."

"You're not even a lawyer," he added. "I mean, except on a *pro hunk* basis."

That was true. But I'd tried to tell Dad; Evil had driven by the Fun Lanes, and Dad's car had been gone. Gladys had said Dad had gone to the court with Marilyn Wilding, and that had given me the idea.

Nick was dead. Marilyn was at the court with Dad. I could go to her house.

I didn't even need to get into the house, really. I just needed to get to the stream with the dead deer in it. I needed a little water sample. If I was right, the water would be toxic.

And maybe my theory was improbable. But it fit the facts.

You're wondering why I didn't call the sheriff.

I had called him, or at least I'd tried. On Evil's phone, standing in front of the records building, and he hadn't been in the office. I didn't have a direct number to call. But the secretary had said he was out, and did I want to leave a message.

And that had made me hesitate. I wasn't so worried about a corrupt deputy anymore, but if I was right, I might have evidence against my own client. Against Dad's client. And if Marilyn Wilding was guilty, so be it. You can't deliberately hide evidence from the police if you're a lawyer, you can't connive with your client to hide a crime.

But if I was wrong, and my guesses got passed around as fact, I could be wrecking my client's reputation.

So I'd asked the secretary to have Sheriff Sutherland call me, and I gave her Evil's phone number. And now we were on our way up to the Wilding place.

Like I said, no one should be there. I just needed to get in and get a water sample, and get that to the sheriff. If there was anything in the water, the prosecutor could worry about admissibility later.

"You know that guy who shot you is still out there," Evil reminded me.

"'Out there' meaning he's alive, not necessarily that he's hanging around the scene of his crimes. I'm betting the flashing lights last night scared him off, if he hadn't already headed out."

"Yeah." Evil nodded slowly. The bandages wrapped around his head gave the gesture a solemn look, as if he were a nodding swami or something. "Still, I'd feel better about this if we were armed, or had the sheriff with us, or even if someone knew where we were."

I shuddered. "I've handled enough pistols in the last two days to last me a long time." I remembered the jerking motions Michael Fellows had made as I'd shot him and shuddered. "And it's probably better if we don't leave a record of where we're going."

"Okay." Evil shook his head. "But for this, you're going to have to watch *The Last of the Mohicans* and the sequel."

I didn't remind Evil that he could just drop me off instead and I'd drive myself. I guess I didn't really want to go back into the Ups alone. "There is no sequel."

"No? Dang." Evil rapped the dashboard of the GSX with his knuckles. "I had such high hopes for *My Left Foot.*"

"*My Left Foot?* I guess you never read the Leatherstocking Tales." I laughed out loud. "What would that even be about?"

Evil shrugged. "Something about moccasins, I guess. Maybe stockings, to hear you talk."

"I want you to know, I'm okay with the fact that you have a crush on Daniel Day-Lewis."

"He's a fine actor." Evil didn't skip a beat. "He's got great hair, which I am particularly conscious of at this time when I may have lost my scalp entirely. And I'm comfortable enough in my own skin to admire a handsome man."

We both fell quiet as he turned the GSX into the Wildings' driveway. My heart beat a little faster, and just as we crested the little bowl and the house came into view, I had an urge to grab the wheel and spin Evil's muscle car around to head back to Howard.

But I didn't grab the wheel, and the driveway was empty.

The driveway forked, which I hadn't noticed before. One fork passed the house and kept going, off to the left. I wondered where it might lead. Evil parked next to the house.

"You said this would be quick," Evil reminded me.

"Yep." We both got out of the car, and then I realized what I hadn't brought with me. "You have anything...to, you know, carry water in?"

Evil laughed out loud. "You mean, did I replace the condom in my wallet? Doggone it, Becky, that's the most romantic thing you ever asked me."

"I really want it to hold water."

"Yeah." He nodded. "And I'm sorry to disappoint you. I have not restocked my emergency canteen."

"Nuts." I looked at the house and thought a moment. There were glasses in the little cabin over the rise, but I didn't want to try to carry an open glass of water back to town. Especially if I was right, and the water was poisonous.

"You know, maybe you ought to think about carrying a condom around in *your* wallet," Evil suggested. "Just to be prepared."

"You'd like that."

"I would be amused. And you never know when it could come in handy."

I didn't see anything useful sitting around in the yard, and I didn't want to waste any more time. I walked up to the front door, wrapped my hand in the front of my own shirt, and grabbed the door handle. Might as well not leave any more fingerprints, just in case.

The knob turned, and the door opened.

If you're from somewhere big, like Denver, you're surprised. Also, you're remembering that I was careful to lock up the Fun Lanes. But a lot of people around here leave their doors unlocked. There's nowhere in Howard to fence stolen goods, and it's a long way for a burglar from anywhere else to drive, for the privilege of breaking and entering. And besides, if a burglar wanted to let himself in by heaving a rock through a window this far into the Ups, there aren't any neighbors in earshot, anyway. Leaving your door open might just save you the expense of having to replace shattered glass.

I'm not saying we don't have crime. I'm just saying we don't always lock the doors to our homes.

"I didn't know this was part of the plan." Evil followed me in through the open door.

"Don't touch anything."

He stuck his hands in his pockets. "How's that?"

"Good move."

"Saw it on a cop show."

Still using my baggy shirt like a glove, I opened the refrigerator and grabbed two bottles of water. "We're going to want to be able to tell these apart," I said, looking at them. "You have a pen?"

"How well you know me. I drive around with a pen, so I can

record my spontaneous observations of people and nature. You know, write a little poetry now and then."

"Smart ass."

"Better than a dumbass. Rip the label off one bottle. That'll tell them apart."

Duh. I ripped off one label and stuffed it in my pocket. Then I emptied both bottles down the sink, bumped the kitchen faucet handle up with one sleeve-shrouded elbow and carefully filled the label-less bottle. "Do *not* drink this." I handed the full bottle to Evil and shut off the water the same way I'd turned it on.

"Got it. The bottle with no label has poisoned water from the house."

"Maybe poisoned. But better safe than sorry."

"That's why I carry a condom. Usually."

"No label, house."

"Right. Now let's go get water from the stream."

"Wait," I said. "I want to take a look at the pipes."

"You mean downstairs? Where the water comes into the house? What do you think you'll see?"

But as he asked, I was already heading deeper into the house. I knew where the stairs were because they'd been on the plans, so I dropped down into the basement. I don't know what I expected to find, but something...I don't know, well-like. Instead, all I found were the usual water heaters in a concrete utility room.

"That's probably your incoming water." Evil tapped one of the pipes. "Actual well's outside."

"You think you could stick poison in there somehow?" I crouched and tugged at an elbow of the pipe.

"It'd be a lot of work." Evil sounded distracted. "Easier just to drop poison in the water heater, don't you think?"

Of course. I looked up at him. He stood in the door of the utility room and peered out. "So collecting water is kind of silly, isn't it?"

He focused on me again. "I would never call you silly, Bucky. Becky. And hey, if the water from the tap is toxic, checking it against the stream water will tell you whether the toxin came from the aquifer, or was inserted somewhere in the house's plumbing. So that's very clever of you."

Ha. "What are you looking at out there?"

"Well, check this out." Evil pointed. I stood and left the utility room so I could follow what he was trying to show me.

Outside the little room was a den. The wall curved behind a sofa in a long gentle slope, and then suddenly turned and straightened out, running thirty feet or so before turning again at a right angle.

And suddenly I saw what Evil saw. "Oh my gosh. That doesn't match the blueprints."

"There's space behind that wall," Evil said, nodding at it. "Kind of a big space, I think. But no door."

No obvious door. "I'm pretty sure the blueprints showed a room."

"What do you think? Secret lever hidden in a bookcase?" Evil looked around.

"I think that's too complicated." The wall in question was a series of wood panels. I pushed on them in sequence, expecting one of them to simply swing inward. Instead, the third panel made a *click* when I pressed it, and then swung open toward me.

The open panel formed a low door. Beyond the door was a room.

I stepped inside. Evil followed me, cursing as he banged his head.

There were no windows and almost no furniture, so I took in the room at a glance. Thick carpet. Amber light bulbs when I hit the switch to turn them on. And a deputy sheriff's uniform, lying on top of a quilt over a king-sized bed.

The bed was king-sized, but otherwise the room appeared to be decorated for children. The quilt was covered with images of bears. Bears in bathing suits, holding balloons in their cute little paws. The same images were hand-painted all over the walls.

I felt like throwing up.

"We gotta leave now." Evil pulled at my elbow and I didn't resist him.

I scanned the kitchen floor on the way back out to be sure we hadn't tracked in any dirt, and then shut the door behind us. The sun was high overhead.

"It's going to be a hot afternoon," I said. I was just making small talk, trying not to think about the fact that I'd been chased, shot at, and then eventually shot, just the day before, in this very place. And that I'd just seen a secret room in the basement of the Wildings' house, a room that contained bears in swimsuits, holding balloons.

A room Sheriff Sutherland had almost certainly not seen.

"It's going to rain," Evil said. "You still want water from the stream?"

"Are you feeling a twinge in your old war wound?"

"Nah." He shook his head. "I can smell the water in the air. Can't you?"

I stopped to look at him. "Are you serious?"

Evil laughed. "No. I checked the forecast this morning. I work on the highways, remember? And I hunt for fun, and I drive a fast car. I always like to know what the weather's going to be."

"Jerk." I kept walking, but I was grateful for his joking. It calmed me down.

"Don't knock old war wounds, though. Storms follow drops in atmospheric pressure. Some animals can sense the pressure differences and know when bad weather's coming. No reason a human being might not be able to feel the same thing, if they had part of their body that was particularly sensitive."

"This is going to sound wrong," I said, stumbling down the slope toward the stream. "But most of the time, I don't give you enough credit for being smart."

Evil shrugged. "I dunno. I'll be lucky to get out of high school, let alone college. You're the smart one. Look at that secret room you just discovered."

"You're smart," I said again, "*and* you know stuff. Lots of stuff. It's just not the stuff I know." I was trying to process what I'd seen in the hidden room. Obviously, Charlie Herbert had been in that room: *bears and balloons*, he had said. So had Michael Fellows, who had

had a menacing conversation on the phone with someone unknown using the phrase *bears in swimming suits.* "You're a good man, Evil Patten."

When had the two men been in the room? And why?

For that matter, the deputy's uniform was there. Did that mean Marilyn's lover Nick was the man I'd seen in the uniform?

I reached the stream and stopped. The deer was still there, dead. I could even see the disturbed stones where I had splashed through the water the day before.

"You almost sound like you're saying good-bye," he said. "As you stand over a corpse. Can't say I like that."

"It's not a corpse." I knelt, upstream of the deer so the animal's body and whatever microbes might be coming out of it wouldn't contaminate my sample. "It's venison."

"Nope, city girl. *Venison* is what you eat. That there is *carrion.*"

I filled the second bottle with water from the stream and stood again. "Label on, stream water."

Evil nodded. "The picture of a mountain stream on the label ought to remind you."

I looked closer at the bottle. "Oh yeah."

"Let's get back to the crime lab, shall we, Batwoman?"

"I think it's Bat*girl*, isn't it?"

"Sexist," Evil said.

We marched slowly back up the hill.

I remembered staggering up this slope at full speed, thighs screaming in pain, just the day before. I remembered the feeling that a rifle was pointed right between my shoulder blades, and I might get shot any second.

I shook it off. I needed to get the water to the sheriff. And I needed to tell him about the room.

Just below the lip of the vale, Evil caught up with me and put his hand on my arm. "Hold on." His voice was low, almost a whisper.

"War wound twinge again?"

He shook his head and put his finger on his lips. "Pretend we're stalking a deer."

"I didn't bring any Budweiser."

"Humor me."

Evil knelt on the slope and I knelt next to him. Each of us holding a bottle of water, we crept to the lip of the vale and looked over.

"Damn," Evil said.

The driveway that we had left empty, but for Evil's GSX, now held three black SUVs. I looked at the license plates: California.

"Well," I whispered. "I can tell you one thing: it isn't the feds."

I felt the first drops of rain hit the back of my left hand.

CHAPTER
21

"We can't leave the car there," Evil said. "I mean, it's in pretty good company with those Porsches, but still."

I only half heard him; I was concentrating on the people who had emerged from the SUVs. Several were big men in dark suits, who looked very Secret Service to me, but what do I know? Assuming Sheriff Sutherland was right and Secret Service agents fell into his category of "feds" who would have special license plates, these guys must be...what? Bodyguards? Mobsters?

They weren't talking into their wrists or anything, but they wore shoulder rigs, and carried guns.

"Porsches?" I said, absently.

"Porsche makes more than two-seater sports cars, you know. Those babies right there are hybrids."

His speech sounded a little slurred, so I looked at Evil. His face was pale.

The rear door of the second car opened and a woman stepped out. She might have been Dad's age, and she was wearing more than Dad's net worth on her person, in the form of a tight, square-shouldered suit and multiple gold rings and bracelets. She wore so much jewelry, it almost didn't feel American.

It certainly didn't feel Howard.

"Don't worry," I whispered back to Evil. "I haven't forgotten your precious Colonel Lee."

"*General* Lee." Evil snorted. "Bo and Luke Duke drove the General Lee, named after Robert E. Lee. I thought your Dad came from, like, Tennessee or something."

"Yeah, but he's on the side of the Union."

"Everybody's on the side of the Union," Evil hissed. "The question is: who's on the side of awesome? And the answer is Bo and Luke Duke, that's who."

"This is not the time, Evil!"

Evil mollified a bit. "And Daisy," he muttered. "And Uncle Jesse."

"We won't leave the General."

"My car is not named the General Lee," Evil said. Which I knew, I was just teasing him. "I mean that if we leave the car, people will know we've been here."

The thought of getting caught refocused my attention. The woman from the car was standing at the door now. Two of the big suited guys flanked her, a couple of steps to her back, with their hands folded across their belts. Several others stood around the driveway and the yard, looking out.

"They *are* bodyguards," I whispered.

Evil squinted past my shoulder. "If they start heading this way, screw the car. Run."

The woman rang the doorbell, and there was no answer. Then she banged on it, hard.

"They don't know we're here," I whispered. "They think your car is Marilyn's."

"Marilyn!" the woman yelled, right as I said the name.

"You know her?" Evil whispered.

I shook my head.

"Marilyn, get out here!"

There was of course no answer. The woman stepped aside and pointed to the door. One of her bodyguards stepped forward and opened the door. The second man followed him inside, and then last of all came the woman.

"What now?" Evil asked.

I struggled with the same question. There were more bodyguards standing around, so we couldn't get to Evil's car without being seen.

We could just walk away, but then it would be obvious we'd been here when Marilyn got back and found Evil's car. I tried to think of a good lie to tell to explain what we were doing on the property. *I thought Dad might be visiting her, and I needed to check with him on the status of his filing the will.* It didn't ring true. On the other hand, sometimes adults would take seriously from me statements that they wouldn't accept from other adults. I get cut some slack for being young, and maybe I could use that.

And of course, Marilyn might get back and find her attention...*occupied* by this woman and her guards. Maybe she wouldn't even realize Evil's car didn't go with the SUVs. I imagined them all having a big argument in the house, and me and Evil sneaking into his muscle car and rolling down the canyon in neutral. But then, in my imagination, all parties started shooting at each other, and we were caught in the middle.

I growled. "We wait."

"Okay," Evil agreed. "And still, if they come this way...run."

At that moment, one of the men facing in our direction turned his face directly toward us. "Freeze," I whispered.

It wasn't enough. He'd seen something.

Pointing toward where our eyes peered through tall grass at him and his colleagues, the man started walking our way.

Evil pulled me flat and then dragged me backward. He started to pull me away, to run down the hill toward Howard, but I pulled him the other way. We both crouched to stay out of sight.

"Bucky!" he hissed.

"That's open country!" I reminded him. "We'll be caught immediately!"

We only had moments before we were seen. Keeping my knees bent and my shoulders as low to the ground as I could, I ran. Higher into the Ups.

Toward Charlie Herbert's place.

Muttering under his breath, Evil followed.

The rain started coming down in earnest.

This is going to sound like an excuse, but it's hard to run with your arm in a cast. You swing your arms when you run, and that's part of your balance. Without arms to swing, it felt as if I was trying to hop really fast. That, the uneven ground, my hiking boots, and the fact that I still felt weak from loss of blood the day before turned my run into a complete shambles.

"Bucky!" Evil had caught up to me and ran at my shoulder. "Can I assume you have a plan?"

"Hide!" I managed to gasp. "Charlie...Herbert's!"

I didn't dare look back, but nobody shouted behind us, and inside a minute we were crashing into a stand of aspens. I tumbled to the ground and lay still, and Evil dropped beside me.

He crept back to the edge of the trees and looked out, his face pressed against a white, scabby aspen trunk.

"See anything?" I whispered. I badly wanted a drink, and I felt I had to say something to remind both of us. "Remember the water is poisoned."

"*Might be* poisoned. Thanks." He was quiet for a minute. "Nothing. I don't think they saw us. Or maybe that guy saw us for a second, but talked himself out of it."

"Or they saw us but they don't care. They're here to see Marilyn."

"Who's *they*?" Evil stayed where he was, watching.

I chewed on that a moment. "My best guess is someone connected to Aaron Wilding. I've read his will, it didn't mention anybody but his wife...so, maybe someone from his company?"

"Condolences, or something? Hey...when I said 'nothing'? Scratch that. A couple of those guys are coming this way. Slowly, but they're coming. You think he died and the company sent someone out to see his wife?"

"Does that sound crazy?" Big companies were outside my area of experience.

Evil shrugged, and started crawling backward to where I lay, in dirt slowly being churned into mud. "Beats me. Let's get out of here."

We stuck to the trees and moved away from Marilyn Wilding's house in a straight line. I went first and Evil followed, and it took me a few minutes to recognize where I was headed. As I realized what I was doing, I stopped and looked back, and Evil said what I was thinking.

"Going to the grow building, huh? Does that feel safe?"

I could see men in the trees behind us. I didn't think they'd seen us, but their presence made me feel unsafe. "It feels *hidden*," I said. "Right now, I'd really like to feel unnoticed."

"You're not Batwoman after all," Evil said. "You're Potwoman, and you want to hide out in the Potcave."

I laughed, if only a little. "You okay with that?"

He nodded, and we headed out again. We found a paved road, and I figured from its angle and curves it had to be the private road connecting Charlie Herbert's house and the pot lab. The Potcave.

I looked toward Herbert's house and wished we could go there to wait out the black SUVs. But it felt too close to the Wilding place. Even the Potcave didn't feel hidden enough, with the road leading straight to it.

"Dang it," I said, moving off the road to keep to trees and brush, "we're going to end up riding a wheelbarrow down to the marina."

"This time you push," Evil said.

I looked down at my cast and snorted. "It's gonna be a short ride."

I looked to Evil, expecting him to chuckle or grin. Instead, he looked even paler than before. Soaked, the white bandage wrapped around his head was starting to look gray, and I couldn't tell whether darker spots were wetter from the rain or darkened by Evil's blood. The rain ran freely down his nose and made him look a little like a gargoyle, spouting water.

"Yeah," Evil said.

Then he collapsed.

"Evil!" I clapped a hand over my own mouth.

I knelt by him on the asphalt in the rain and felt his pulse. It was there, a little weak and maybe a little irregular. Concussion, I thought. Or exhaustion or shock? He'd banged his head in the house, maybe that had triggered something. It was my fault, whatever was wrong. We should have stayed home, watched a movie, and taken our meds.

The Potcave...how far was it? I turned and looked, and saw that we'd nearly made the entire hike. I wasted a moment trying to drag Evil off the road, but with only one working arm, it just wasn't going to happen.

I turned and ran for the cave.

It felt as if it took forever, but it can't have taken more than a minute of sloshing and jogging through the rain to the little parking lot. The truck was still there. The keys...were the keys inside the truck? I thought maybe they were, but even if I drove the truck back, what was I going to do, park it over Evil to keep the rain off?

I pushed the door of the cave open and went inside. It didn't look disturbed from yesterday, though surely Sheriff Sutherland and his deputies must have searched it. Surely, at some point, the sheriff...or somebody...would have to come confiscate the marijuana, but it hadn't happened yet.

I found a short stack of fire blankets in the corner—I'd ridden in the wheelbarrow under one the day before. I threw two of them over my shoulder. That was a struggle in itself but then, because I was afraid and I couldn't think of anything smarter to do, I also picked up an ax.

It was more of a hatchet than an ax, really. I guess it must have been there for use in a fire emergency, or maybe it was just a gardening tool. But I felt the edge and it was sharp, so with the hatchet in my left hand and two blankets over my shoulder, I turned and jogged out into the rain again—

And stopped.

One of the two men stood there. He was tall, with a big chest and a face like a broiled pork butt. His suit jacket was soaked and he smelled of sweat and cheap cologne, from ten feet away.

And he had a pistol pointed at me.

I registered the pistol, saw that it was an M1911, a bit of a connoisseur's pistol, these days. It was a pistol that suggested the guy thought he was a badass.

"We got your friend," the big guy said. "He ain't conscious, but he's alive, for now. And I think you better start explaining yourself."

"I just...explain what?"

"Why were you spying on us back there? You work for Marilyn Wilding? You work for Indra?"

Indra? I was cold enough to be almost numb, but something about that word seemed familiar. Maybe it was a corporation? Was that the name of the company Aaron Wilding owned? In fact, I did work for Marilyn Wilding, but it didn't seem like a safe thing to admit.

"We're hiking," I said. I'm not a great liar, so I hoped that fatigue and the rain would help me out. "We saw you guys...and you looked scary."

"Yeah?" The big man chuckled. He raised his aim from my chest to my forehead. "I look scary to you now?"

Thunk.

As if it had suddenly sprouted there, a length of rebar appeared, poking out of the man's sternum.

CHAPTER
22

I didn't scream.

I'd like to say that was a reflection of my gutsiness and pluck. Really, though, I was just too tired.

The guy with the iron spike in his chest toppled sideways, collapsing to his knees and then sinking onto his side as dark blood soaked the front of his shirt. He shuddered as he fell, his fingers curling into claws. I felt my breath squeezing in and out of my throat like a six-inch-thick cable grating through the eye of a sewing needle.

Then someone behind me pushed me, and I stumbled forward into the rain.

"Hey!"

The shouting voice didn't come from behind me, from the Potcave. It came from his companion, the second man. He stood over Evil like I stood over his friend, and he pointed at me as he shouted.

"Dock!" he shouted again. Dock must be the guy on the ground. The dead guy, I thought. "You!"

That meant me. I staggered and almost fell over, dropping the fire blankets, and then the second man rushed my way. He had a pistol out, a Beretta like Dad's, and he pointed it at me.

"Run!" I yelled. I was yelling at the guy pointing a gun at me. As I shouted, I sprinted away from the Potcave, toward the trees on the other side of the little parking lot.

"Hold it!" the guy with the gun shouted. He turned, following me with his line of sight, and I braced myself for the bullet.

It didn't come. Instead, I heard a meaty *thwack* and then the softer *thud* of a body collapsing to the ground. At the edge of the trees I caught a pine branch and let myself swing, off balance, around the tree's trunk, to get a look at what had happened behind me.

The second man lay on the ground, with an ax in his head. The ax I'd just dropped.

Standing over him was Michael Fellows. This was a guy who'd sat in Dad's office two days earlier with *big city* written all over him. Now he leaned in the doorway of a backwoods marijuana farm, stained bandages wrapped around his chest and shoulder, and a wild look in his eyes. He was battered, but standing.

And in the mud between us were two pistols.

I dove for the guns.

Cursing, he fell forward, too.

I landed on one of the pistols, across the body of the dead man with the rebar stuck in his chest. Fellows scrambled toward the second pistol, which had fallen from the grip of the other gunman. He dove with outstretched fingers—

And I swatted my hand sideways, knocking the gun out of his grasp.

I rolled back, pulling the pistol with me. I was afraid I'd shoot myself in the confusion, but I managed to roll completely over at least once and wind up on my back, with the weapon in my hands.

Fellows sprang up and raced for the second gun.

"Stop there!" I yelled. To make my point, I fired my pistol at the sky.

The gun clicked, but didn't fire. Maybe mud stopping the pistol from cycling?

He'd have the other gun in seconds. I racked the slide and tried again.

Nothing.

"No!" I yelled. I tried to scramble to my feet, I grabbed the hatchet and yanked, but couldn't pull it out of the corpse's head. I choked back sour bile.

Michael Fellows picked up the second pistol, and only then did I realize that the pistol lay just a few feet from Evil Patten. I felt very, very cold.

Fellows didn't point the gun at me. He pointed it at Evil.

"I think you know I'm willing to shoot your friend," he said. "In fact, I kind of owe him."

"You owe *me*." I immediately regretted my words, because I didn't want to get shot any more than I wanted to see Evil take a bullet. But I had to say something to slow Fellows down. "I'm the one who shot you."

Fellows chuckled, a soft, dry sound. "Good point. Technically, I only owe your friend a hard head butt. But I like to repay my debts with interest."

"If you do that," I said, "you'll never get the will."

Fellows's eyes narrowed. "Throw away the gun!"

I obeyed. My hand shook.

Fellows glared at me. "Keep talking."

"My dad has it." This was at least half a lie. By now Dad had probably filed the will with the court.

"Which one?" Fellows asked. He watched me closely.

I tried not to show that a light was going on in my head. There was more than one will, of course. The most recent one would be the will the court would enforce, but it couldn't enforce a will it didn't know about.

But what did Fellows want? Did he want the will I had taken from him, or some other will I knew nothing about?

Why did he care about what happened to Aaron Wilding's property? And what did he want to happen?

"I'm not sure." That wasn't really a lie. "Dad's the lawyer. I'm just an office manager, really."

"You seemed to think you were more than just an office manager the other day." He showed me white teeth and his voice took on an amused note. "Grilled me about Indian law and serving process on cowboys, as I remember."

I shrugged. "Just being cocky, I guess."

"It's very important that Marilyn not inherit," Fellows said slowly. "She's wicked."

It was easy to agree with him on that point, since I thought it was pretty likely that Marilyn had poisoned her husband. Also, she had a secret room in her house, and I was starting to think she might have had Charlie Herbert beat up there. I still didn't know how Fellows knew about the room. Of course, I had no real proof of Marilyn's guilt, not yet, and the one thing I knew for certain was that Michael Fellows had shot a man dead, in the back. And killed these other two men right in front of me. And kidnapped Evil.

"Tell me more," I urged him.

"I don't care about me. Well, maybe I do, but the more important thing is that Marilyn not inherit."

"Okay."

"Tell me where the will is."

"Dad has it. Probably his office. It's possible he's filed the will with the court by now."

Fellows cursed. He looked up the hill toward the house, out of sight. "Sooner or later, more of her men will come looking for these two."

I didn't like the thought of that, though at this point it seemed as if I was between a rock and a hard place. "Let me go. I can find out about the will. I can...come back and tell you what I find."

"You won't come back. You'll call your sheriff friend."

"You've got a hostage." I pointed to Evil and tried not to sob. He lay still and the rain puddled around his body.

Fellows shook his head. "We stick together. We're going to find the will, and you're not leaving my sight."

"Can we throw a blanket over my friend?" I asked. "Or maybe take him inside the...grow room? He's hurt, and he doesn't deserve to die."

Fellows looked down at Evil and almost seemed surprised. "Yeah. Let's put him in the truck."

Fellows did the work; that guy was strong, especially for someone who'd been shot just the day before and, like me, only seemed to have the use of one arm. He knelt, dragged Evil up onto his shoulders in a fireman's carry, stood, and then dumped him into the cab of the pickup truck. Then he flashed the truck keys and the pistol at me, shooting a glance up the hill.

"Get in," he said.

"You remember the road doesn't go anywhere," I reminded him. "Just up to Charlie Herbert's place."

"That place never belonged to Charlie Herbert," Michael Fellows said. He slid behind the wheel of the truck and waited for me.

He had Evil now.

I picked up the two bottles of water and the fire blankets. I didn't look at the cab of the truck, but I knew Fellows was following me in his mirrors. I stayed away from the pistol and the ax.

Feet squelching in the mud, I stepped around the truck to the shotgun-side door and let myself in. I put the two bottles in the truck's two cup holders in the dashboard.

The one with the label picturing a stream came from the stream, I reminded myself. The stream where the deer had died. The one with no label on it had come from the house.

Which had a secret, demented, room in it, a room decorated with bears in swimsuits, holding balloons.

I shivered from the cold. I draped one blanket over Evil and the second over my lap.

"Keep your hands in sight," Fellows said. I shivered again.

I checked Evil's pulse. He was cold, and his pulse a little irregular, but he was alive.

"What if we drop him off at the Urgent Care first?" I suggested.

"Eventually. First, we have to get off this mountain. Seat belt."

Why did *he* care that I was strapped in?

I'd barely managed to buckle myself in when Michael Fellows gunned the pickup truck and swerved sideways into the trees.

Evil bounced on the seat. He wasn't buckled in, and I tried to pin him in place by pressing my body against him. He groaned.

Michael Fellows tapped the butt of his pistol on the truck door. "Hands where I can see them." The fact that he was driving with one arm, and holding a pistol in the same hand that held the steering wheel, made me nervous. I imagined the truck hitting a rock and Michael Fellows accidentally shooting me, like Samuel L. Jackson shot that guy in the back seat in *Pulp Fiction*.

I put my hands where he could see them.

The truck bounced over a fallen log and caromed back and forth across a ragged spill of boulders. Then it hit a slope of grass and started to slide.

I didn't scream then, either, but I grabbed the dashboard with one hand and Evil with the other and I squeaked pretty loud.

"I guess the sheriff didn't find you." My vocals cords felt tight and my voice was a little unnaturally high.

"It's a big mountain. All I had to do was hold still for a while. They didn't have dogs or anything."

"They still have people out looking on the roads," I said. I wasn't one hundred percent sure why I was telling him this. Maybe it was to gain his trust. Maybe if he thought I was on his side, he'd let Evil go. Drop him off with the doctor. "I mean, I don't want to get caught in a shootout."

"Guess we better not use roads, then."

Fellows was pretty good at driving off-road, as it happened, even with one arm. He had an eye for the patches of rock that would rip the underside of the truck to pieces and he skidded around them easily, sometimes slaloming like a skier in the dust, grass, and mud. The slope was steep and the truck seemed to be falling, nose-first, toward Howard.

"Where are we going?" I asked.

He said nothing, didn't even look at me. But I knew. Of course I knew; I'd set him up.

The Fun Lanes.

We hit dirt roads I didn't recognize, coming down out of the Ups. Fellows took some of them, and some of them he skipped right over. He chose his path without hesitation—he knew the slopes intimately.

The barbed wire fence that marked the edge of the Wilding Property, he didn't even slow down for. The snapping of wire was almost melodic, like the sound of a guitar being smashed on stage. The bottles of possibly poisoned water jumped at the impact, then went back to rattling back and forth.

We entered Howard proper past a few trailers I didn't know. I saw the Dog Ears pass to my left and we crossed Reservoir Road, which meant I wasn't too far from Sheriff Sutherland's house. I had a momentary fantasy of jumping from the truck and racing to Wood Duck Island—but that wasn't going to happen. Fellows had Evil as a hostage, and even if he didn't, I couldn't outrun him on foot.

Finally, he skidded to a halt by a knot of pine trees I'd seen before a million times, but never up close; we were just across the river from the Fun Lanes. I sat still and kept my hands where he could see them.

"Shall I check if anyone's in the office?" I asked.

"Your dad's car's not there," Fellows said. "Just that woman's, and a couple of beaters I don't recognize."

"The Grand Marquis belongs to Gladys." I didn't know whether the smarter thing was to avoid giving Fellows information I didn't have to give him, or to try to humanize potential victims to slow him down. "The others are probably people bowling."

"Bowling," Michael Fellows said. "I'd forgotten."

Pointing with his pistol, he backed me out of the truck. I took the two bottles with me, and the fire blankets. That was enough to make it hard to stand, exhausted as I was. Once outside, I looked around, hoping to see someone who might notice us, but there was no one.

Then Fellows slung Evil across his shoulder again and prodded me in the direction of the Fun Lanes.

"Take us in by the back door," he told me.

CHAPTER
23

I entered the office first, but Fellows came in right on my heels, his pistol on the back of my neck. Dad wasn't there, and Fellows shut the door behind us.

"We keep coming back to the same places," I said. "I interviewed you here."

"Good times." Fellows pointed at the corner of the office with his gun. "Put the blankets down."

I did as I was told, and he slid Evil to the floor on the blankets. Following further directions, I stood in another corner and waited.

Fellows peered through the front door of the office into the Fun Lanes. I heard hooting and some bad singing along to a Kid Rock anthem, and then Fellows pulled the door shut.

"So?" He gestured at the New Files cabinets. "Find the will."

I set the water on the desk and looked. I was going through the motions with a heavy heart, because I knew I wouldn't find anything. Dad had already filed the will. He was probably still at the courthouse, unless maybe he had accompanied Marilyn Wilding home.

But I made a show of pulling the fat *WILDING* file from the cabinet and setting it on the desktop. "I would expect the will to be in a folder here in the front of the file," I said. "Matters get put into the file in chronological order from back to front, so you can stick a new matter for an existing client right in the front of that client's folder. Once the file gets too full, you stick the stuff in the back of the file into the Old Files cabinets."

"That sounds as half-assed as could be."

"And yet it works. Mostly. Here, the most recent thing in the file is...looks like a DUI Dad handled for Aaron Wilding, a year or two ago." I couldn't help snickering. "Pot, maybe?"

"What does that mean? Where's the will?"

I sighed, knowing I'd have to explain what I had known all along must be the case. "It means the will is probably filed with the court now."

"The court..." Fellows gestured with his pistol, "sits in one of those trailers downtown."

"Yeah." I shouldn't have found anything amusing in that, but I did. "Both courts are in trailers downtown, actually. The district court judge is Judge Ybarra. She says she won't waste county money on a fancy building the county doesn't really need, just to boost her ego. Dad says she worries if she moves her court into a fancier building, some of Howard's Latino populations—migrant workers, for example—might find it harder to approach her. And Sam Barlow, the old magistrate, can't very well move his little court into a new brick building when the district court's in a trailer. So that's Howard County justice for you...dispensed from a trailer."

I had no business spilling all that to Michael Fellows, but I didn't intend to. He mentioned the trailers, and suddenly I felt like I had to talk. Like there was something really important or interesting about those trailers.

Only I couldn't quite remember what it was, even with all the spilling the beans.

Two trailers. Two courts in two trailers.

Fellows shook his head. "Check again. Maybe it got misplaced."

You've got the pistol, I almost said, but there was no need to provoke him. Instead, I just dug through the files again, looking. "Can we take Evil to Urgent Care?" I asked, my fingers walking from one file folder to the next with short, precise steps. "I'm worried about him."

I was worried about myself, too. My hand was shaking, and my lips and the tip of my nose both felt numb.

"Find the will." Fellows jabbed his gun in the direction of the Old Files cabinets, in the odd corner of the room created where the bar's walk-in refrigerator jutted out, disturbing the otherwise rectangular space. "What about those? Are those the Old Files?"

I shrugged. "I don't think the will's that old, but I can look."

"Don't make excuses," Michael Fellows said. "And don't fail."

The Old Files were organized by the same logic as the New Files: alphabetical, more or less. I had little hope, so I was pleasantly surprised when I found a folder marked *WILDING*. It was lurking behind *WINDOWS*, rather than in front of it, but there you go... alphabetical, more or less.

Still, the folders in the file seemed irrelevant. A boundary agreement, a threatening letter to a contractor. "It's not...wait a minute." I pulled a folder out from deep in the file. "No, that's not it."

Fellows crowded close to me. "It says 'will' on it."

"Yeah, but look at the date." I pointed. "This is twenty years old."

Fellows frowned. "Pre-Marilyn."

"Exactly. This is not the one I saw. That you had...taken from here." I pulled the old will out to look at it and confirm. Sure enough, it was an entirely different document, and Aaron Wilding's heirs at the time were two people named *Rainbow* and...

"Indra?" I said.

"What?" Fellows said.

And then I froze.

Don't freeze up, don't freeze up, I told myself.

"The heirs on this will," I said. My head swam. "Rainbow and Indra Wilding."

"Huh."

He'd recovered quickly. But when Michael Fellows had said 'what,' it hadn't been the 'what' of 'what are you talking about,' but the 'what' of 'what do you want from me,' the kind of 'what' you say in answer to another person saying your name.

As in: *Hey, Bucky?*

What?

The Howard County Register was still on Dad's desk, open to Aaron Wilding's obituary. My eyes jumped to the photo of the dead man, and I silently cursed myself for not noticing it earlier.

Michael Fellows had Aaron Wilding's hair, his eyes, and his nose.

There was no Michael Fellows. This was Indra Wilding. That kind of sounded vaguely like a girl's name, but maybe it was Indian or something. His sister's name, after all, was *Rainbow*, and his dad was a fruity millionaire from California.

And Indra Wilding probably wasn't here as somebody's agent. He was here on his own account. He wanted the will...why? Because he thought he was getting screwed?

Because he hated his father's new, young wife. I almost laughed out loud at the thought; it was like Howard County had its own little fairy tale, complete with wicked stepmother, and I was caught up in the middle of it.

Two trailers. Nuts, why was that ringing such a bell?

"If the new will isn't filed," Indra Wilding said, "and this one gets filed instead?"

"The executor files the will with the court and publishes notice. If no one comes up with a later will, this would be the will that would get executed."

"What if the more recent will...disappeared from the court?"

I tried to imagine. "Boy, it depends," I finally said. "If it got far enough that there was a good record of it, or if there were witnesses to the making, it might not matter that the original disappeared. But if the filing hasn't been recorded for some reason, if it's just waiting in Judge Ybarra's inbox...then maybe." I almost mentioned that the filed will was a certified copy, and that Sheriff Sutherland had the original in his evidence room, but then I had visions of Indra Wilding barging in the front door of the sheriff's office with a gun to my head, demanding the key to the evidence room.

That was a scenario I could do without.

Indra looked at the clock. "How far are we from closing time?"

I shrugged. "We could close now. It'd be early for us, but it wouldn't be the first time we'd closed before the hours posted on the door. This is a small town, people understand when you have a personal emergency."

Indra thought about that. "Here's what we're going to do," he finally said. "You text your dad and tell him you'll close up here, not to worry. Then you send the old lady home."

"I don't think I'd call Gladys an old lady. At least, not while she was armed."

"Right now, I'm the one who's armed." Indra Wilding's face cooled and he pointed his pistol at the floor between my feet.

"Yeah. Sorry."

"We wait here until it's dark. Then we go break into the court and get that will back. Understood?"

I nodded. "I'll need to use Evil's phone. I...lost mine yesterday."

"Funny." Indra dug in his pocket and produced my phone. It was dirty, and had a crack across the face, but it was definitely mine. I touched its screen: the battery icon was red, but the phone wasn't dead yet. "I found it."

"Okay."

"Be careful what you type." Indra stepped behind me. "I'm watching."

I wished at that moment I had code words with Dad, if you know what I mean. A secret word I could type into the text message that would look harmless but would in fact be a cry for help. Like, maybe the code word could be *onions*, so I'd type: *Dad, don't worry about coming by the office. I'll lock up and then bring home the onions*, and he'd know there was something wrong.

But we didn't have a code word, and if I had tried to write any nonsense about onions to my dad, I was pretty sure Indra Wilding would have shot me.

Dad, I typed. *I'm at the office. I'll close up here, and see you at home later.*

There was no immediate answer, and then Indra took back my phone.

"Right." He nodded. "Now call Gladys over here, and send her home."

He positioned himself to one side of the door and pressed his body flat against the wall. He kept his pistol pointed at me. I was getting awfully tired of having a gun pointed at me. Evil lay in the corner of the room behind the door, so he'd be invisible to Gladys unless I opened the door all the way, which of course I wouldn't do.

I opened the door, stood in it, and waved to Gladys. "Hey, Gladys!" I yelled. "Got a minute?"

The kids who had been bowling were on their way out the door, which was lucky timing. Or unlucky, maybe.

"Hit the front door as you pass, will you?" I called as Gladys marched past the lanes.

I stood in the doorway. It was little unnatural, but it meant Indra would see me and hear me, and Gladys couldn't see into the office.

"You thinking of closing up early?" she said. Then she chuckled, seeing how wet I was. "It's raining, I guess?"

"Yeah," I said, answering both questions. "Dad wants me to get some sleep."

"He's right. Go home, and I'll close up."

Oops. "No, I've got a few minutes of paperwork and then I'll get the till and lock up. I'll come in and hit the urinals and wipe spilled pop off the tables in the morning. You've had long days, too."

"Well, not like you have. But I admit I've been worried."

"Lock the bar door on the way out, would you?"

"You sure about this?"

Part of me wanted to scream for help and run. If mine had been the only life at risk, I might have done it. But I had Gladys to think about too, and Evil lay helpless on the floor. If I ran, either or both of them might get shot.

I nodded. "Good night!"

Gladys was efficient when she wanted to be. Three minutes later, the doors were all locked and she was gone.

"Good." Indra relaxed, pointed his gun at the floor again. "Now we turn off the lights and wait."

"In the dark?" But I knew what he was thinking; lights could only attract attention. So I shut off the lights, opened the door connecting the office to the Fun Lanes, and sat down next to Evil. He was still breathing.

"I'll help you on one condition," I said.

I couldn't see Indra in the dark; he sat in a shadowed corner. But I heard him laugh. "Oh?"

"We get Evil to Urgent Care."

"Which one of us is going to carry him all that way...you or me?"

My heart sank. "Then we leave him here and call 911."

"After we're done at the court," Indra countered.

It was the best I could do. I nodded, and tucked Evil's blankets around him tighter. I felt his forehead; he was feverish. I bit my lip.

There was a bright side in what he was saying. It implied we'd be walking to the court, and Evil would have to stay here at the Fun Lanes.

Which meant that Indra Wilding, for once, wouldn't have a hostage to use against me. He wouldn't have any leverage over me other than the possibility that he might shoot me. I steeled myself to the likelihood that I would have to run that risk. He'd miss, I told myself. It's dark outside, and he's still injured, and he has to be sleep deprived, too. Where had he slept the night before...a tree?

But I couldn't quite bring myself to feel optimistic about my chances.

I dozed a little, leaning against the wall. It was a shallow sleep, and I didn't dream, but I did wake up with confused thoughts of trailers and breaking and entering. I shook my head to clear it.

"You ready to go?" Indra asked.

I stood up and stretched. I hurt, and I was overdue to take my antibiotic. Evil and I both were, and I thought again how much I wanted to get him to the doctor.

"Let's get this over with," I said.

I walked out the door first, stretching my imagination. I needed a solution here, some kind of practical but surprising tool or remedy that would stun Indra Wilding, or hide me from him, or notify Sheriff Sutherland. Something weird, I thought, like Evil's condoms that could hold water or be used as a flotation device.

That's it, I thought. That's what I needed to figure out.

In this situation, what would Evil do?

CHAPTER
24

We dropped down into the river and followed it. The rain had stopped, and the gathering darkness suggested that the sun was going down; this far north, in the summer, that makes it late. I walked first, pushing through the gnarled and poking pine branches, and Indra Wilding followed.

"I didn't want to kill anybody," he said, as we cut through a ragged stand of pine. "Especially not a clever person like you. I respect the trick with the balloon."

"It was a condom," I said.

"What?"

"Surprised me, too. And before you get to thinking I'm that kind of girl, the guy whose condom and whose trick it was is lying unconscious on the floor back there."

"You should give yourself more credit."

"Believe me, I take all the credit I'm due and then some. Look, Mr. Fellows—"

"Don't jerk me around."

"What?" I stopped and looked back at him. He was a thin shadow in the darkness.

"You know who I am."

Nuts. There went one advantage; knowing more than my captor realized I knew.

"You're Indra Wilding," I said. "See? Taking credit."

"Keep walking."

I kept walking.

"And I didn't kill Charlie," he added. "Not that you'll believe me. Not that it matters."

"The room," I said. I wasn't quite sure how to bring this up. "I saw the room."

"Which one?"

"Bears. Bears with swimming suits."

Indra said nothing.

"I hope all the killing is done," I said. "Whatever it is you want, I hope you get it and get out of here."

"What I want is *justice*."

I had a lot of snappy comebacks to that one. I bit down hard and held them all in. No point getting myself shot by pointing out that his justice seemed to have amounted to little more than murder.

"You don't like Marilyn." I chose my words carefully—if I was right, and he had it in for his stepmother, then calling her *Marilyn Wilding* or *Mrs. Wilding* might only aggravate him.

"You *are* clever. What gave me away?" His voice was acid, and his question was totally rhetorical.

"So who's the other woman?" I asked. "The one in the fancy suit, with the bodyguards?"

"I'm disappointed. I'd have thought you could guess by now."

"So she has to be Rainbow." I laughed a little. "She doesn't really look like a Rainbow. A Rainbow ought to be, I don't know, finger painting, or teaching yoga classes."

"Or growing pot?"

"I guess. Yeah." I stopped and looked at him again. "Is this all about the pot? 'Cause this seems like a lot of mayhem over a little weed."

He punched me in the face.

I wasn't expecting it. The sudden blow hit me square in the jaw and I dropped to the ground. I held up my good arm to protect my face, and though I don't like to admit it, I whimpered.

"We're not friends, Bucky McCrae." Indra stood over me, the moonlight glinting off his pistol so it looked like a single silver talon, projecting from his hand. "You're bright, but you're also my prisoner. When the time comes, you may be my hostage, to keep the sheriff and his boys on their best behavior. Understand this: if necessary, I will kill you."

So much for my attempts to disarm him by being friendly.

I nodded, he stepped back, and I climbed to my feet. I was off-balance physically because of the cast, and now Indra's punch had put me off-balance mentally, too. I couldn't think of anything useful to say, so I turned and plodded on.

The eastward curve of the river was opening more space on our right, and that space was filling up with Howard. We couldn't see it from the river bottom, except for occasional glances, but those glances were enough to tell me where we were: the brick back of Tuck's Bullets and Blades; the tall wood-slat fencing that enclosed Matteson's, the butcher; the bright green shingles of ImagiNation, where *Magic: the Gathering* players from four states convened on a monthly basis to hit each other with fireballs and transformation potions.

Boy, I could really have used a fireball or a metamorphosis myself. My jaw hurt. My broken arm hurt. The night chill was setting in, and I felt it in my bones. Also, I was getting angrier with each step, and by the time we reached downtown I was spitting mad.

Judge Ybarra's court isn't a trailer like you'd pull around on the back of a truck, it's more a cheap, temporary, smallish building. Its exterior is covered with a kind of fake pebbling that somebody thought looked really great in the 1970s, but has been universally hated since, and its brown-painted wood frame shines out at the edges. It's got stairs up the front and a ramp next to the stairs, to accommodate anybody who might find stairs tricky.

The lights were off. This was by no means a given, since sometimes Judge Ybarra runs her hearings late, or works with her clerks hammering out a legal opinion into the wee hours. But not tonight. Lucky me.

Indra looked around. The Judge's court sat between

McAllister's, a cheap burger bar catering to locals and fishermen from out of state, and Veterans' Park, which is a handful of tall trees, a curly slide two stories tall, and an acre of grass. The park was quiet. McAllister's was loud, but it was minding its own business and starting to get a bit of a buzz, so nobody looked our way.

"Is there a back door?" Indra asked me.

I nodded. Inside, the trailer is divided into a waiting and processing room, a courtroom, and the Judge's chambers. I knew the chambers had their own door, because I'd delivered memoranda there more than once, when the Judge wanted something directly from Dad, or the clerks and the office staff were out to lunch. I pointed around the side.

"You first."

I made my way to the Judge's door. This faced a small reserved-spaces-only parking lot behind the building, lit only by the yellowish glow thrown by the windows of McAllister's. The door was at the top of three concrete steps.

I stopped at the bottom of the steps. "It'll be locked." This was not someone's house out in the sticks, this was a government building.

"Step aside," Indra said. When I had done so, he waggled his pistol at me by way of admonition. "Don't move."

He tucked his pistol into the back of his pants. From his pocket he then produced a big folding knife, single blade. He grinned at me as he opened it with one hand; all I could see of his face were his white teeth. "This is not the manufacturer's recommended use," he whispered, and he jammed the blade deep into the wood of the door frame near the knob.

He dug for nearly a minute. I considered running away, but every few seconds he turned to glare at me. I was standing in an open parking lot, and I'd get nowhere. I stood still and shivered.

"You went to military school, didn't you?"

"You know who I am, it's no secret. Yes." Indra kept digging. "Spent a few years in the Army. Army got me through college. Was looking at the JAG Corps—Army lawyers—but lost interest. The practice of law just isn't really my thing."

"Your thing is revenge."

He didn't answer.

When Indra had finished, a pile of wood splinters lay heaped on the top step, nearly invisible from five feet away. The bolt of the door's lock gleamed, newly exposed. He put away his knife, opened the door, and then pulled out the gun again.

"Go find the will," Indra told me, nudging the door further open with his toes.

I entered the Judge's chambers. My feet were heavy. "I can't see. Leave the door open."

Indra stayed by the door, but he shifted to one side to stop blocking the light. "Don't get any ideas about running. I still have the gun."

"And the knife. And I have a broken arm." *And a big bruise on my jaw,* I didn't add. At least it wasn't broken.

He didn't say anything.

Boldness would win, or nothing would. I stepped inside and walked to the Judge's desk. I walked fast, counting on my memories of the room. Those were none too specific—I remembered the big desk, and the potted plant on the floor next to it reasonably clearly, but there was a refrigerator in here somewhere too, and I couldn't quite see in my mind's eye where that was.

But I needed to act before my eyes adjusted to the darkness, because if my eyes hadn't adjusted, then Indra's probably hadn't, either.

"Maybe the desk." I worried I'd said it too loud. He might think I was telegraphing to hide my movements.

I slammed into the edge of the desk. "Oomph!"

Indra laughed, but the move had been on purpose. In banging into the desk, I knocked the desktop phone to the floor.

In Howard, the cell reception can sometimes be spotty. And when one of the cell towers goes down, it can take the big cell providers a couple of days to get a repair crew up from Boise or over from Yakima to fix it. So we still have landlines here, and not fancy Voice Over IP landlines either, I'm talking copper. And especially we still have landlines in our government buildings.

"Aw, crap," I said.

The dial tone was loud in the darkness. With the phone on the floor between the plant—it was a ficus, a little miniature tree—and the desk, I grabbed the handset and jammed the top half of it, the part that cradles up against a caller's ear, deep down into the dirt in the ficus's pot.

I was counting on the dirt to muffle the dial tone, and then the beeping as I pressed numbers, and it worked. The phone went silent, then I dialed nine-one-one by feel alone and stood up. To Indra it must have looked and sounded as if I'd knocked the phone off the hook, and then hung it back up again.

But meanwhile, a call was going through to the emergency switchboard. And since the part of the handset that cradles against the caller's mouth was exposed, the switchboard operator should be able to hear what Indra and I said.

The switchboard would transfer the call to Sheriff Sutherland's office, but only if I gave them a reason not to simply hang up. They might try to talk to me, but hopefully the dirt would mute the operator's voice.

"You think you can get out of town without being caught?" I said. "There aren't that many roads."

"Shut up and find the will."

"I'm looking." I actually did look. My eyes were adjusting, and I dug through the papers on top of the Judge's desk. It was slow going, because in the darkness it took longer to read everything, but if I turned the pages toward the door and focused I could make out the text. The papers were filings of various kinds, motions, and other court papers, but none of them had Dad's name on them.

"Look faster."

"Judge Ybarra has a lot going on," I said. "But I don't see the will here. Can we call Urgent Care now, and ask them to send an ambulance to the Fun Lanes?"

"Shut up," Indra growled. "Not yet."

"Evil's alone in my dad's office," I said. "He's hurt, he may be in shock, and if he does wake up all alone there in the dark, he'll be disoriented and scared." I didn't mean to, but I teared up a little as I talked about Evil. That was good, though. That probably helped hide how on-the-nose my words were.

"Shut up about your boyfriend!" Indra snapped. "Now where else can we look?"

I could see Indra looking around the outside of the trailer. It occurred to me, too late, that if I took too long he might turn the lights on to help me...at which point, he'd see what I'd done with the phone.

And then probably shoot me.

"New filings aren't given directly to Judge Ybarra, anyway. They're put into an inbox in the front office," I said. He didn't really care about the detail, and I didn't really care whether he knew or not. I was explaining these things in the hope that the switchboard operator or a deputy sheriff would hear what I was saying and realize where I was. "And they're entered into a log, and date-stamped."

"I guess you better go look at that log, then." Indra Wilding stalked my direction, herding me like a sheep into the front half of the trailer.

I crossed the actual courtroom, which wasn't all that big. You know how in the movies, the courtrooms are always huge marble chambers like a bank or a Greek temple, with columns and a mezzanine from which the common folk watch, waiting for a great victory for justice? Well, Judge Ybarra's courtroom looked more like the nursery in a low-rent church. It had flat industrial carpet, a desk, two tables, and a few rows of folding chairs. Without Judge Ybarra in the room, it felt like you could push the chairs aside, chalk a hopscotch grid on the carpet, and start skipping for nickels.

With Judge Ybarra in the room, it could feel like the lion's den.

The waiting and processing room had a counter with two chairs for court employees to work at, and benches for people waiting their turn. On the counter was the logbook, and beside it a stack of filings.

"Here's the log." I picked it up and scooted closer to the window, where light from McAllister's filtered through the slats of Venetian blinds. My finger found the entry. "Yeah, this filing has to be it." I started reading the file number, but Indra Wilding didn't wait. Diving into the stack of court papers on the counter, he shoved each into the thin light coming through the blinds until the sight of one made him cackle victoriously.

He waved the paper at me, crumpling it in his fist. "Done!"

I wasn't sure about that. There was a record that *something* had been filed. And we probably had a scanned copy of the will on a hard drive somewhere, and Marilyn Wilding might have a copy...but I wasn't going to argue.

I was just glad that in the darkness, he hadn't noticed that he was joyfully destroying a copy, and not the original will.

Also, improbably, I remembered at that moment Sheriff Sutherland's account of the world being full of dipshits, and every once in a while someone following the logic of morons, breaking into a bank thinking he could burn his mortgage and be debt-free. That was Indra Wilding. He was deadly and he might even be cunning, but on a pretty basic level he was a complete dipshit.

That heartened me, a little.

He was still hooting and crowing about his success when something outside the window caught Indra Wilding's eye.

"Dammit." He shoved the will into his pocket. "Cops."

CHAPTER
25

Should I just run?

I eyed the front door. It was only ten feet from me, but there was a counter in the way I'd have to hop, and then I'd have to get the door unlocked—

Indra didn't leave me the time to decide. He grabbed my hand and dragged me toward the door by which we'd entered.

I rattled out the back door and hit the ground with a shock to both ankles. Wordlessly, Indra dragged me right, toward McAllister's. Before we were halfway there, he jerked me sideways again, pulling me left this time, and dragging me down into a ditch.

My call had worked. If someone from the sheriff department had come here, that could only mean they had listened to my call. Which meant they must also be sending someone to check on Evil, or they would be in a minute, once they saw the door forced, which would confirm what they'd heard on the phone.

If Evil was still alive, he'd be safe.

This was more than I could say for myself.

"Shh," Indra said softly. In case I didn't get the message, he pressed the barrel of his pistol to the back of my neck. It felt like an ice cube.

He looked over the lip of the ditch and watched the courthouse. I lay down inside the depression and saw nothing, but I heard the scrape of boots on the gravel of the parking lot, and then the click-talk-click patterns of police handhelds.

"Howard one-eight here."

"Howard one-eight," I heard dispatch answer.

"I have visual confirmation of a forced entry. Unit for code two."

I knew enough cop-radio-speak to know that *unit for code two* meant that the deputy wanted backup. So I'd done it. I'd alerted the sheriff department under Indra's nose. But my heart was hammering way too fast to enjoy my success.

Besides, it wasn't too late for Indra to simply shoot me.

"Rebecca?" the deputy shouted. His voice sounded a little muffled, like maybe he was inside the trailer now.

Indra surged suddenly to his feet. I had a terrible vision of him rushing forward to shoot a deputy, or two deputies, and dropping them dead right there in the parking lot. Instead, he pulled me and we ran the other way.

I was sweating profusely, which I only realized because my running, slow as it was, turned that slick sheen of sweat into a casing of ice. I shivered.

We crossed a vacant lot, that was supposed to have turned into a McDonald's more than ten years earlier, only the owner's financing fell through in one of the stock market busts of the aughts. The *FOR SALE BY OWNER* sign had been sitting in the weeds as long as I could remember. The great thing about the lot was supposed to have been its location right next to St. Joe's, one of Howard's two high schools. But the McDonald's didn't happen and no one since had found the lot interesting enough to step in and pick up the project.

Indra dragged me several more blocks. We were in downtown Howard now, so there were sidewalks, but we didn't use them. He stuck to the shadows of trees, and ran behind buildings, and he turned us in a slow loop down Third Street, which is all little old-style Howard bungalows, and then brought us out on the outdoor basketball courts of St. Joe's.

I stood in the shadow of a leaning basketball standard with no net on the rusted hoop, catching my breath. Across the big front lawn of St. Joe's, speckled with tall weedy grass, and over Veterans' Park, I could see Judge Ybarra's courtroom. Two trucks from the sheriff department were now parked in front of the trailer, and the lights were on inside the building. I could see silhouettes through the windows that suggested people moving.

I didn't hear ambulance sirens, though. I tried to think through the route. Would an ambulance have to pass within earshot of me to get from the Urgent Care to the Fun Lanes? Or would the ambulance even use its sirens? Maybe it wouldn't need to. Maybe it would drive at flow of traffic, not sure yet whether there even was an injured person to pick up. Maybe the paramedics on the scene could help Evil enough they wouldn't need to use the sirens.

I crossed my fingers and looked up at the statue of St. Joseph who stood over the nearest door to the school. He was bearded and robed, and I wasn't really sure which Joseph the saint was. Joseph, as in Joseph and Mary? But wasn't there another Joseph, who let Jesus use his own tomb? Maybe there were others. I hadn't really grown up on saints, but neither of those guys seemed like an obvious choice to have a school named after him.

Neither one seemed like a natural patron of hostages, either, or people lying unconscious on the floor of a bowling alley. Plus, I had no idea what kind of prayer you were supposed to say to a saint. Really, the McCraes had never been a praying household, and less so since Mom had left. Still, I crossed my fingers and thought, because I didn't dare say it out loud: *St. Joseph, get us both out of this and I'll...* What would St. Joseph want? *I'll let kids from St. Joe bowl free for a week.*

Whatever else he was, presumably St. Joseph was the patron saint of the kids studying at his school.

I realized that Indra didn't know I'd sneakily sent an ambulance, and I needed to keep playing my part. "Can we call the Urgent Care now? Then you can take Charlie Herbert's truck and get out of town. Now's probably the right time to do it, with the sheriff department distracted. I think you and I are done."

Indra Wilding looked at me with flat eyes. "Yes. You and I are done."

I didn't like the tone of his voice. He prodded me with his pistol, and for once I wished there were a whole lot more traffic in Howard at night. Especially foot traffic. I would have been grateful for a passerby to notice this man pushing me around with his pistol, but no such luck.

"Where are we going?" I asked.

"Back to the river," he said. "And the truck. I can't leave you here in town, so you're going to come with me and I'll drop you off somewhere down the road. Far enough from a phone so you can't do me any harm."

It was a lie, and I knew it. He had no intention of helping Evil, and he had no intention of letting me free. Indra Wilding was going to kill me. He hadn't punched me in the face to control me, he'd punched me in the face to remind himself that he had to be brutal to me, treat me like an enemy.

"Okay," I said.

Then I ran.

Indra cursed. I sprinted past him to force him to lose precious time turning to come after me, but there was no way I was faster than him, especially with my arm in a cast and my balance thrown off. I had precious seconds at best, and I gambled on McAllister's. I ran toward the burger bar as fast as my exhausted legs would carry me, but when I hit the road, I heard the squealing of tires.

A black SUV slammed on its brakes and skidded to a halt right in front of me, so close that I bounced off its hood and almost fell down. Two others pulled up behind it.

I wondered where Indra was, but as I staggered away from the first SUV, rough hands grabbed me and dragged me back. My vision swung wildly as my body practically flew through the air, but I didn't see Indra.

Instead, I saw a big-shouldered man in a suit, and then I was stuffed into the back seat of the SUV and the door was slammed shut behind me.

And the car drove on.

For a few long seconds, I couldn't make out anything, except a greenish glow that must be the light of the car's dashboard instrumentation.

"Rainbow?" I croaked.

"I don't know what you're talking about, kid." The words sounded like the words of a mobster, but the accent wasn't Brooklyn, or at least it wasn't the Brooklyn accent I recognized from movies and TV. It could have been a Spokane accent, or Pocatello—just mid-American western flat. "I didn't see any rainbow today. Just rain."

"Who told you my name?"

This second voice belonged to a woman, and I recognized it. It was Rainbow Wilding's voice. I sat up, and my eyes adjusted enough that I could see her sitting in the back seat beside me, still wearing her expensive suit. Closer up, I realized that she wasn't as old as I had taken her for, not as old as my Dad. Older than her brother Indra by a few years, though.

"Nobody told me. I guessed." I wondered whether I could trust her. She traveled with rough men, but that didn't mean she was a crook.

"Not out of thin air."

I sighed. "I read a will."

"You're the lawyer's kid."

"I don't really think of myself as a kid."

"Neither did I when I was sixteen. I was wrong. You read my father's will. Which one?"

I trembled with adrenaline, and I knew that as soon as that artificial kick passed through my system, I'd collapse from fatigue. "I read two of them. Or anyway, I skimmed two of them."

"Dated when?" I couldn't see Rainbow Wilding's face in the darkness, except for one cheek and ear that were bathed in spectral green dashboard light, which made her look a bit like a detached and floating ghost's head. "This is important."

In the front sat two of her muscle men. The one in the shotgun seat, who I thought was the one who had yanked me into the car in the first place, leaned back and stared at me, his face veiled in the darkness of the SUV.

"One about ten years ago," I said, struggling to remember the date.

"And the other more recent?" she snapped.

More recent? "No," I said slowly. "The other was about twenty years old."

Rainbow snorted. "How many wills did my father *write?*"

"It's what people do," I said. "They update their wills, you know, when their life situation changes. Like when they...remarry, for instance."

"Thanks for the lecture." Rainbow didn't mean it. "Now tell me what you saw up on the mountain."

"Up on what mountain?" I said feebly. The guy in the seat in front of me leaned in closer. He smelled stale and sweaty, and there were onions on his breath.

"You were hiding outside Marilyn's house. Don't lie. I know the car there isn't hers, it belongs to a kid named Ronald Patten. You and Ronald were there, watching. Tell me *exactly* what you saw."

How did they know the car belonged to Evil? Were these cops? Maybe Rainbow Wilding traveled with bodyguards because she was a politician of some kind. I had a terrible sinking feeling. I hadn't been rescued; I'd been snatched from the jaws of one predator by a pack of a different species, but I still had teeth at my throat.

And then I realized what had been niggling at the back of my mind all evening.

"You're looking for a third will," I said.

Rainbow didn't move, just kept looking at me. In the dim light her eyes looked like a lizard's. "Go on."

"It's more recent." This much, Rainbow herself had virtually told me. Now I started guessing. "Charlie Herbert must have witnessed it."

A hiss of breath in the darkness told me my guess had struck home. "Have you seen it?"

"No, but I know where it is."

"Don't give me any nonsense about Charlie's shack." Rainbow's voice carried an unstated threat. "Or the little weed factory, either. We've searched both places quite thoroughly." I remembered her two dead thugs, one with a rebar spear in his sternum and the other with a hatchet to the head. I didn't mean to, but I shuddered.

"No," I said. "It's actually here, in town. We're quite close."

"Your father's office."

"No, Dad has the twenty-year-old will. And he had the ten-year-old will too, until he filed it with the District Court today. But I know where the most recent will is, and I can get it for you."

"Go on."

"But these guys are scaring me." I pointed at the two men. "I'll bring you the will, but these guys disappear."

"You think I'll just let you go, and hope you come back? We still haven't finished talking about what you might have seen up at Marilyn's place."

"You can come with me." She didn't seem to be jumping at that idea, so I threw out another. "Or I'll take along one of your bruisers, only first he gives me his pistol."

"No way," the man in the shotgun seat harrumphed.

But Rainbow Wilding cocked her head to one side and looked at me. She was silent for a moment, and I thought the expression I was seeing on her face might just be a hint of a smile.

"Burt," she said firmly. "Give her your gun."

The man called Burt muttered something in a language I didn't know. But he reached into his jacket and pulled out a Glock, which he handed to me. I took it.

"Show me your ankles, Burt," I said.

"That's my only piece."

"Ankles."

Burt muttered again, but he lifted up his cuffs and showed me both ankles, lifting his feet off the floor to do it. By now my eyes had adjusted enough that by the dashboard lights I could see that he wasn't wearing an ankle holster on either leg. "Satisfied?"

"Yep," I said.

"Go with her, get the will, and let her go," Rainbow Wilding said to Burt.

I ejected the magazine to make sure the pistol wasn't empty, then reseated it. For once, I'd be the one who was armed. "Let's go, Burt," I said.

CHAPTER
26

Burt and I stepped out into the light of a single street lamp and two of the three SUVs pulled away, taking Rainbow with them. They left Burt a single vehicle and Rainbow's instruction, "Call when you've got it."

I waited for a moment to give them time to disappear, and in the meantime looked at Burt's face.

He had strong eyebrows, a square jaw, and wide open eyes, all of which gave his face a very honest look. It might have been a reassuring look for him to have, except that Burt's face also looked excited and a little angry. I decided to try being honest with him.

At least partially.

"Indra Wilding was chasing me," I said. "I think he wants to kill me."

"Good thing you got a gun," Burt shot back. "Tell you what, if I see him coming, I'll point him out and step out of the way so you can shoot him. Or maybe I'll just throw myself to the ground and shriek."

"I thought you'd rather be warned. You don't need to be so sarcastic."

"Just doing my job, kid," Burt said. "Which, by the way, is also what my pals Dock and Steve were doing. Their jobs. Only when they went to figure out who was hiding in the tall grass and spying on them, they got killed for their trouble."

"That wasn't me."

"Yeah, I don't see you a shoving an iron pole into a grown man's chest or sinking an ax into a guy's head. Frankly, I don't see you shooting anybody, either. I get that kids out here know their guns and all, but they mostly shoot tin cans and raccoons. Shooting a human being is an entirely different proposition. I think if I really wanted to take that gun back, I could just yank it out of your hands. But in the meantime, you're dangerous. So forgive me if I'm not all excited to be walking around the streets of Hicktown here without a weapon."

"Why don't you just take the gun away from me, if you think it's so easy, and you're so uncomfortable without it?"

"I'm doing my job, like I said. And right now, my job is to follow you to wherever this will is stashed and get it. Afterward," Burt's sneer flashed into a cruel grin, "we'll see."

"This way." I didn't like it. Despite his open face, Burt didn't feel straight to me, and I wanted to test him, catch him up. Marilyn's orders had seemed straightforward, but maybe Burt had other plans.

Maybe, it occurred to me, Burt was playing a different game. After all, when I'd heard Indra Wilding talking on the phone in the little A-frame cabin, it had sounded as if he was talking not to Rainbow, but to someone in Rainbow's entourage. *Just stay away*, Indra had said, and *keep her out of this*.

I started walking toward Sam Barlow's trailer.

"You know we could drive," Burt said.

"It isn't far." Being in the SUV only made me feel conspicuous, and what I wanted to feel right now was discreet. Burt didn't press the point.

Sam's court was held in a trailer not too different from Judge Ybarra's. Probably I should call him *Magistrate Barlow*, but that doesn't feel right, Sam's not that kind of guy. Sam's the kind of guy who fishes a lot, who buys everybody at the bar a round of drinks when he shows up, and who is surprisingly good at chess. His curving mustache and pointed little beard make him look like an old Spanish don, but the dons never got this far north, and his relaxed grin and slow conversational pace make you want to call him *Sam*, even when he's forty years older than you. He's everybody's favorite uncle, Sam Barlow, and he's the county magistrate—that means he runs a minor court that can handle certain small matters, mostly to keep the little stuff from clogging up Judge Ybarra's District Court. Traffic tickets, licensing disputes, small claims, all that kind of stuff, you end up in front of Sam.

The night Charlie Herbert had died, his last words, he'd said something about how he'd gone to the wrong trailer. I hadn't understood what he meant then, or how he'd come to be there, but I was starting to be able to fill in the gaps. Charlie had been in the Wildings' secret room, and someone had manhandled him. Probably, I guessed, that someone was Marilyn's lover Nick, and probably at some point he'd stolen a deputy's uniform and worn it as a way to get Charlie to trust him. Which must mean that Charlie hadn't recognized Nick, so if Nick was Marilyn's lover, he hadn't been living with the Wildings. In fact, unless Charlie was just so stoned out of his mind he didn't recognize people, it must be the case that Marilyn had done the beating up without Nick, and then Charlie had escaped, so Nick had stolen a deputy's uniform and gone after Charlie. Because if Charlie recognized the guy who'd been pummeling him, he wasn't going to trust him, no matter what uniform he wore. Maybe Nick had also been the one who had burgled Judge Ybarra's court. Maybe Charlie had told him he'd given the will to the Judge. Or maybe he'd told Marilyn and she'd done the burgling. Only she didn't seem like the type, not with those nails.

I had a good guess about what Charlie Herbert had meant by two trailers now too, and what had happened with the last will and testament written by Aaron Wilding, the truly final one. It was a will Charlie had probably witnessed, and Aaron had probably asked him to give it to the court. Charlie had gone and stuffed it under the door of the court he was familiar with—Sam Barlow's magistrate court. That was where Charlie would have been brought if he'd been busted for speeding, for example, or fishing without a license. Charlie may not even have realized that there *was* a second court, until after he'd left the will, which had to have happened this week.

Because Sam Barlow was out fishing this week. So he hadn't seen the will, and no one else had either, because when Sam took off, so did his clerks. And at some point, Charlie had realized that he'd put the will in the wrong place. Maybe he'd been at the Fun Lanes that night because he was trying to tell Dad what he'd done. And Nick had found him there. In any case, what had been on Charlie's mind in his dying moments was the fact that he had screwed up. Aaron Wilding had trusted him to witness and then deliver Wilding's true last will and testament, and Charlie had taken it to the wrong trailer.

Anyway, that was my guess. I didn't explain any of this to Burt. I just walked back around St. Joe's, keeping my eyes open and peering deeply into every shadow in search of Indra Wilding.

"You stick this document in your locker at school?" Burt asked.

"We're not going into the school." And then I had an idea. "It's all bears in swimsuits, anyway," I mumbled

Burt stopped. "What the hell did you just say, kid?"

That was it. Burt had heard the phrase before. It didn't have to have been from Indra, but odds were, he was the source. My breath caught in my throat, but I tried to act natural. "I just come here for swimming. This isn't my regular school."

Burt squinted at me. "A town the size of a pothole and it has two high schools?"

"Kids come into town from half the county to go to school," I explained. "This is St. Joseph's. Howard High is the other high school." I pointed vaguely in the direction of Howard.

He didn't really care. "So where are we going?"

I didn't want to tell him. I half-expected Burt to cheerfully cut my throat once he had his hands on the will, either because Rainbow had secretly instructed him to or because he was double-dealing as Indra's covert ally. "We'll be there in a minute."

Past the rickety stadium seating that ran along the side of the track, we hit Sam's trailer. It was roughly the size and layout of Judge Ybarra's, the principal differences being that Sam had better furniture—it was handcrafted, and I thought maybe he even made it himself—and his walls were covered with mounted fish.

From the outside, it was still a pebble-covered box with a locked front door. I stopped.

"For real?" Burt asked.

"I'm not a hundred percent sure. But probably."

"What is this, like, the detention annex for the high school or something?"

"It isn't fancy," I said. "But it's the county's magistrate court. I'm pretty sure Charlie Herbert brought the will here by mistake."

"Yeah?"

I nodded. "I think he was trying to explain that to me when he died. Only I just figured it out tonight."

Burt looked around. On one side of us was St. Joe's, which blocked out the lights of town, and on the other a street lined with old cottonwoods and living room lights just starting to wink out.

Burt exhaled through pursed lips, then nodded. "Okay then," he said, and he kicked in Sam Barlow's door.

The door gave way immediately. That was good, because the kick was loud, and I didn't know for sure where Indra was, and I didn't really want him to hear the noise and come find me. If, that is, he wasn't already following us. I scanned around the trashcans and stairwells that made up this side of St. Joe's, but didn't see him.

There on the cheap carpet, just inside the door as if it had been stuffed under, lay a manila envelope. On the front were scrawled the words *JUDGE BARLOW*.

"Technically he's not a judge," I said.

"Like I give a crap." Burt stooped to pick up the envelope. "This it?"

"It's got to be."

"I'm not paid for 'got to be.'" Burt pinched together the brad that closed the envelope, opened the flap, and shook out the contents. "This is the last will and testament of Aaron Wilding," he read. "Dated just a week ago."

I felt a rush of vindication. It felt like relief coming in, but as it passed through me my stress levels were no lower. I could easily wind up right and dead.

"So who gets everything?" I asked. "What was the fuss all about?"

"Fuss?" Burt asked.

"In the last will, Wilding left everything to his wife. I see now that he did that because there was a previous will, that he'd made when he was single, leaving everything to his kids. And I guess he decided...they didn't need it, and she did. Or he loved her more than he loved them, or whatever. So he changed his mind again, right? Maybe he found out his wife was cheating on him, or maybe he just got a wild hair. And whatever he did, it was worth killing over to somebody. Maybe to lots of people."

Burt's eyes narrowed. "Like who?"

"Indra Wilding, for one," I said. "I think he knew there was at least one more recent will, maybe he knew there were two, and he wanted to get rid of them so he could inherit again."

"Yeah? Who else?"

I suddenly realized that I had come very close to telling him that Rainbow Wilding also had incentive to commit murder. Or that I suspected him of mixed loyalties. My grip on the Glock felt sweaty. "Well, clearly not your boss," I said. "She's pretty wealthy as is, it's hard to imagine she would care about a little grow house full of stinkweed." I hoped I was right about that. "But there's Marilyn and her boyfriend. Marilyn stood to inherit everything, which I don't know how much that is but it must be a lot if people are willing to go to all this trouble. And maybe she could only inherit if Wilding didn't change the will."

Having said all that, I realized I didn't really know what Rainbow Wilding was doing in Howard. If she really was rich, and she really didn't care about inheriting her father's fortune, why not just stay away?

"You're a thinker, all right." Burt handed me the will.

My left hand held the pistol, so I took the will gingerly between two fingers of my right hand. The sling's position put the will a little further from my face than was comfortable for reading, but I could make out the words. I skimmed them.

"Nobody inherits," I said. "He wants to set up a wildlife trust."

I looked to Burt to gauge his reaction—did he know what Rainbow Wilding was doing here? Would he show rage, disappointment, satisfaction? Would he take this will and try to destroy it?

Before I could see anything in the darkness, I heard the sound of gunfire. Not one shot but several, *Bang! Bang! Bang!*

Burt staggered away from the door and sat down in a chair. It wasn't voluntary; blood poured from his shoulder.

I threw myself back from the door and peeked out the front window, just in time to see the muzzle flash of another shot.

Bang!

The bullet smashed into the monitor of an old desktop computer sitting on the receptionist's desk in Sam's front office. The monitor sparked and jumped, and then an ozone reek filled the small room.

I fired three blind shots out the front door, *bang! bang! bang!*, then slammed it shut and dropped to the floor, keeping a careful eye on the window above me.

"Burt!" I hissed.

What he mumbled back to me was unprintable.

"Sorry," I said. "There's a back door. We can—"

And then I stopped. There was a back door, but Indra would probably assume there was a back door, too, seeing a trailer the same size and shape as the one we'd broken into an hour earlier. Wouldn't he run around to the back, to stop us slipping away, or to break in and catch us by surprise? Shouldn't I break out the front instead, and run as fast as I could?

Or call? Sam's office had phones, I could call for help and just wait. How long would it take the sheriff or one of his deputies to get here? Surely only a few minutes. They were just a couple of blocks away. They might already be on their way now...

"Kid," Burt murmured.

I looked at him. He held a pistol in his hand, a little snub-nosed revolver, and it was pointed at me.

"Give me the will." His eyes were slits.

"Sure."

I stood up. Please, I thought, don't let Indra Wilding be standing in front of the window or he'll see me right now and shoot me dead. My shoulders were stiff as boards, I half expected to catch a bullet.

But I didn't.

And then I threw myself sideways out the window.

CHAPTER 27

My ears filled with the crash of breaking glass. For a horrible moment, I imagined myself landing wrong in the shards, cutting my own throat or slicing an eye open.

But it wasn't a long moment, because then I hit the ground. I landed on my shoulder with a loud *crack*, and lightning flashes of pain shot down my arm.

I heard gunshots. They sounded far away.

If the shooter was aiming at me, he missed.

I rolled onto my knees, whimpering, then staggered up to my feet and ran. By sheer force of concentration, I was still holding on to both the will and the pistol.

Judge Ybarra's court, I thought. If I could just get around St. Joe's, I'd get to Judge Ybarra's, and the deputies there would help me.

I ran toward the nearest edge of the school. Each footfall was excruciating; the ground felt like a boxer, striking the soles of my feet.

But there were no more shots. Maybe Indra and Burt had shot each other, I thought, my heart full of wild hope.

I passed a big black walnut tree, and my feet were kicked out from under me.

I hit the ground and lost my grip on both the will and the pistol. Something hit the back of my head, slamming my face into the dirt, and then I was dragged to my feet. I gasped for breath and it sounded a bit like sobbing.

"It turns out we're not quite done with each other, Rebecca McCrae."

My captor was Indra Wilding. He held me by the back of my shirt and shook me.

"Is this the will you and your new boyfriend were talking about?"

I was dizzy, but I saw he had both the Glock and the will now.

I nodded. "I thought he was *your* boyfriend, though."

Indra laughed. "Good. Now all we need to do is catch a ride."

"You don't need me," I said.

"Oh yes I do. *For now.*"

I wished I was bigger, and weighed more. Then it might have been harder for Indra Wilding to drag me like he did, around the corner of St. Joe's, behind McAllister's, and back into Judge Ybarra's parking lot. I felt like a stray cat being thrown off the property, and I had an image of Indra stuffing me into a sack and tossing me in the river.

There was a sheriff department pickup truck parked behind the courtroom trailer, the kind with big saddlebags full of tools in the bed and an extended cab split down the middle by a steel mesh so the deputies could keep prisoners in the back seat. A deputy with a cowboy hat stood in the open door of the truck, writing on a clipboard with his back turned to us.

I opened my mouth to shout a warning—

And Indra shifted his grip, clamping a hand over my mouth. He held me with one arm around my neck, and with his other hand he kept the Glock pressed against my temple. If his wounded arm hurt as much as mine did, he must be in excruciating pain.

But excruciating pain didn't mean he would miss.

"Mmmph," I mumbled, but mostly I sucked in air through my nostrils, just trying to breathe.

"Turn around slowly," Indra said, when we were close enough to be heard. He dragged me forward, my toes scraping the asphalt.

The deputy turned around. Only it wasn't a deputy. It was Sheriff Sutherland.

He scowled, the facial expression that's scared many a Howard teenager into pulling his pants up and driving straight home. He leaned forward into his frown, which made his shoulders look even broader than they really were.

"I assume you're here to turn yourself in," he said. "'Cause otherwise, you'd have been well advised to stay the hell out of my sight, pal. And you really would have been well advised not to sneak up on me with my friend's daughter in a half Nelson like some dickhead amateur luchador."

"Shut up and give me the keys."

Sheriff Sutherland didn't budge. "You understand the seriousness of what you're doing, right? I mean, whatever else we can charge you with, and I have to tell you the county prosecutor is a vindictive son of a bitch who absolutely wants every offender in jail for life, you're now throwing in a couple of counts of kidnapping. And on top of that, I'm really going to have to kick your ass."

"Three," Indra Wilding said, "two..."

Sheriff Sutherland held up his keys. I saw veins in both temples throbbing.

"Set them on top of the truck. And your belt. And your ankle piece, too."

Sheriff Sutherland slowly cooperated. His eagle stare never left Indra's face. "Bucky," he said calmly, "if this clown ever takes the gun off you, bite him."

"Now put the handcuffs on your wrists."

The sheriff growled slightly in the back of his throat, but he cuffed himself.

"Get in the back."

"Let Rebecca go."

"Rebecca is going to drive."

Indra released me, but kept the pistol pointed in my direction. Scooping up the sheriff's guns and belt, he pushed Sutherland into the back seat of the truck and locked him in, taking his big hat for good measure. Then he handed me the keys.

I climbed into the driver's seat and Indra took shotgun. I had to scoot the sheriff's seat forward and up to fit me, and when I finally took the wheel and turned the key in the ignition, awkwardly because I had to do it with my left hand, I was shaking.

"Where to?" I said the words as calmly as I could manage. It wasn't very calm.

"My father's house. You know the way."

I put the truck into gear and turned south, heading toward the Dog Ears and the Ups. I tried to focus on next steps, and how to catch Indra Wilding by surprise and get a gun away from him. Instead, I found myself thinking of Evil, and regretting that I wouldn't be driving past the Fun Lanes or the Urgent Care, so I could see whether someone was taking care of him.

"Is Evil okay?" I looked at Sheriff Sutherland in the mirror.

The sheriff nodded. He looked like a caged bear on the other side of the quarter-inch-thick wire mesh, teeth grinding together and eyes shooting death wishes at Indra Wilding. "They got him to Urgent Care, thanks to your dad."

"Thanks to Dad?" I hadn't expected to hear that.

"Yep. He got a text from you, and remembered your cell phone had never turned up, so he figured out there was something fishy going on at the Fun Lanes. We sent a deputy and an ambulance."

Wow. Dad.

"Evil will be okay. Shock, exhaustion, dehydration, but I think we got to him in time. You kids ought to know to take it easier the day after some jerk shoots you or bangs you on the head with a shovel. I'm surprised *you're* still conscious."

"Say what you want," Indra hissed. "We all know it's only talk."

As we turned past the Dog Ears, I noticed that there were headlights behind me. Just a single car, and it was too dark to tell what kind of car it was. But the roads were empty enough that I noticed.

And hoped.

"So what's the deal, champ?" Sheriff Sutherland asked Indra. "You say your *father's house*. Does that make you a Wilding?"

I had forgotten that I'd reached that conclusion only recently.

"Sheriff Sutherland," I said, looking at him in the rearview mirror, "meet Indra Wilding. Aaron Wilding's son, and once one of his heirs."

Indra said nothing.

"That what all this bullcrap is about?" Sheriff Sutherland shook his head. "*Money?* I couldn't imagine a stupider reason to shoot someone."

I didn't say anything, but part of me wanted to point out that he might feel that way because he had plenty of cash. *I* could imagine lots of stupider reasons than money for shooting somebody. Anger, envy, and hate were all completely pointless reasons to kill another human being—money could be spent to buy security, good health, education, peace.

Indra snorted.

"So we're your hostages, right?" the sheriff pressed. "You got the official truck, so you'll get waved right past any checkpoints, that was a pretty good move. Mind you, if anybody tries to reach me on the radio and I don't respond, they're going to get suspicious. And then they might start stopping sheriff department vehicles. So either you ought to get out of the county as soon as possible, right now, before anybody starts asking questions, or you better get my cooperation."

Indra's sneer flattened into a suspicious glare. "A minute ago, you were going to kick my ass."

"Oh, I'm still going to kick your ass, believe me. I get you in my jail cell, you're going to have an astonishing number of accidents—slip and bang your face on the toilet, crush your fingers in the door, accidentally get a size thirteen boot up your butt cheeks. But in the meantime, I want you not to hurt Rebecca. So let her go, and I'll drive you out of the county. Heck, I'll drive you to Canada if you want. I'll drive you right to the border on dirt roads where there's nobody to check your passport, you can't get a better deal than that. And nobody will ask you questions at any point, because you'll be with me."

"You know I've killed people."

"So have I."

Indra scratched his chin. "Hold on to that thought." Turning to me, he added: "Kill the lights."

I pulled over and turned off the headlights. We were just shy of the turnoff to the Wilding house. The car behind me slowed, then passed.

In the moonlight, it looked like an SUV. My heart sank. That wasn't the cavalry. It was more hostile Indians. And I know that's not politically correct, but it's what I thought. Cut me some slack—I was under a lot of pressure.

"Get slowly up the driveway," Indra directed me, and I did, past the left turn and past Evil's GSX that was still parked there.

The H3 that was canary yellow by day looked brown under the quarter moon. "Stop here," Indra said. We were still well short of the house. "And get out. Not you," he added, looking at Sheriff Sutherland.

"Checking in with your co-conspirator?" the sheriff challenged him.

Indra just snorted again and followed me out into the night. Inside the house, only a couple of lights were on—bedroom and kitchen, I thought. I didn't see Marilyn, but she must be here.

"Walk straight up to the door in the side of the garage," Indra told me. "No sudden moves, and you'll see your boyfriend again."

"He's not my boyfriend."

"Break my heart."

The garage door was on the straight exterior wall of the house, and I noticed now as I approached that this side had very few windows. I reached the door and stopped, and Indra came right behind me. "See?" he grinned. "No motion-activated lights on this side of the house. Oops. That's what you get for taking all that south-facing windows crap too seriously."

"What are you going to do?"

"The sheriff is right. I should be getting out of here as fast as possible. But I haven't done the one thing I really came here to do yet. So we're making a short stop here, but it will only be a minute."

He tested the doorknob, but it didn't turn. A quick shoulder thrown against the door knocked it open, though, and he pushed me in ahead of him.

In the garage were a Tesla Model S and a charging station; that must be Aaron Wilding's car. There was also space for the H3, and lots of sporting equipment—kayaks, backpacks, a pair of snowmobiles sitting on a trailer, and so on.

Indra pushed me toward the two steps up and the door into the house. I could see them by the strong glow of the garage door opener button, set into the wall right next to the door.

He prodded me and I opened the door and walked through.

I found myself standing in a narrow hall. The wooden walls and stone-tiled floor matched what I'd seen before in the Wilding house interior, but I was disoriented enough that I wasn't sure where I was relative to the kitchen or the bathroom I'd used. Light shone around the frame of a doorway to my right.

"Shh," Indra Wilding said as he pushed me toward the light.

It was like a creepy horror film, and I was walking down the dark passage to the mysterious, unexplained light that kept appearing at night in the unused attic. Only there was no ghost behind the door, no demon, it was Marilyn Wilding. The monster was on my side.

Money didn't seem to be what Indra was after. So it had to be revenge. He hated Marilyn, and he was going to do something to hurt her.

And what did he hate Marilyn for? What was the odd secret room with all its bears for? Why was it meaningful for Indra Wilding?

"Marilyn!" I yelled.

Indra cursed under his breath and I felt his foot kick me suddenly in the backside. I staggered forward, knocking the door open as I crashed through it.

On the other side of the door was a sitting room or a library. I saw bookcases and a TV screen, and I saw Marilyn staring at me over the barrel of a shotgun as I tumbled to the floor and lost sight of her in my spinning.

"Rebecca McCrae?" I heard her ask.

Bang! Bang! Bang!

The shots were not from Marilyn Wilding and her shotgun. They came from Indra, and Marilyn Wilding re-entered my vision as a corpse, thudding to the floor beside me.

CHAPTER
28

I staggered out to the truck. You'd think seeing another murder might have left me in shock, but instead my mind raced at a million miles an hour. Indra Wilding had killed his stepmother right in front of me.

It was my fault. No, not really, but I *felt* as if it was my fault— Marilyn had been expecting Indra to come for her, and she had been armed. But when I had shouted to warn her, it had knocked her off-guard instead, and Indra had killed her.

She had expected him to come kill her, and he had done it. What was between them, exactly? What had driven Indra Wilding to murder?

And now he was going to kill me.

I needed a way out.

If I ran, I'd be leaving Sheriff Sutherland behind. He sat in the back seat of his truck, glaring at Indra through the wire mesh that contained him as we came out of the house.

I got into the truck first and shut the door.

While Indra circled the hood to get in on his side, gun pointed at me through the windshield, the sheriff spoke in a low voice. "My hands aren't cuffed. That jackass didn't test the tightness, so I just left them loose and I've pulled my hands through. There's a Leatherman in the cup holder. If you can shove that back to me through the cage, I can get myself out of the truck."

Then Indra pulled the door open, and Sheriff Sutherland raised his voice. "Marilyn's dead now, isn't she?"

"She deserved it."

"I don't see how you think you can benefit from this. You've cut your way through this town like a bad samurai movie, leaving corpses all over. You think you can just put a suit on now, walk into court like nothing happened, and inherit the ranch?"

"I'm not going to inherit." Indra pointed to the little road forking away from the driveway; it wasn't the one that led to Charlie Herbert's house, because that exited the other side of the vale. "Drive," he said to me.

"So what's this about, then?" the sheriff asked. "Revenge?"

"*Revenge* makes it sound like I'm the bad guy."

"I don't know about good guys and bad guys," Sheriff Sutherland said. "At least, not in my professional capacity. I know about people who obey the law, and people who don't. Guess which category you fall into."

"I'm justice," Indra said.

Sheriff Sutherland snorted.

"The ancient Greeks knew that the polis, the city-state, couldn't guarantee justice. They thought it was up to the gods. When someone needed punishing and there was no good human agency to do it, no king or no judge, the gods sent furies after that person."

"Yeah? What was Charlie Herbert's big sin? Dope? Being a loner? Not shaving?"

"I didn't kill Charlie," Indra said. He looked out the window at pines trees crawling past in the darkness. "I rather liked him."

If I'd had two usable hands, I'd have snatched the Leatherman at that moment. But I was driving with my left, and couldn't reach across my own body to grab the little tool. I bit my lip and kept driving.

"So who was your accomplice?"

"I don't have an accomplice. I have only an oath-breaking sister who is trying to stop me, and enemies."

"Nick," I said. "The second man who was in dad's office the other night was wearing a deputy's uniform. He's the one who shot Charlie. It was Nick, wasn't it? He was about the right size, with dark, curly hair. He knew there was a second will, a will that disinherited Marilyn, and he was trying to stop Charlie from delivering it. Or maybe he was trying to scare Charlie into revealing where it was, and he accidentally killed him. And then you shot him."

"Well, I know you didn't come here to kill the boy toy," the sheriff grunted. "He was innocent when you got here."

"He wasn't innocent," Indra said. "But he wasn't my accomplice either, and I didn't come here to kill him. I came here to kill his lover, and now I've done it."

The road crested a small rise and straightened out. Indra looked out the window again, and I saw my moment. Bracing the steering wheel with my left knee, I snaked my left arm across my body and grabbed the Leatherman.

The sheriff might have seen it. He didn't let on.

"Your justice has a pretty scattershot aim," the sheriff said. "You shot Bucky here. Banged that kid Patten over the head. Killed your mother's boyfriend."

"She wasn't my mother." Indra Wilding's voice was bitter.

The trees faded from sight at the edges of the headlights' glow. We were in a big meadow, and ahead I saw the dark outline of a boxy building and a smooth path in front of it. Then I realized where we were.

"This is an air strip," I said.

Sheriff Sutherland kept right on talking. "You killed a couple of men today, too. Real commando style, impaled one right in the center of the chest and just about chopped the other one's head off. You don't seem like justice to me so much as a rabid animal, running crazy and biting everyone it can get its teeth on."

"Maybe I'm not rabid," Indra said. "Maybe I'm the dog who's been kicked too many times and finally bites back."

"Bullcrap," the sheriff said. "You waited until your dad was dead, and then you came up here and started killing people. You didn't want to inherit, so...what? You wanted to stop Marilyn Wilding from inheriting? What did she do, take away your pony? Make fun of your name?"

"Indra is a storm god," Indra said. "He's the god of victory, and the bringer of the sun, like Yahweh in the Bible. He is the mighty one, who makes war, who frees the oppressed. He brings justice."

"Jeez," Sheriff Sutherland said. "I wish your dad had named you *Grover*."

"She didn't take away my pony. Until my dad sent me away to boarding school, she abused me."

I felt very tiny. The road I followed blended into the beginning of the paved airstrip itself, in a pool of asphalt around the corner of the hanger. In the glare of the headlights, I saw a big garage-style door, only bigger, that the airplanes must go through, and the smaller entrance on the side. I put the truck into park.

"Oh," I said. "Bears and swimsuits."

Indra looked at me sharply. "Bears and swimsuits. You saw."

I just nodded.

"*Abused*." The challenging, belligerent tone of Sheriff Sutherland's voice dropped away, and now he just sounded serious. "Let's be clear about this. Do you mean she *beat* you? Didn't let you take the family car out on prom night?"

"I mean she raped me." Indra's voice was cold, but in the reflected light of the headlights I saw a trail of tears down both cheeks. "She and the boyfriends she always had, right from the beginning. Nick wasn't the first, and he wouldn't have been the last. Marilyn used me, and she gave me to her friends."

"*Bears and swimsuits* means what?" Sheriff Sutherland asked.

"There's a room," I told him. "You missed it because it's behind a secret door."

"I see you've been busy," the sheriff said.

"It's a room where bad things happened." Indra's jaw was clenched so tight I could barely understand his words.

I choked. "What about your dad?"

Indra nodded. "Eventually he sent me away. He sent Rainbow away first, once he realized what was going on."

"But he didn't turn Marilyn in?"

"He loved her. He was a very smart man, about many things. But he was stupid about women. And about his heart."

"You know what you've done is still murder." Sheriff Sutherland's voice sounded different, and it took me a second to recognize what it was.

Compassion.

He sounded sorry for Indra Wilding.

"Justice will come for me too. Justice comes for everyone." Indra looked at me. "Get out of the car."

Then he turned and opened his door.

I pivoted and shoved the Leatherman through the mesh into the back seat. I didn't hear it hit the floor, so maybe the sheriff caught it, but I wasn't looking. Instead, I turned the car off and stepped out.

I left the keys in the ignition. I didn't know what Sheriff Sutherland could do with a Leatherman, but he seemed to have a plan. Maybe the truck would be useful to him.

The night was getting cold—a stiff breeze blew down across the Ups and toward Howard.

"I don't know how to fly a plane," I said.

"I do." Indra pointed the Glock at me. "Come on, into the hangar."

I walked the way he indicated, but slowly. "Well then, go. You don't need me."

"I *do* need you," he said. "Until I'm sure I'm safe and no one's following me, you're my insurance policy."

"You mean hostage."

"Po-tay-to, po-tah-to."

"That's not funny. You're joking about my life."

"You're right," Indra agreed. "None of this is funny. None of this is funny at all."

He opened the door to the hangar and pushed me inside.

It was dark as pitch inside, but Indra knew his way. He walked straight to a light switch on the wall and flicked on long rows of overhead fluorescent lights. At the same panel in the wall, he also hit a button that started a motor overhead. The motor growled and whined, and the hangar's big bay door started climbing up.

There was an airplane in the hangar. I don't know airplanes any more than I know yachts or steam trains, so all I can tell you is it was small, and had a single propeller on the nose.

"Get in," Indra said. He opened the door, dropped down a small ladder, and then hoisted me up into the cab of the plane by my belt.

I scooted across the pilot's seat to the shotgun seat on the right.

"Grab that strap." Indra pointed.

I looked; the strap was a loop of vinyl on the right side, like you'd hang onto to brace yourself for turbulence. "Across my body?" I asked.

"I didn't say it would be comfortable." Indra poked me with the Glock.

I grabbed the strap.

From his pocket he pulled out a clear plastic zip tie. It was industrial-sized, more like a rope than a zip tie. Setting his pistol on the seat and kneeling next to it, he threaded the zip tie around my wrist and through the hand strap, tying me in place. Then he yanked the zip tie tight. Even shifting my weight around onto my right hip, it still felt as if my left shoulder was being slowly pulled from its socket.

Indra shut the door behind him and started manipulating the plane controls.

"What are you doing?" I asked him.

"Checking ailerons and fuel gauges," Indra snarled. "Warming the carburetor, getting ready to take off. Why? You have an opinion on how I operate the plane all of a sudden?"

I shut up.

"Hey!" A shout broke into the gentle *clicks* and *whooshes* made by the plane controls as Indra got the vehicle ready for take-off. I knew the voice. It was Rainbow's man, Burt. I tried to turn and look, but couldn't crane my head past my shoulder.

In response, Indra started shooting. Glass shattered, and then I heard answering fire from Burt's gun.

The plane shuddered as bullets hit it.

"You promised!" Burt shouted. "Half, you said!"

"I lied!" Indra shouted back.

I heard another racket of answering fire from the Glock, and then a *click* as its magazine came up empty.

The thud of feet running across concrete.

"Stop!" I yelled. I knew what Burt must not have realized.

Bang! Bang! Bang!

Indra Wilding had more than one gun.

I heard a heavier thud and a clatter, and I knew that Burt was dead.

"Idiot," Indra snarled. "That was completely unnecessary."

"Then why did you shoot him?" I meant to ask it calmly, but it came out with a slightly manic edge to my voice. "Wasn't he your ally? Your partner?"

"*Rainbow* was my partner!" Indra shouted. His voice was much louder than it needed to be to be heard over the sounds of the plane. "We swore, the night before she left home, that when Dad died we'd come back and kill that bitch!"

"But then you called her and she backed out," I realized.

"Said she was older and wiser," Indra snorted. "So I played along. And Burt was supposed to keep her out of the scene, at least until I had arranged things for us. For her. He stopped being my ally when he showed up and went after the will."

The plane moved forward.

"What would he want the will for?" I asked.

"Who cares?" Indra shot back. "Blackmail? Hold it against me? Sell the will to Marilyn?" He laughed, his voice falling apart in a maniacal cackle. "It doesn't matter now!"

I couldn't bear looking out the right window at nothing, so I

226 | D. J. BUTLER

twisted in my seat. Kneeling and facing backward, I could see Indra, driving the plane forward onto the runway with a grim smile on his face.

"FAA regulations require you to wear a seatbelt," he said. "Or so I've been told."

I looked past him, and at what I saw, my heart jumped into my mouth.

The sheriff's truck was rumbling forward. Its headlights were off, but I could see it clearly in the light coming from the hangar. Indra might not have noticed it, focused as he was on the runway.

And beyond the truck, coming up from the Wilding house, were the headlights of two cars. As the first slowed and turned to drive onto the airstrip, it was clearly silhouetted in the headlights of its companion. It was a black SUV.

CHAPTER
29

The plane bumped and jostled from side to side a bit, like a jock shouldering his way through a crowded hallway. Indra turned the plane and rolled forward, and then the lights of the hangar were behind us, and ahead was a long meadow, barely visible under the shrinking moon.

"You can't even see the runway," I said.

Indra shrugged. "I think I know where it is."

"And if you're wrong?"

"Then I crash and burn into the trees. Isn't that a fitting end for a specter of divine justice? Like a meteorite, that crashes to earth, does the work of heaven, and is itself consumed."

"What does that make me? Stardust?"

"It makes you a necessary sacrifice."

"You've been reading too much," I said, "and the wrong kind of books."

"You really ought to sit down. But suit yourself." Indra clicked his own shoulder belt into place and accelerated down the runway.

I yanked at my hand, trying to squeeze it out of the zip tie, but no luck. Spiraling back into a sitting position, I tried to put my shoulder belt on with my broken arm, but no luck there, either.

At least I could see ahead of the plane. If death was going to take me in the form of a stand of pines trees, I'd see it coming.

But I didn't see death. Instead, I saw the sheriff's truck.

The pickup swerved out in front of us, several car lengths ahead. And then Sheriff Sutherland hit his brakes, and the truck slowed... heading straight back toward our propeller.

"He's trying to force us off the road." Indra shook his head. "What a waste of time."

It didn't feel like a waste of time to me. It felt like madness. I practically crawled up the wall of the cabin, trying to back away from the approaching pickup.

"Stop!" I shouted.

Indra laughed and accelerated.

The truck came closer...

Indra laughed louder...

And the sheriff swerved left, off the runway. He was again out of my field of vision, pinned against the right wall as I was, and I had a sudden terrible image of his truck crashing into a tree or boulder beside the airstrip and bursting into flame.

"That's why you buy insurance," Indra said. "See?"

I unwound myself back into kneeling position. Since I couldn't work the shoulder belt anyway, I might as well see what was happening.

The SUVs were behind. One of them had stopped at the hangar and I saw people entering the building. It was too far away, and we were rattling too much, for me to make out if Rainbow Wilding was one of them. The second SUV chased after us.

But just behind the plane came the sheriff's truck. I could tell the truck from the SUV because, just as I looked at it, the sheriff hit his sirens and flashing lights.

In response, Indra accelerated. We started to pull away from the sheriff.

"Please," I said.

"Really?!" Indra laughed. "You think I can stop now, and just let you out? Ha!"

He was right. There had been a point of no return somewhere, and he was past it. Maybe it had been the first death, Nick's. Or maybe before that, Evil's kidnapping. Maybe the point of no return had been years ago.

It didn't matter now.

The sheriff's truck burst forward and right, pulling up alongside the plane. As he pulled even with me and below me, I saw him through his window—his hat was off, he was hunkered over the wheel, and the big-toothed snarl on his face made him look like an animal. But a friendly one.

He looked up as he passed and nodded at me.

I knew what he wanted. And I didn't think I could do it.

The truck pulled forward, slightly, but then paced us. Its bed was underneath and just outside the door on my side of the plane.

I looked under my armpit and saw the end of the runway approaching, fast. Beyond its end the meadow continued a short distance, ending in a dark meandering line in the grass that might be a creek. Beyond that line stood pine trees.

I needed a knife. Or wire cutters. I needed to somehow cut the thick zip tie around my wrist. Of course, even if I'd had a knife, I wouldn't have been able to use it. My right arm was in a cast, and there was no way I could bend it around to get to the wrist strap to which I was tied.

I stood. In the cabin, that meant pressing my head and shoulders against the ceiling.

"Sit down," Indra growled. He pushed me.

I fell back, but not back onto the seat. One knee fell down between the seats, and my left knee was bent up, my left foot on the cabin floor. I was positioned like I was waiting to take a football snap, with my left hand up in the air, to signal when I had the ball.

Only this was no game.

Sliding around onto my right knee, I raised my left foot, and I just managed to get it onto the handle of my door. Dragging my foot down, I brought the door handle with it.

The door opened.

Wind had already been whistling in the cockpit because of the window Indra had shot out. Now it became a huge *whoosh*.

"Sit down!"

There was a note of panic in Indra's voice, and he punched me as he screamed. The punch hit me right at the base of the skull, what they call a rabbit punch. My vision went black for a moment, and I swooned.

But then I came back, and I lurched forward. I was awkward and off balance, but I had only one shot. Kicking with both my legs, I threw myself out of the open door.

I fell, but only the length of my arm.

The zip tie caught me. I screamed. My shoulder felt like it was going to disconnect completely from my body. I slammed against the side of the plane.

Cold liquid splashed on my shirt. It smelled strongly of gasoline, and I realized a stream was sputtering out of the plane.

Indra swerved left and right. Sheriff Sutherland tried to swerve with him, but for long moments I saw speeding asphalt flash beneath my feet.

The zip tie didn't break. But the handle I was tied to suddenly did. I fell—

And slammed into the truck.

I didn't quite land in the bed. One leg hit the side of the pickup's bed as I crashed into it, and I screamed again, feeling my leg break. My back landed flat, mercifully, and then my head bounced off the plastic liner of the truck's bed.

Sheriff Sutherland braked.

I slammed up against the steel toolbox bolted in just behind the truck's back seat, and then the truck spun. I crunched into one wall of the bed, and then the other as the sheriff fishtailed.

Then I bounced and flipped like a pancake done on one side. Overhead, I saw Indra Wilding's plane take off. The truck skidded as if it was hydroplaning, and then fell and stopped with a loud *splash*.

Water jumped up over me in a wave, but then receded, leaving me lying on my back. Cold, wet, out of breath, broken. Smelling like gasoline.

And alive.

"Bucky!"

The sheriff made sloshing sounds as he jumped from the cab of the truck. We'd stopped in the creek, I guessed.

He poked his head over the edge of the truck bed and jammed two fingers up against my throat, feeling for my pulse.

"Bucky?"

"Unnnnh," I managed to say. It felt pretty articulate, all things considered.

"How are you feeling?"

"Unnnnnnnnnh," I repeated, with more Ns this time.

Sheriff Sutherland climbed up his truck's rear tire and jumped into the back of the truck with me. "Talk to me," he said, and then he started frisking me, checking for broken bones or major bleeding.

"He won't get far," I said.

Sheriff Sutherland chuckled. "That what you're really worried about right now?"

"He's got at least one hole in his fuel tank," I said. "Maybe more."

"He's got a hole in his head," the sheriff said. "Poor stupid bastard."

"You feel for him?" Then I screamed wordlessly as the sheriff touched my leg. He nodded and kept prodding.

"Broken," he said. "Bad. Yeah, I feel for him."

"He killed a lot of people."

"Let me tell you a secret about the law, Bucky," he said.

"I'm listening." I gritted my teeth against the pain and tried not to black out.

"Sheriffs have some discretion about what we investigate. And prosecutors have some discretion about whom they prosecute. And judges have some discretion in their decisions. Do you know why?"

I tried to shrug, but even moving that tiny amount hurt too much. "Tell me."

"Mercy," he said. "Law is a blunt instrument. And sometimes, when the law and the facts tell you that, strictly speaking, a person is supposed to be thrown in jail, mercy, compassion, and just reasonable humanity tell you that that's not the best outcome for the case."

"You're saying you would have looked the other way. For Indra Wilding."

"Nope. He's killed way too many people, so as soon as I'm sure you're not bleeding to death I'm going to call the office and get the word out on his escape. But I'm saying, some of it was understandable. And I'd have felt bad about investigating him, and handing him over to the county prosecutor."

"And if he'd shot Marilyn Wilding when he was sixteen years old, and she and her boyfriends were using him as a human sex toy?"

The sheriff nodded. "I'd have been really tempted to look the other way."

He opened the toolbox and took a blanket from it, wrapping the blanket around me.

"Let's get you into the cab," he said.

He dropped the tailgate but then stopped.

One of the two SUVs pulled up. It parked politely, aiming its headlights away from us, and I could see well enough to realize it was Rainbow Wilding who got out of the back seat.

"I guess you know I have a lot of questions to ask you," the sheriff called to her.

"If you want to arrest me," she said, "I'm here to turn myself in."

"Are you confessing to a crime?"

"No."

"You planning to leave Howard anytime soon?"

"I've got a hotel room. I'll be here as long as you need me."

"Then I guess I don't need to arrest you." The sheriff paused. "Is that true, all the stuff your brother told me?"

"He came here to kill our stepmother. If he told you what I think he told you then yes, it was true, and as far as I'm concerned, she deserved death."

"You come here to kill her, too?"

"I guessed what Indra was planning. I came here to stop him."

"You just said she deserved to die."

Rainbow hesitated before answering. "Yes. But Indra didn't deserve to kill."

"I guess I know what you mean." Sheriff Sutherland turned and looked at me, then back at Rainbow. "If one of your bodyguards would help me get this young lady into the cab of my truck, I'd be grateful."

Rainbow waved her hand, and a big man I hadn't noticed, standing in the shadow of the SUV, came forward and climbed up the tire to join Sheriff Sutherland and me in the truck bed.

"Be careful," the sheriff said. "She's got a broken leg, at *least*."

Rainbow's bodyguard grunted. The two men knelt beside me to link arms under my knees and behind my back.

"On the count of three," Sheriff Sutherland said.

CHAPTER
30

The hospital was in Yakima, a couple hours' drive away. I'd been there before, for stitches in my lip when I'd fallen out of a tree house as a kid, but it had been a while. A bearded nurse in teal scrubs and rubber-soled shoes gave us directions to Evil's room.

He was propped up on pillows and watching the TV over the door when I came in, hobbling on two crutches with one leg and one arm in a cast.

"Rebecca," he said.

I gave him a one-armed hug and managed not to fall on top of him. Dad stood in the door and looked around innocently.

Evil hit the button to summon a nurse. "Tell me what happened."

"Jeez, I...a lot of stuff."

He accepted that with a nod. "That guy Michael Fellows was the killer."

"His name was Indra Wilding. And there were two killers, actually. Or maybe three." I updated Evil about Nick and Marilyn, Marilyn's history of exploiting her stepchildren, Rainbow Wilding and her double-dealing thug Burt, my jump from the plane, and Indra Wilding's disappearance.

"You solved the mystery," Evil said.

"No. No, I didn't. I figured out a few things along the way, and I followed a lot of wrong trails, too, but mostly I just survived the experience. For now, though...that's enough."

"And have they found the guy yet? Indra Wilding?"

"Nope. Not him, and not the plane. There's a lot of wilderness out there, so the most likely thing is he just crashed, and no one will ever see him again. But they're still looking."

"So what's going to happen to Aaron Wilding's money? And all that pot, for instance?"

I laughed. "Well, Dad filed the most recent will with Judge Ybarra this morning. Turns out Indra left it in the sheriff's truck. So it'll have to go through probate, but odds are it will be executed, which means the executor will have to set up a trust, appoint a trustee, and so forth."

"A wilderness fund."

"Yep."

"This from the guy who hated hunters. I feel like I just helped Darth Vader find the rebel base. What's this fund going to do, run around buying up land and fencing it off? Make the world safe again for mule deer?"

I shrugged. "The trustee will decide ultimately. But the will doesn't say anything about hunting. I think it's going to buy private land and return it to wilderness. Probably starting by returning the Wilding property to wilderness."

Evil knitted his brows. "You mean this trustee might take down the barbed wire?"

I shrugged again. "Might."

"What about the water? Someone will need to check the groundwater...you know, in case you were right about the aquifer. Was the Wildings' water poisoned, after all?"

"I don't even know," I said. "The sheriff's having it tested. If it was poisoned, then Marilyn and Nick probably conspired to kill her husband. Either way...does it matter now?"

"Might matter to the *deer*," Evil said. "And to any hunter who takes water from that stream."

"Good point," I agreed.

A nurse came in and started unhooking Evil from the IV bag that had been rehydrating and medicating him.

Evil exhaled. "Well, I think I still have about a million questions."

"So does Sheriff Sutherland. But he's starting to sort it out. In the meantime, I brought you this."

I handed him a DVD of *The Last of the Mohicans.*

Evil whistled. "I guess I better come over tonight and watch this, before it has to get turned back in."

"Nope," I said, "that's your copy. Lucky for you, the Walmart here in Yakima had it in stock."

Evil grinned, but his eyes were a little moist. "Thanks, Rebecca. And, Mr. McCrae?"

"Yeah?" Dad pulled up from his very close inspection of an unplugged monitor in the corner of the room. He looked a little surprised not to be called *Jim.*

"Thanks for the ride home."

"No rush." Dad snorted and waved his hand. "We're ready to go when you are."

I followed Dad out into the hall so Evil could get dressed.

"Well," I pointed out, "you lost a client."

"Yeah," he agreed. "On the other hand, I do a little trustee work. Maybe the court will appoint me to run the trust." He grinned. "Maybe the court will appoint *you.*"

"Me? I wouldn't know the first thing about how to manage that money."

Dad looked at me with a sly grin on his face. "Somehow, I think you'd manage."

"I hope one of us gets it," I said. "I forgot to tell you this, but I sort of promised St. Joseph I'd let the kids at his school bowl free for a week."

"You promised who? The school administrators?"

"Uh...I promised the saint."

"That's just fine." Dad laughed. "As long as you didn't promise him his kids could *eat* for free."

Evil emerged from his room limping. He held a prescription clutched in his hand. "We could pick up a portable DVD player, watch the film on the ride home. I bet that Walmart sells them."

"You're anxious," I said. Dad moved to get his arm under Evil's shoulder, and help him down the hall.

"It's a great movie."

We headed for the elevator.

"You know you're not my boyfriend," I said.

"You've been clear about that," he said. "But you can't blame a guy for trying."

"Nope," I agreed, matching my pace with theirs as we slowly made our way out of the hospital. "I don't blame you at all."

ABOUT THE AUTHOR

D.J. (Dave) Butler has been a lawyer, a consultant, an editor, and a corporate trainer. His other novels include Witchy Eye, Witchy Winter, and Witchy Kingdom from Baen Books, as well as The Cunning Man, co-written with Aaron Michael Ritchey, and the pseudofantasy thriller, In the Palace of Shadow and Joy. He also writes for children: the steampunk fantasy adventure tales The Kidnap Plot, the Giant's Seat, and The Library Machine are published by Knopf. Other novels include City of the Saints from WordFire Press.

ALSO BY D. J. BUTLER

The Witchy War
Witchy Eye
Witchy Winter
Witchy Kingdom
Serpent Daughter

Tales of Indrajit & Fix
In the Palace of Shadow and Joy

The Cunning Man

City of the Saints

The Buza System
Crecheling
Urbane

The Extraordinary Journeys of Clockwork Charlie
The Kidnap Plot
The Giant's Seat
The Library Machine

This has been an
Immortal Production

www.ingramcontent.com/pod-product-compliance
Lightning Source LLC
Chambersburg PA
CBHW050349190726
48284CB00007BB/2210